INTERMEDIATE GRAMMAR, USAGE and COMPOSITION

M.L. TICKOO, M.A. (Lond.), PH.D. (Lond.)
A.E. SUBRAMANIAN, M.A., L.T. (Madras)
P.R. SUBRAMANIAM, M.A., L.T. (Madras)

AF543350

Orient BlackSwan

INTERMEDIATE GRAMMAR USAGE AND COMPOSITION

ORIENT BLACKSWAN PRIVATE LIMITED

Registered Office
3-6-752 Himayatnagar, Hyderabad 500 029 (A.P.), INDIA
e-mail: centraloffice@orientblackswan.com

Other Offices
Bangalore, Bhopal, Bhubaneshwar, Chennai, Ernakulam, Guwahati, Hyderabad, Jaipur, Kolkata, Lucknow, Mumbai, New Delhi, Noida, Patna

© Orient Blackswan Private Limited

First published by Orient Longman Pvt. Ltd. 1976
Reprinted 1978, 1982 (twice), 1983, 1986, 1988, 1989, 1991, 1996, 2001, 2002, 2005, 2007, 2008

First Orient Blackswan impression 2009
Reprinted 2010, 2011, 2012

ISBN 978 81 250 1033 3

Printed in India at
B. B. Press
Delhi

Published by
Orient Blackswan Private Limited
1/24 Asaf Ali Road, New Delhi 110 002
e-mail: delhi@orientblackswan.com

PREFACE

A pedagogic grammar is prepared for the specific needs of learners at one particular stage. This one is meant for the intermediate learner who has come through ten years of schooling, and is designed to answer a set of fully-defined linguistic needs, which this one attempts to do.

In preparing the book we were governed by a third important consideration—that grammar is learnt through repetitive use and thoughtful involvement on the part of the learner. Throughout the book therefore the learner is being helped to arrive at the essential rules through examples of living English. And each such rule is followed by exercises that provide him opportunities to use it in meaningful sentences. This is thus a learner's practice book and not just a book of grammatical rules.

The book covers, in suitable depth and detail, items commonly covered at this level. In doing so it does not, however, lose sight of an important characteristic of current English—that certain aspects of its structure can be better learned as parts of larger topics than in isolation. We have treated these aspects (viz. synthesis, transformation and correction of sentences) at a number of appropriate places throughout the book.

The composition section has been divided into four chapters. Each chapter gives guidance in the skills that are involved and each provides specimen materials, hints and suggestions suited to the intermediate learner. Each one also sets tasks for the learner. In setting these tasks we have, on the one hand, stayed away from themes that are much too abstract or far too removed from his experience and, on the other, attempted to provide enough challenge to stimulate his interest and attention and make him strive for his best.

It is our hope that the book will go a long way in giving the learner valuable insights into the system and structure of modern English and in putting him on his feet in written English.

M.L. Tickoo
A.E. Subramanian
P.R. Subramaniam

CONTENTS

1 THE SENTENCE

1 The Subject and the Predicate

A When we say something in any language, we say it in groups of words which are called sentences. We make a sentence by putting words together in a certain order.

Here are some sentences in English:

A	B
Mr Kumar	is a teacher.
He	teaches in the high school.
The school	has over a thousand pupils.
It	is a good school.
Mr Kumar's students	like him very much.
Mrs Kumar, who is also a teacher,	works in a primary school.
The children of that school	wear uniforms.

Each of these sentences has two parts. The first part, under column A, is called the **subject**. The second part, under column B, is called the **predicate**. Every grammatical sentence usually has a subject part and a predicate part. In each of the sentences given above the predicate part has a verb which says what the subject is, has, does, etc. For example, in the first sentence above, the predicate part *is a teacher* says what Mr Kumar is.

B Looking at the subject part you will find that it can be:

1 the name of a person: *Mr Kumar, Mrs Kumar.*
2 a pronoun: *he, it.*
3 a noun with a possessive adjective or an article before it: *his* students, *the* school.
4 a noun or pronoun with a phrase qualifying it: ***the children of that school.***

5 a noun with a clause qualifying it: Mrs Kumar, *who is also a teacher.*

The subject is a noun or a pronoun with or without other words going with it.

C Now look at these sentences:

There are a number of boys waiting outside.
There is nothing more healthy for a child than mother's milk.
There is a letter for you on your table.
There happened a sudden revolution in the country.

In these sentences the word *There* is in the subject position, although it is not a noun or pronoun. It is said to be the 'grammatical' or the 'dummy' subject. The real subject in each of the sentences above is the noun that comes after the verb.

D Looking at the predicate part of the sentences given at the beginning under columns A and B, you find that it can have

1 a verb with a noun complement: *is a teacher*
2 a verb with an adverb phrase: *teaches in the high school, works in a primary school*
3 a verb with a complement: *is a good school*
4 a verb with an object: *teaches science*
5 a verb with an object and an adverbial phrase: *like him* (object) *very much* (adverbial phrase)

The predicate is the verb and the words — object, complement, adverb, adverb phrase, etc. — that go with it.

Exercises

1

Underline the subject parts in the following sentences:

1 The train arrived.

2 Rajeev, the famous football player, got off the train.
3 He was the captain of his team.
4 The last match had made him famous.
5 There was a large crowd on the platform to receive the team.
6 Rajeev's friends and admirers were there.
7 They gave the team a rousing welcome.
8 One of them garlanded Rajeev.

2

Underline the predicate parts in the following sentences:

1 Aeroplanes fly over my house frequently.
2 They make a deafening noise.
3 I don't like this noise.
4 No one in the house does.
5 We are shortly moving out of this house.
6 We are moving to a house on the outskirts of the city.
7 The house commands a beautiful view.
8 The house is furnished.
9 It has a beautiful garden around it.

2 Kinds of Sentences

A *Statements*

Look at these sentences:

Mr Kumar teaches science.
Varanasi is on the banks of the Ganga.
India became independent on 15th August, 1947.

Sentences of this kind state facts, describe things, or report events. They are called **statements**. Since they make certain assertions or declarations, they are also called 'assertive' or 'declarative' sentences.

B *Commands*

Look at these sentences:

Take these files away.
Please get me a cup of coffee.
Be neither a borrower nor a lender.
Go and read in the library.

These sentences express an order, a request, advice, a **direction, a suggestion, a command, etc. Sentences of this type are called by the common name commands, although** they are not all of them commands. They are also called 'imperative sentences'. The subject in these sentences is *you*, but it is not expressed.

Look at these sentences:

Let the boys assemble in the hall for the lecture.
Let's start at once.

These are also imperative sentences, but the 'commands' are expressed in an indirect way. In imperative sentences beginning with *let*, as seen in the examples above, the subject is not omitted but expressed, and it is either in the first person or the third.

C *Questions*

Look at these sentences:

Can I help you?
What do we have for dinner?
Where do you live?
Is the train late?

Sentences of this kind are used to make enquiries and are called **questions** or **interrogative sentences**. Note the question mark (?) at the end of each of these sentences.

D *Exclamations*

Look at these sentences:

How fast time flies!
What a beautiful view we have from here!
What a wonderful piece of luck!
What a tragic end!

Sentences of this kind express surprise, admiration, pity, sorrow and other feelings in an emphatic way. They are called **exclamations** or **exclamatory sentences.**

Note that at the end of each of these sentences, there is an exclamation mark (!).

E *Affirmative and Negative Sentences*

You will have seen that all the sentences given as examples are statements, commands, questions and exclamations. They affirm something or state something in a positive way. They are **affirmative** sentences. But look at these sentences:

He is not a reliable man.
I cannot complete this work today.
They don't understand our difficulties.
I have never watched a test-match.

These are also statements but they use words such as *not* and *never* and are negative in meaning. They are called **negative** sentences.

Commands can also be negative.

Example:

Don't touch the exhibits.

Sentences of this kind are called *negative commands* or prohibitions. Here are some questions which are negative:

Hasn't he got a car?
Why didn't you come in time?

Sentences of this kind are called *negative questions.*

2 PARTS OF SPEECH: IDENTIFICATION

In a sentence, as we have already seen, there is a subject part and a predicate part. In each part there are a number of smaller parts. Each of these smaller parts is a word which has a certain function in the sentence, that is, it does work of a certain kind. Depending on this function, a word is said to belong to a particular **part of speech**.

English words belong to eight parts of speech: Noun, Pronoun, Adjective, Verb, Adverb, Preposition, Conjunction, and Interjection.

1 Nouns

Look at these sentences and the words that are put in italics.

> *Jawaharlal Nehru* was the first *Prime Minister* of *India.*
> *India* won its *independence* from foriegn *rule* in the *year* 1947.
> *India* exports *tea* and *sugar* to foreign *countries.*
> A *classroom* has a *table*, a *chair* for the *teacher*, and *benches* and *desks* for the *students.*

The words in italics name persons, places, things, etc. These words are naming words and are called **nouns.**

Exercise 1

Pick out the nouns in the following passage:

Our sun is, in fact, a rather unimportant member of a huge system of stars, or galaxy, consisting of at least a hundred thousand million stars. We can see a part of this galaxy stretching across the sky as a pale white band of stars, called the Milky Way. In India it is sometimes called the heavenly Ganga.

2 Pronouns

Look at the words in italics in these sentences:

> Mr Kumar is a teacher. *He* teaches science.
> Mrs Kumar is a teacher too. *She* teaches in a primary school.
> Mr Kumar's school has over five hundred pupils. *It* was started a hundred years ago.
> Mr Kumar has two children. *They* go to school.
> *Both* are boys. *One* goes to a high school. The *other* goes to a primary school.
> Mr Kumar's school has a large number of teachers; *some* are men and the *others*, women.

My brother and *I* go to college. *We* go by bus every day.
My uncle sent *me* a present on my birthday.
My uncle and *I* went to the Ajanta Caves last month. A guide took *us* round.
My brother is weak in mathematics. A tutor teaches *him* at home.
My mother took ill last week. '*You* have neglected your health,' the doctor told *her*.
Mice and rats eat up a lot of foodgrain. *We* should get rid of *them*.

In these sentences the words in italics stand for nouns, and are called **pronouns**.

Exercise 2

Pick out the pronouns in the following sentences and say which noun each of them stands for.

1 My brother is an engineer. He works in Bombay.
2 My sister is a teacher. She teaches in a school in Bombay.
3 The boys are going on a picnic. They want me to go with them.
4 I planted these two coconut trees five years ago. One has started yielding coconuts. The other hasn't.
5 The boys were to pay their fees today. But only some have paid.

3 Adjectives

Look at the words in italics in the sentences given below:

a Our team played a *splendid* game.
b A *big* crowd watched the game.
c He spoke for *fifty* minutes.
d *Every* sentence that he spoke was listened to with *great* attention.

The words in italics describe or 'qualify' the nouns that come after them. Words of this kind are called **adjectives**.

Sometimes adjectives which qualify the subject of a sentence also come after the predicate. They are then said to be 'subject complements'. Here are some examples:

> The paper has turned *brown.*
> King Dasarath became very *old.*
> The questions were very *difficult.*

Exercise 3

Pick out the adjectives in the following passage:

> Tourists go to Gingee to see the ruins of some old fortifications which stand on three hills. There is an old fort on the top of one of the hills, which can be reached only by a narrow bridge that lies across a deep moat. A great wall, now broken in many places, runs around the three hills and a deep moat, now dry, runs alongside the wall. The fortifications, built by the Rajput kings who ruled over Gingee a long time ago, are fine examples of engineering skill.

4 Verbs

Look at the words in italics in these sentences:

> Mr Kumar *teaches* science.
> He *has taught* the subject for twenty-five years.
> He *is* a capable teacher.

The words in italics are **verbs**. Verbs express what the subject of the sentence is, or does, or has, or what is done to it. We shall study verbs in detail in a later section.

Exercise 4

Pick out the verbs in the following sentences:

1 The enemy made an attack on the fort and captured it.
2 I don't believe that ghosts exist.
3 The teachers are discussing the examination results.

4 We have invited all the old boys to dinner on College Day.
5 He will work in a hospital in London.

5 Adverbs

Look at the words in italics in these sentences:

I walked *very fast*.
I am *extremely* tired and I need a rest.
He comes to see me *daily*. He came *yesterday*.
He is sure to come *today*.

The words in italics modify verbs. They are called **adverbs.** Adverbs can also modify adjectives:

I am *deeply grateful* to you for your help.

They can modify other adverbs too:

He spoke *extremely well*.

Exercise 5

Pick out the adverbs in the following sentences:

1 The soldiers fought bravely and drove back the enemy.
2 The children walked fast, but their grandfather walked slowly.
3 I gave the child a chocolate. She took it and smiled sweetly.
4 We are quite happy with our new flat.
5 It has been raining here very heavily for the last two days.

6 Prepositions

Look at the words in italics in these sentences:

Work *in* the school begins *at* 10 a.m.
We killed the snake *with* a stick.
The boys lay down *on* the grass.
I shall see you *after* ten o'clock.
We went *across* the river *in* a steam launch.

The words in italics are called **prepositions** because they normally stand or take *position* before (pre) a noun. The preposition is said to 'govern' the noun that follows it. The noun is said to be the 'object' of the preposition.

Besides single-word prepositions, there are also phrases which do the work of prepositions and are called 'phrase prepositions'. We shall study the uses of prepositions in detail in a later section.

Exercise 6

Pick out the single-word prepositions in the following sentences:

1 John attends service in the Church on all Sundays.
2 The train for Delhi leaves at 9 p.m.
3 This bus comes from Nagpur and is going to Jabalpur.
4 This river flows through three states before it flows into the sea.
5 We got a ticket for the show without any difficulty.
6 Tell me all about the accident.

7 Conjunctions

Look at the words in italics in these sentences:

Ravi *and* his sister go to the same college.
Please give me a notebook *and* a pencil.
I want a pen *or* a pencil.
Is that colour green *or* blue?

The words in italics join words or groups of words (phrases). They are called **conjunctions** or **connectors**. Conjunctions are also used to join sentences:

The teacher read the essay ***and*** was impressed by it.
You have to work very hard *or* you won't be able to make up for the lost time.

The conjunctions in the examples above are single words. There are also phrases and pairs of words which are used as conjunctions:

Give me *either* a pen *or* a pencil.
I want *neither* coffee *nor* tea.

He is *not only* bright in his studies *but also* very good at sports and games.

He is very good at studies *as well as* sports and games.

There are also other words (such as *if*, *when*, *although*, *as*, *since*, *that*) which do the work of conjunctions. We shall study them in a later section.

Exercise 7

Pick out the conjunctions in the following sentences:

1 He was tired and hungry, yet he went on with the work.
2 We have to invite him in person, or he won't come.
3 He didn't come to college today, nor has he sent a leave-letter.
4 The weather was very cold, still he preferred to bathe in cold water.
5 Most boys want to study either medicine or some branch of technology.

8 Interjections

Look at the words in italics in the sentences below:

Oh! What a thing to happen!
Alas! What will the poor man do now?
Hush! Don't say a word of this to anyone.

Such words express a strong or sudden feeling — surprise, joy, fear, sadness, etc. They are called **interjections.** They are not grammatically connected with the rest of the sentence. Usually, exclamation marks are put after them. Here are some other words used as interjections:

Ah! Hurrah! Well! well! Dear! dear!

3 THE NOUN PHRASE

Look at these sentences:

Subject	Predicate
Birds	fly.
Vidyasagar	was a man of great learning.
A bicycle	has two wheels.
My box	has been stolen.
That man	is my neighbour.
Some boys	came to see me yesterday.
The cold	was unbearable last winter.

Each of the subjects above is a noun with or without another word before it. The words used before the nouns (e.g. *the*, *some*, *a*, *that*, *my*) belong to a class of words called *determiners*. (We shall study this class of words in a later section of this chapter.)

A noun with or without a determiner is called a **noun phrase**. It can occur both in the subject part of a sentence and in the predicate part. It can be expanded to include single word adjectives, adjectival phrases and adjectival clauses. The noun is therefore the key or 'head' word in a noun phrase. Let us find out more about nouns and their function.

Nouns

Nouns are divided into three main kinds by writers of modern grammar:

Proper nouns
Countable nouns
Uncountable nouns

Proper Nouns:

All *names* by which persons, places, rivers, mountains, and things are called **are proper nouns.**

Examples:

Persons: *Mr Joshi, Hamid, Kamala*
Places: *Delhi, Madras, Trivandrum*
Rivers and Mountains: *The Ganga, The Himalayas.*

A proper noun begins with a capital letter. But some names always have the article 'the' before them: *The Ganga, The United States of America.*

Countable Nouns:

Countable nouns are nouns that we can count: *boy, table, cup, pen, house, gentleman,* etc.

The classes of nouns known as 'common nouns' (boy, table, etc.) and 'collective nouns' (flock, regiment, herd, troop, party, etc.) can be included in the larger class of countable nouns.

Number:

Countable nouns can occur in two forms: *singular* and *plural.*

Look at the group of words below:

a book	my bicycle	that hill
an ant	our team	this book
the table	their hostel	any boy

The noun in each of the phrases above is in the *singular* form. We use the singular form of the countable noun when we refer to a single (one) item; and in every case we put one of the determiners before it.

Look at these sentences:

These *boys* are from my village.
My *books* have been stolen.
Cows eat grass.
Lions do not eat grass.

The nouns in italics are in the *plural* form. We use the plural form of the countable noun when we refer to *more than one.* In some sentences plural nouns require a determiner before them, and in others they don't, as seen in the examples above.

Gender:

Look at these sentences:

1 Raju said that *he* had lent *his* bicycle to Mohan, and Mohan had promised to return *it* to *him* the next day.

2 Meena said that *she* had lent *her* umbrella to Kamala, and Kamala had promised to return *it* to *her* the next day.

In sentence (1) *he*, *his* and *him* refer to Raju, and *it* refers to the bicycle. In sentence (2) *she* and the first *her* refer to Meena, and *it* refers to the umbrella.

He, *his* and *him* are said to be in the *masculine gender* and we use these pronouns to refer to 'males'.

She and *her* are said to be in the *feminine gender* and we use these pronouns to refer to 'females'.

It is said to be in the *neuter gender*, and we use it to refer to a thing which is neuter, that is, which is neither 'male' nor 'female'. **It is also used to refer to an animal or bird when its sex is not being thought of.**

I, *me*, *we*, *us*, *you*, *they*, *them* are used to refer to both the genders, masculine and feminine, and they are said to be in the *common gender*.

Forms of Genders:

1 Some nouns add the suffix /*ess*/ to form their feminine gender. If the noun ends in /*e*/, it drops the /*e*/ when /*ess*/ is added. In some nouns there is also a change in spelling.

a prince	—	princess	god	—	goddess
b wait*er*	—	wait*r*ess	ac*tor*	—	ac*tr*ess
tig*er*	—	tig*r*ess	emp*eror*	—	em*p*ress

2 A few nouns indicate the gender change by prefixing the pronoun *he* or *she*.

he–goat/she–goat   he–wolf/she–wolf

3 Some nouns take special endings to mark the feminine gender.

hero — heroine   viceroy — vicereine

4 A number of nouns go in pairs, one noun referring to the male of the class, and the other to the female.

bachelor	—	maid	uncle	—	aunt
brother	—	sister	boy	—	girl
cock	—	hen	dog	—	bitch
father	—	mother	horse	—	mare
husband	—	wife	king	—	queen
lord	—	lady	man	—	woman
nephew	—	niece	son	—	daughter

5 Some nouns are common to both the male and female members of the class. Here are a few examples:

cousin	child	cook	doctor
driver	friend	parent	teacher

6 Note the feminine genders of the compound nouns given below:

son-in-law	—	daughter-in-law
grandfather	—	grandmother
washerman	—	washerwoman
men teachers	—	women teachers
men students	—	women students.

Uncountable Nouns:

1 Uncountable nouns name things which we cannot count or usually don't count. We cannot use *a* or *an* (in the sense of 'one') or the numbers *one*, *two*, *three*, etc., before such nouns. These are also called 'mass' nouns.

2 Uncountable nouns fall into the following groups:

a Things which are considered in mass or quantity and not in numbers: rice, wheat, sugar, salt, sand, hair, grass, dust, etc.

b Materials: paper, wood, cloth, earth, gold, silver, etc.

c Liquids: water, milk, oil, ink, ghee, honey, etc.

d Gases: air, hydrogen, oxygen, smoke, mist, steam, etc.

e Natural phenomena: heat, cold, electricity, lightning, sunlight, etc.

f ' Abstract ' nouns naming states, qualities, **processes,** actions, ideas, etc.: Example: courage, friendship, happiness, freedom, attention, childhood, honesty, enjoyment.
[*Note:* A number of names of qualities, states, actions, etc. are, however countable: punishments, joys, sorrows, miseries, etc.].

g Branches of learning: Economics, Mathematics, Politics.

3 There are some uncountable nouns which we refer to in parts. When we do so, we use them with expressions such as *a piece of*, *a grain of*, *a kilo of*, etc. Here are some uncountable nouns expressed in this way:

a piece of chalk	a flash of lightning	a piece of furniture
a drop of water	a block of ice	a loaf of bread
a cake of soap	a slice of bread	a log of wood
a grain of sand	a metre of cloth	a cup of tea
a kilo of rice	a litre of petrol	a glass of water

These expressions have their plural forms: pieces of chalk, loaves of bread, flashes of lightning, **etc.**

Exercise 1

Say whether the nouns italicized in the following sentences are countable or uncountable:

1 These *benches* and *chairs* are made of *wood.*
2 The *wood* comes from the *forests* of Kerala.
3 Mr Taranath was a famous *sportsman* in his youth.
4 Hamlet was not a *man* of quick decision.
5 No one had the *nerve* to walk into the Principal's *room.*
6 It is the *power* of *speech* that distinguishes man from *animals.*
7 Mr John read an interesting *paper* at the English Teachers' *Conference.*
8 Your *health* needs *attention.*
9 Wash this *glass*; it is not clean.
10 He is a strict *vegetarian.* He doesn't eat any *meat.*

Determiners

There is a group of words which are used before nouns to fix or define the nouns in some way or other. These words are called *determiners*. **There are sixteen of them and no two of them can be put before a noun side by side.** Here is a list of determiners:

i Demonstratives: *this, that, these, those.*
ii Possessives: *my, your, his, her, its, our, their.*
iii *some, any*
iv Articles: The indefinite articles—*a* or *an.*
The definite article—*the.*

1 *Demonstratives*

Look at these sentences:

This house was built by my grandfather.
These trees were planted by him.
That house over there is my uncle's.
Those buildings you see beyond are the police lines.

The words in italics point to or demonstrate things (house, trees, buildings) or pick them out. **They are called demonstratives and are one class of determiners. *This* and *that* are singular; *these* and *those* are plural.**

2 *Possessives*

Look at these sentences:

That is *my* umbrella.
Its handle is black.
Kamala forgot to take *her* handbag with her.
Let me see *your* notebook.
Our school closes tomorrow for the vacation.
I will look into *their* complaints tomorrow.
He had *his* house whitewashed.

The words in italics are possessive forms of pronouns. They are another class of determiners. They can be used before both singular and plural nouns: *my book, my books; her bag, her bags*; etc. They can also be used before uncountable nouns: *my milk, her courage, their patriotism*, etc.

3 *Some* and *any*

Look at these sentences:

I sat down to write *some* letters.
Some books are missing from the library.
Have you *any books* on architecture in the library?
Sorry we haven't *any books* on architecture.

Some and *any* are determiners in the above sentences.

When *some* is used with a countable noun in the plural, it means an unknown or indefinite number.

Some persons were hurt in the accident.
Some articles have been stolen from the house.

When *some* is used with an uncountable noun, it means an indefinite quantity.

I would like to buy a notebook and some paper.
He brought a pen and some ink.

***Any* is rarely used in affirmative sentences. It is generally used only in negative and interrogative sentences.**

There isn't any sugar in the house.
I have bread, but I haven't any biscuits.
Is there any milk in the jug?

Exercise 2

Fill in the blanks with *some* or *any:*

1 There are ——— history books written in Hindi in the library. There aren't ——— geography books.
2 We saw ——— boys there; we didn't see ——— girls.
3 There aren't ——— hippos in the zoo; there are ——— rhinos.
4 The tourists visited ——— temples; they didn't visit ——— other places of interest.
5 I don't want to eat ——— more rice. I would like to have ——— more bananas.

The Genitive

Look at this sentence:

John's sons go to school.

In this sentence *John's* is said to be the genitive form of John. The genitive is shown by the ' apostrophe *s* ' i.e. /'s/.

Look at this sentence:

The roof of the house was blown off in the storm.

In this sentence, *of the house* is the genitive of *house*. There are therefore, two kinds of genitives, the /*'s*/ genitive and the /*of*/ genitive.

The forms of the /'s/ genitive

The /'s/ genitive has two forms: apostrophe *s* /'s/ and *s* apostrophe /s'/.

a With singular nouns /'s/ is added to form the genitive:

the boy's bag, John's sons,
the king's death, the cat's paws,
James's children, the girl's dance.

b With plural nouns not ending in /s/, /'s/ is added:

children's toys men's rooms

c Only an apostrophe /'/ is added to plural nouns ending in /s/.

birds' nests, boys' school, students' clubs

d Only an apostrophe /'/ is added to singular nouns which contain two or more /s/ sounds in the last syllable:

Jesus' parables Moses' laws

e Only an apostrophe is added when the word *sake* follows a word ending in /s/ sound:

for conscience' sake for goodness' sake

f **In the case of a phrase having two or more nouns taken together /'s/ is added to the last noun:**

The *King of Nepal's* palace, My *son-in-law's* house, in a *month or two's* time, an *hour and a half's* walk.

g When two nouns are in apposition, the /'s/ is added to the second noun:

Alexander the Great's conquests.
Moti the carpenter's shop.

Choice of the /'s/ genitive

Generally speaking the */'s/* genitive is used in the case of animate nouns, in particular persons; it is also used in the case of animals when they are given personal characteristics. In the case of inanimate objects the */of/* genitive is used.

Choice of the /of/ genitive

The */of/* genitive is used with nouns denoting lower animals and inanimate nouns.

the bite of a mosquito	the hood of the cobra
the doors of the house	the depth of the well

In these expressions we have both the /'s/ genitive and the */of/* genitive:

a friend of my father's = one of my father's friends
a work of Keats's = one of Keats's works

Note that the first noun (friend, work) is a noun with an indefinite article before it, and the second noun (father, Keats) is a person. We cannot say:

the friend of my father's.
a leg of the table's.

Exercise 3

Put together the following pairs of nouns using the /'s/ genitive or the */of/* genitive:

Pratap, car; a day, work; this month, income; the girls, school; cow, milk; India frontiers; house, window; a month, holiday; stone, throw; a day, wages; conference, participants; Gandhiji, statue; the picture, the frame; my father, properties; elephant, memory.

4 ARTICLES

The words *a*, *an* and *the* are called **Articles**. *The* is called *the* **definite article** and *a* and *an* are called **indefinite articles**.

Examples:

a pen, a book, a uniform.
an egg, an elephant, an hour.

The article /a/ is used when the sound following it is a consonant. The article /an/ is used when the sound following it is a vowel. The word *uniform* begins with a *vowel* letter /u/ in spelling, but with a *consonant sound* when spoken. Hence *a uniform*. The word *hour* begins with a consonant /h/ in spelling, but with a vowel sound when spoken. Hence *an hour*.

The Uses of the Indefinite Article

1 A hunter saw a bird in a tree.
An aeroplane flew over just now.

The singular nouns introduced in these sentences have not been referred to before, that is, nothing has been said about them earlier. We use an indefinite article before a noun when it is newly introduced.

2 A child cries when he is hungry.
A helicopter can take off vertically.

In these sentences the indefinite article is used before a noun which is meant to be an example of a class of things.

3 He drove the car at sixty kilometres an hour.
Rice costs four rupees a kilo.

In these sentences the indefinite article is used in expressions of price, speed, etc. *A* or *an* in such expressions means *per* or *each*.

4 Birds of a feather flock together.
Two of a trade seldom see eye to eye.

In these sentences *a* means *the same*.

5 The indefinite article is used in exclamations before a singular countable noun:
What a beautiful building!
What a strange sight!

6 A Mr Thomas called when you were away.
A Miss Smith rang an hour ago.

The article *a* is used in these sentences before names. *A Mr Thomas* means *a man called Mr Thomas* and implies that he is a stranger to the speaker.

7 Look at the use of the indefinite article before a proper noun in these sentences:
He is a Shylock in his financial dealings.
Only a Newton can answer this question.

A *Shylock* means a person with the qualities of Shylock.

A *Newton* means a person with the intellect of Newton.

The Uses of the Definite Article

1 A man went for a walk with his dog. The man fell into a well and the dog began to bark. A passer-by pulled the man out of the well.

In the sentences above, *the* is used with nouns that have already been mentioned and are referred to again.

2 The bicycle is the comman man's vehicle.
The lion is a fierce wild animal.

In these sentences the definite article is used with a singular countable noun which stands for a whole class.

3 The teacher wrote an outline of a story on the blackboard.
The Principal is not in town.

In these sentences the definite article is used before a noun which is the only one of its kind in a given situation. This *the* is called the 'unique' *the*.

4 The tall man is the Minister for Health.
The beggar in that corner is a policeman in disguise.

In these sentences the definite article is used before a noun which is specified or made definite by the addition of a qualifying word, phrase or clause: *tall, in that corner.*

5 There is a school for the deaf in this city.
The rich should help the poor.

Here, the article *the* is used before an adjective to turn it into a noun with a plural meaning.

the rich = rich people
the poor = poor people
the deaf = deaf persons

6 *The* is placed before the names of mountains, rivers, oceans, seas, groups of islands, etc.:

The Himalayas, The Baltic Sea, The Ganga, The Laccadives, The Indian Ocean.

7 *The* is used to refer to a whole family:
the Nehrus, the Kennedys.

8 Note the use of *the* with proper nouns in the following sentences:

He is the Tagore of Telugu poetry.
Hercules is the Bhima of Greek mythology.

These sentences mean:

He is to Telugu poetry what Tagore was to Bengali poetry.

Hercules in Greek mythology is a character like Bhima in the Mahabharata.

9 *The* is used before adjectives in the superlative degree when we make comparisons.

Mont Blanc is the highest mountain in Europe.
He owns the most expensive car in the city.

Omission of Articles

1 *Happiness* is what everyone longs for.
Patience is a great virtue.

Happiness and *patience* are abstract nouns and they do not take an article before them.

But look at the following sentences:

We must work for the happiness of all sections in society.
The patience that he showed was remarkable.

The abstract nouns *happiness* and *patience* in the sentences above take articles before them because they are made specific by the phrases that follow them.

2 Iron is the most useful of all metals.
Air and water are indispensable to man.

The article is not used before mass nouns. But mass nouns take the definite article when they are made specific by the phrase or clause that follows them :

The air in the room is very warm.
The water in our well is not fit for drinking.

3 Note the omission of the article in the sentences in column (1) and their use in column (2) below:

(1)	(2)
Rahul goes to school/ college.	The postman comes to the school at 11 o'clock every day.
David goes to church every Sunday.	Leela went to the church to listen to the music.
The injured man was in hospital for a week.	His friends went to the hospital every day to see him.

The article is not used before nouns such as school, church, bed, hospital, when their primary purpose (study, attending service, treatment for illness, etc.) is referred to, as in column (1). But it is used when these nouns are referred to as places, as in column (2).

4 Man is a social being.
Is woman really the weaker sex?

The article is omitted before *man* and *woman* when used in a general sense.

5 In the examples given below the article is omitted before both the nouns used in pairs:

They are brother and sister.
Father and son are both blind.
The play was interesting from beginning to end.

6 The article *the* is omitted before the nouns in the phrases below:

He invited me to lunch/tea/dinner.

7 Collective nouns such as *humanity*, *labour*, *mankind*, *posterity*, *society*, don't usually take an article.

Society must be concerned with all its sections.
The saint's daily prayer was for the welfare of humanity.

8 What sort of person is he?
What type of house does he live in?

The article is omitted after expressions such as *sort of*, *type of*, *kind of*, *manner of*.

9 The article is not used in these phrases:

by bus	by plane	by messenger	by car
by sea	by post	on foot	by train

Exercise 1

Fill in the blanks with *a*, *an* or *the*:

1 Has ——— postman brought anything for me? I am expecting ——— letter from my uncle.

2 There is ——— public meeting in ——— City Hall this evening. ——— speaker has come from Delhi.

3 'Can you tell me how to get to ——— railway station?'

'Yes, take the first turning on the left, walk past ——— post-office and take the second turning on ——— right. ——— station is just about 200 metres down that road.'

4 There is ——— red book and ——— green book on ——— table in ——— library. Will you bring me ——— green one please?

5 ——— fire broke out in ——— next street yesterday evening. ——— fire-brigade were fighting it till ——— early hours of this morning.

Exercise 2

Put in *a*, *an*, or *the* wherever necessary and rewrite each sentence:

1 He is poor man. He has wife and children to support.
2 His eldest child is boy of ten; youngest is girl of two.
3 Everyone likes kind of salesman who is polite to customers.
4 Andamans are group of islands in Bay of Bengal.
5 We travelled by plane at night, flying very high. The view from sky was splendid. It was thrilling experience.
6 What happens to all money he earns is a mystery to us.
7 I went to borrow book from library, but librarian was on leave.
8 A number of accidents in city were reported in papers last week. Man was run over by lorry. Woman lost her life in fire. Student fell from moving bus.

5 PRONOUNS

Look at this passage:

> Mr Chaturvedi is a district judge. Mr Chaturvedi is due to retire in March. The staff are planning to give Mr Chaturvedi a fitting send-off. The staff also propose to have Mr Chaturvedi's portrait unveiled.

We can see that this passage makes tedious and clumsy reading. Why? Because Mr Chaturvedi's name is repeated so many times.

Now read the following:

> Mr Chaturvedi is a district judge. *He* is due to retire in March. The staff are planning to give *him*

a fitting send-off. They also propose to have *his* portrait unveiled.

The passage now reads better. Why? Because the repetition of Mr Chaturvedi's name has been avoided by the use of the words *he*, *him*, *his*. Words of this kind are called **pronouns**. Pronouns stand for nouns.

Pronouns are of different kinds.

Personal Pronouns

1 Personal pronouns are those pronouns which stand for what are called the three *persons* in English grammar.

	Singular	*Plural*
First person: the person(s) speaking	I	We
Second person: the person(s) spoken to	you	you
Third person: (an) other person(s) or thing(s)	he, she it	they

The personal pronouns, except *you* and *it*, have one form when they are subjects, and another form when they are objects or when they come after prepositions.

Subject	*Object*	*Subject*	*Object*
I	me	they	them
we	us	you	you
he	him	it	it
she	her		

2 Names of animals taken in general are usually treated as neuter nouns and are referred to by *it*.

The camel has a hump on *its* back.

When the sex of an animal is not specified, it is referred to by the masculine pronoun.

We saw a lion at a distance. He was staring at us with a steady gaze.

When the sex is thought of or specified, or when the word denotes sex, the appropriate pronoun (masculine or feminine) is used.

We saw a lioness in the forest. There were five cubs near *her*.

3 Names of lifeless objects are usually neuter, but nouns denoting cars, locomotives, ships, aircraft, etc. are often referred to by feminine pronouns.

> 'Is the Bombay train late today?' 'Yes, *she* is.'
> The *I.S.S. Jaladurga* arrived in port this morning. *She* has brought a cargo of rice from Burma.

4 *She* and *her* are sometimes used with reference to lifeless things such as the moon, the sea, the earth and one's country, and ideas such as Nature, Fortune, Science, Liberty, Mercy, Peace, etc.

> Nature has blessed our country with all *her* bounty.
> Peace has *her* victories no less renowned than war.

5 You and I will have to do the work.
He and I are working on a project.
You and he are both welcome.

Note the order in which the two pronouns have been used in each of these sentences. *I* follows *you* and *he*; *he* follows *you*.

Possessive Pronouns

Study the possessive forms (in the second and third columns) of the personal pronouns in the first column:

I	—	my	—	mine
we	—	our	—	ours
you	—	your	—	yours
he	—	his	—	his
she	—	her	—	hers
they	—	their	—	theirs
it	—	its	—	..

The forms *my*, *our*, *your*, *his*, *her*, *its* and *their* are determiners. They are also called possessive adjectives. The forms in the third column function like pronouns and are called **possessive pronouns.**

Examples of use:

> Please lend me your pen. *Mine* has no ink in it. (*Mine* here means *my pen*).

This is Mr Gobind's house. *Ours* is at the end of this street.

It is my turn now; *yours* is over.

The form *its* is used only as a determiner and not as a pronoun.

This lock is for the box. Here is *its* key.

We don't say, 'This key is *its*.'

Here are some idiomatic uses of pronouns:

1 His is a special case.
(*His* here means *his case*).

2 With kind regards, Yours sincerely, etc.
(Used at the *end of* letters).

3 He has a small house of his own.

The use of 'it'

1 *It* and *its* are used to refer to lifeless things.

2 *It* may refer to animals; it suggests less familiarity than *he* or *she*.

The bird is flying to its nest.

3 It may refer to the whole of a preceding statement.

He has failed again. I expected it. (=his failing again)

4 *It* can be an impersonal pronoun, supplying a subject for various verbs.

It is ten o'clock now.
It is my turn now.

5 *It* is common as an introductory subject, standing for a clause, an infinitive or a gerund.

It is not clear *why he wants to resign.*
It is better *to leave* him to himself.
It is no use *asking* him the reason.

6 Look at these sentences:

It is I who wanted it.
It is they who wanted it.
It is Ram who broke the news to me.

It is used here as an introductory subject to emphasise the noun or pronoun following: *I, they, Ram.* *It* in such sentences can stand for all numbers, all genders and all persons.

Exercise 1

Fill in the blanks with appropriate personal pronouns, each in its correct form. Some of the blanks are to be filled in with determiners, i.e. *my*, *your*, etc.

1 Ravi, Sashi and Shyam visited ———. I had tea with ———. ——— left after an hour.

2 Ravi and ——— are in the same class. We sit on the same bench.

3 'We expect *you* and ——— wife at the wedding. Don't disappoint ———.'
'I shall certainly come, but I am sorry ——— wife can't. ——— is leaving for Bombay tonight.'

4 RAVI: Could ——— lend me your motor bicycle, Shyam?
SHYAM: What happened to ——— ?
RAVI: ——— is with the mechanic for repairs. I will get ——— back only tomorrow.
SHYAM: What is wrong with it?
RAVI: ——— chain has snapped.

5 Asha and Uma have invited a friend of ——— to dinner. They have told ——— mother about it.

Pronouns: 'self' form

1 *Reflexive Pronouns*

Look at these sentences:

I have to blame *myself* for this mistake.
He washed *himself* at a roadside well.
Put *yourself* in my position and say what you would do.
They found *themselves* in great difficulty.

In the sentences above, *myself*, *himself*, *yourself*, and *themselves* are 'self' forms of pronouns, used as objects of verbs and they are called *reflexive pronouns*. In each sentence the object and the subject are the same person or thing. In such sentences the objects are put in the *self* forms.

Here is the full list of reflexive pronouns.

		Singular	*Plural*
First person	..	myself	ourselves
Second person	..	yourself	yourselves
Third person	..	himself herself itself	themselves

The reflexive pronoun is also used as the object of a preposition.

He said *to himself* that he had made a mistake.
Don't talk *about yourself* all the time.

Exercise 2

Fill in the blanks with the appropriate '*self*' forms:

1 'I am not thinking of ——— alone. I am thinking of others in the family as well.'
2 The boy wanted all the sweets for ———.
3 Raj and Prem dressed ——— and went to the park.
4 'How dirty you look, Ravi! Go and wash ———.'
5 The wounded lion dragged ——— to his cave.
6 They were always quarrelling among ———.

2 *Emphatic use of 'self' forms*

I offered to drive the car *myself*.
How can you break the rules that you *yourself* have made?

The *self* forms are used in the sentences above to emphasise the nouns they stand for. *I myself* means *I and no one else*; *You yourself* means *you and not anyone else*; The *self* forms used in this way are called *emphatic pronouns*.

Note that the *self* form is never used as the subject of a sentence. Emphatic pronouns emphasise nouns and pronouns which are the subjects of sentences. They do not normally emphasise pronouns in the object position. For instance, we cannot say: *I saw him himself.* However we can say: *I saw the Manager himself.*

Emphatic pronouns are not used to emphasise items such as adverbs. *I shall see him today/tomorrow itself* is not good English.

Exercise 3

Read these sentences:

He repaired his bicycle.
He did not ask anyone to do it.

We can express the idea in these two sentences in one sentence, in the following way:

He repaired his bicycle himself.

Express in one sentence the idea contained in each of the following pairs of sentences, using a suitable *self* form, as shown above.

1 Let us harvest the rice.
Let us not expect anyone to help us.

2 You do the work.
Don't expect anyone to help you.

3 He painted the windows.
He did not ask anyone to do it.

4 I will clean these rooms.
I won't take anybody's help.

5 They built a fence round the house.
They did not seek anyone's help.

Demonstrative Pronouns

Look at these sentences:

This is the bicycle that I bought yesterday.
That is Mr Kannan's house.
The books I bought are *these.*
These saris are less expensive than *those.*

In these sentences *this*, *that*, *these* and *those* are used not as determiners, but as *demonstrative pronouns.*

This stands for *this bicycle.*
That stands for *that house.*
These stands for *these books.*
Those stands for *those saris.*

A demonstrative pronoun may also stand for a whole sentence.

Remember *this*; you have to pay your fees before the tenth of each month.

Indefinite Pronouns

Look at these sentences:

Some are born great; *some* achieve greatness.
'Are there any letters yet to be typed?' 'No, there aren't *any*.'
Anyone can take a horse to the water, but no *one* can make it drink.
'*Someone* called when you were away; he didn't tell me his name.'
None of the boys answered the question.

The words in italics in these sentences are called *indefinite pronouns*. Indefinite pronouns stand for persons or things whose number and identity are not defined.

Other indefinite pronouns are: *somebody*, *anybody*, *anything*, *something* (*the*) *other*, *others*, *another*, *nobody*, *nothing*.

The indefinite pronoun *one* has the meaning of *anyone* in the following example:

What can one do when two doctors give opposite advice?

Pronouns of Number and Quantity

Look at these sentences:

Of the ten guests *seven* were men and *three* were women.
Ten candidates sat for the test; *all* passed.
Not *all* of these are good books; *many* of them are just trash.

The question was so difficult that *none* of the boys could answer it.

Much has been said about overpopulation in the country.

The words in italics are *pronouns of number* or *pronouns of quantity*. The other pronouns in the class are: *more*, *most*, *both*, *few*, *a few*, *little*, *a little*, *several*.

Distributive Pronouns

Look at the pronouns **italicized** below:

Each of Mr Thakur's sons got a share of his property.

Either of the applicants can be appointed temporarily.

Neither of them is qualified for a permanent appointment.

Everyone has his own problems.

Not *everybody* has the time to read books.

The pronouns in italics are called *distributive pronouns*. They are so called because they refer to persons or things considered individually, that is one at a time, and not collectively.

The distributive pronouns are in the singular number. They are therefore followed by singular verbs.

Each may be put in the beginning, middle or end position in a sentence.

Each of Mr Thakur's four sons got a share of his property.

The four sons of Mr Thakur got each a share of his property.

The four sons of Mr Thakur got Rs. 50,000 each.

Reciprocal Pronouns

Look at these sentences:

The two boys helped *each other*.

The members of the family quarrelled with *one another*.

Each other and *one another* express a mutual or reciprocal relationship. They are considered as single units, and are called *reciprocal pronouns* or 'compound personal pronouns'.

Each other is usually used to refer to two persons or things and *one another* to more than two persons or things.

Interrogative Pronouns

Who is the chief guest for College Day?
Which is the road to the hospital?
To *whom* did you give the money? (*Who* did you give the money to?)
Whose is this bicycle?
What have you to say about my suggestion?

The words in italics in these interrogative sentences are called *interrogative pronouns*, because they are used in questions.

The uses of interrogative pronouns

1 *Who*, *whose* and *whom* are used when referring to persons:

Who teaches you English?
Whose is this pen?
Whom did you borrow this book from?

In questions like the last one, we usually use *who* in place of *whom*.

Who did you borrow this book from?
Who are you looking for?

2 *Which* is used when referring to persons and things.

Which of you is Mr Kumar's son?
Which is your seat?

3 *What* is used when referring to things, professions, ideas, words, etc.

What is this idol made of?
What is the meaning of *homogeneous*?
What do you call an unmarried man?
What is your uncle?

Whose, *which* and *what* are also used as interrogative adjectives:

Whose bicycle is this?
Which pen do you like?
What reasons have you for your conduct?

Relative Pronouns

Look at these sentences:

> The gentleman *who* stands there is our new postmaster.
> The parcel *which* my uncle sent me reached me yesterday.
> This is the gentleman *whose* guest I was in Calcutta.
> The boy *whom* I recommended will be seeing you tomorrow.
> The car *that* I bought last month is already giving trouble.

In these sentences *who, which, whose, whom* and *that* are pronouns standing for the nouns before them. The nouns are called *antecedents* and the pronouns are called *relative pronouns.* They relate the adjectival clauses to the main clauses. The forms *which* and *that* are used both in the subject and object positions. The form *who* is used in the subject position and *who* as well as *whom* is used in the object position. The form *whose* is the possessive of *who* and *which.*

Who, whose and *whom* are used generally when the antecedents are persons and occasionally, when, they are pet animals. *Which* is used when the antecedents are animals and inanimate things. *That* is used for persons as well as things.

You can find more about relative pronouns in a later section dealing with relative clauses.

Exercise 4

Fill in the blanks with suitable relative pronouns in their appropriate forms:

1 Tell me the name of the boy ——— won the first prize in the music competition.
2 I am eager to buy back the house ——— my father sold away ten years ago.
3 Uneasy lies the head ——— wears a crown.
4 That is the man ——— pocket was picked.
5 Which is the boy to ——— you lent your bicycle?
6 The two men ——— had escaped from the prison were captured this morning.
7 The warden has a master key with ——— he can open all the rooms in the hostel.

6 ADJECTIVES

Look at these sentences:

A *huge* crowd gathered to hear the Chief Minister.

The Chief Minister made a *long* and *impressive* speech.

Huge, *long* and *impressive* are **adjectives.** Note that they occur between the determiner and the noun: a *huge* crowd, *a* long and impressive *speech*.

A Kinds of Adjectives

1 *Descriptive adjectives*

A *blind* beggar comes to my door every day.
A *cool* breeze blew from the sea.

The adjectives in italics say something about the condition, or quality of the nouns that follow them. Adjectives of this kind are called *descriptive adjectives*.

Descriptive adjectives are of four kinds:

a *Adjectives of quality* indicate the following:

shape: round, square, circular, etc.
size: long, narrow, thick, thin, etc.
colour: red, blue, dark, light, etc.
taste: sweet, bitter, sour, etc.
condition: good, bad, dirty, empty, weak, etc.
behaviour: kind, cruel, gentle, etc.
feeling: hard, cold, smooth, etc.
general impression: pleasant, beautiful, great, etc.

This list, however, is not exhaustive. Several other categories can be added to it. Some adjectives, e.g. *good*, *bad*, *enjoyable*, can belong to more than one kind listed above.

b *Proper* adjectives are formed from proper nouns, by adding certain suffixes or by making some internal changes:

Indian Burmese English

c A noun functioning as an adjective is called an *epithet* adjective:

passenger train; *car* factory; *clay* model; *master* key.

d Present and past participles functioning as adjectives are called *participial* adjectives:

a *sleeping* dog; a *wounded* soldier; *running* water.

2 *Limiting Adjectives*

Look at these sentences:

Bhaskar and Rahim live in the *same* room.
Nirmala bought *two* saris.
These are *my* books.

The words in italics are examples of *limiting adjectives.* They are so called because they limit the scope of the noun. Adjectives of this kind can be sub-divided as follows:

a *Emphasising Adjectives*

This is the *very* man that the police have been looking for.
They saw the *same* film three times.
I saw the accident with my *own* eyes.

b *Quantitative Adjectives*

i Indefinite adjectives:

They played the match on *a* rainy day.
One day a riot broke out in the village.
[This *one* is not a numeral adjective.]
Some words are missing in this paragraph.
I have hardly *any* money.
There are *no* apples in that shop.
Have I made *many* mistakes in the essay?
We haven't *much* time at our disposal.
We have only *a little* time.

[*Note:* ***Many*** **and** ***much*** **are not often used as objects** of affirmative verbs. They are usually replaced by *a lot of* with countables and *a lot of/a great deal of* with uncountables.]

You have made a lot of mistakes in your answers.
We have a lot of/a great deal of time to get there.

All the adjectives listed above except *a* and *no* can be used as pronouns.

ii *little and few*

Look at these sentences:

There is *little* sense in what he says.
Few towns have such a public theatre.

Little and *few* mean ' *almost no* ' or ' *hardly any*'. ' Little sense ' means ' almost no sense ' or ' hardly any sense '; ' few towns ' means ' almost no towns ' or ' hardly any towns '.

Look at these sentences:

I have *a little* milk to spare, I can make some coffee for you.
They have now added *a few* Sanskrit books to the library.

In these sentences *a little* and *a few* mean *not much* and *not many*, but their meaning is positive rather than negative.

c *Pronominal Adjectives*

i Possessive adjectives: *his book*, *their* house, *its* tail, etc.

ii Demonstrative adjectives: *that* man, *those* books, *this* report, etc.

iii Distributive adjectives: *each* boy, *every* town, *either* side, *neither* answer.

Both *each* and *every* mean ' all '. But whereas *each* and *every* refer to persons or things considered individually, *all* refers to persons or things considered as a group.

Either road will take you to the college.

In this sentence *either* refers to any one of two roads. But in the sentence

Trees were planted on either side of the road,

' either side ' means ' both the sides '.

Neither answer was correct

means ' Both the answers were wrong.'

iv Interrogative adjectives: *what* comments, *which* question, *whose* suggestion, *how many* votes, *how much* sugar, etc.

v Relative adjectives:

The man *whose* house we wanted to buy is here.
This is the lady *whose* boxes were stolen.

Certain grammatical items that function as adjectives

There are a number of other grammatical items which can function as adjectives.

a *Gerunds*: *dining* table, *walking* stick, *bathing* ghat, etc. The words in italics are different from participial adjectives in their meaning. *A walking stick*, for example, means not a stick that walks, but a stick used for walking.

b *Adverbs*: *upward* trend, *backward* classes, *outward* appearances etc.

c *Compound participles*: *old-fashioned* tie, *panic-stricken* people, a *hard-hearted* man.

d Here are some more examples of several words put together to form compound adjectives:

a duty-free article   my next-door neighbour

B Adjective: Attributive and Predicative Use

1 Look at these sentences:

That girl has *lovely* eyes.
Mr Jaleel is a *clever* lawyer.

The words in italics are adjectives which state the attributes of the nouns that follow. They usually appear between the determiner and the noun.

Now look at these sentences:

Mr Jaleel is *clever.*
Kamala is very *pretty.*

The adjectives in these sentences come after the verbs in the sentences and form part of the predicate. They are subject complements, since they are related to the subjects.

Look at these sentences:

He made his wife *miserable.*
I found him *efficient.*

In these sentences too the adjectives are used predicatively, but they are object complements because they relate to the objects in the sentence.

Some adjectives are not used attributively.

We say: He is ill.
We do not say: He is an ill man.

Similarly

We say: The child was afraid.
We do not say: He was an afraid child. (We should say: He was a frightened child.)

Ill, however, is used attributively in the following examples.

ill health, ill will, ill temper, ill luck.

Note that the following words are adjectives though they look like adverbs.

manly (manly behaviour), kingly (kingly generosity), friendly (friendly treatment), kindly (adj. & adv.) (kindly attitude). womanly (womanly modesty), heavenly (heavenly bliss), earthly (earthly possessions).

2 *Positions of Adjectives*

Adjectives usually stand before the nouns they qualify, but sometimes they are put after the nouns.

a We discussed all matters, *secular and religious.*
We serve all people, *big or small, rich or poor.*

Note that the adjectives coming after the nouns in these sentences are separated by commas from the rest of the sentence. This is so when there are two or more of them. When there is only one adjective following the noun, no comma separates it from the noun.

This is the only *answer possible.*

b Adjectives qualifying indefinite and distributive pronouns always come after them:

He always does *something useful* in his spare time.
Anyone interested is welcome to the meeting.
Everything necessary will be done.

3 *Adjectives: Order of use*

When a number of adjectives are used to qualify a noun they have to appear in a certain order. The order is:

all/both, pronominal adjectives, adjectives of number, adjectives of quality, shape, size and colour, proper adjectives, epithet adjectives.

Examples:

a long blue ribbon (not 'a blue long ribbon')
three beautiful round red bowls
my very useful heavy black steel trunk
all my favourite new American gramophone records.

Exercise 1

Fill in the blanks with suitable adjectives:

1 A: Can you tell me —— road will take me to the college?
B: You see those two roads. —— road will take you there. You can take the one or the other.

2 Warden: Have you —— complaints against the food?
Student: We have —— complaints at all against the food. What we ask for is —— changes in the timings.

3 There weren't —— grammar mistakes in your composition; there were just one or two. But there were far too —— spelling mistakes.

4 The weather was very bad and —— people attended the meeting.

5 —— man is perfect. —— man has some fault or other.

4 *Adjectives used as other parts of speech*

a *The deaf* and *the dumb* deserve our sympathy.
The wounded were rushed to hospital.

Some adjectives such as those above are turned into nouns by putting the definite article before them. Other examples: the rich, the poor, the accused, the following.

b *Much* has been said about the large scale pollution of the earth.
Little is known about the true origin of the universe.

The words in italics are adjectives used as pronouns.

C Comparison of Adjectives

1 *Degree of Comparison*

When we talk about qualities or quantities or numbers of different persons or things, we often compare them.

Look at these sentences:

a Mohan is a tall boy.
b Ashok is taller than Mohan.
c Kannan is the tallest of all in the group.

In these sentences the tallness or height of three boys, Mohan, Ashok and Kannan, is the point of comparison. In sentence (a) you are just told that Mohan is tall, but no comparison is made with the height of anyone else. An adjective used without any comparison is said to be in the *positive degree.*

In sentence (b) comparison is made between the heights of Ashok and Mohan and the word *taller* is used to indicate this. An adjective like *taller,* used to compare only two persons, things or qualities, is said to be in the *comparative degree.* It is usually followed by *than.*

In sentence (c) more than two boys are compared and the word *tallest* is used to indicate that of all the boys in the group Kannan has the greatest height. An adjective form like *tallest,* used to compare more than two persons or things or qualities, is said to be in the *superlative degree.* It is usually preceded by the definite article *the.*

Look at this sentence:

Raju is stronger than Balu.

Note that what the sentence does is only to compare the strength of Raju with that of Balu. It does not necessarily mean that Balu is very strong.

Similarly,

It is safer to send important letters by registered post than by ordinary post.

The comparison here implies that ordinary post is not so safe as registered post.

2 *Formation of Degrees of Comparison*

a Adjectives of one syllable and a few adjectives of two syllables which do not end in /e/ form the comparative degree by adding /er/ to the positive form. They form the superlative degree by adding /est/.

Positive	*Comparative*	*Superlative*
high	higher	highest
tall	taller	tallest

b When an adjective ends in /e/ only /r/ and /st/ are added.

Positive	*Comparative*	*Superlative*
brave	braver	bravest
sure	surer	surest

c When an adjective ends in a single consonant with a short vowel before it, the final consonant is doubled and /er/ and /est/ are added.

Positive	*Comparative*	*Superlative*
hot	hotter	hottest
thin	thinner	thinnest

d When an adjective ends in /y/ and is preceded by a consonant the /y/ changes into /i/ and then /er/ and /est/ are added.

Positive	*Comparative*	*Superlative*
easy	easier	easiest
holy	holier	holiest

e If instead of a consonant a vowel comes before /y/ then /y/ is not changed to /i/.

Positive	*Comparative*	*Superlative*
gay	gayer	gayest
gray	grayer	grayest

f Adjectives of two syllables which do not take /-er/ or /-est/, and those of more than two syllables form the comparative degree by taking *more* and the superlative degree by taking *most* before them.

Positive	*Comparative*	*Superlative*
beautiful	more beautiful	most beautiful
difficult	more difficult	most difficult

g There are certain irregular ways of forming the comparative and superlative degrees which you have to commit to memory.

Positive	*Comparative*	*Superlative*
good	better	best
bad, ill	worse	worst
little	less	least
many, much	more	most
far	farther	farthest
	further	furthest
old	older	oldest (of people & things)
		eldest (of people only)
northern	—	northernmost
top	—	topmost
bottom	—	bottommost

h There are a number of adjectives which are not gradable, that is, they do not usually have any degrees of comparison.

round, perfect, unique.

i Some comparative adjectives are followed by *to* in place of *than*.

This wood is superior to that.
This cloth is inferior to that.
Mr Kamath is senior to Mr Pai.
Mr Pai is junior to Mr Kamath.

These adjectives have only their comparative form.

j Look at these sentences:

We had a most enjoyable time.
His behaviour was most unfortunate.

In these sentences the superlative is used either with the article /a/ or with no article. It is not used with the article *the*. There is no idea of comparison in these sentences. The first sentence means, for instance We had an extremely enjoyable time. A superlative of this kind is called ' the superlative of eminence'.

3 *Constructions with Comparisons*

a When we make a comparison with the positive form of an adjective, we use ' as, ... as,' if the sentence is affirmative.

Raju is as tall as Ravi.

When the sentence is negative we use ' not so/as . . . . . as.'

Kamala is not so/as tall as Asha.

When we use the comparative form of an adjective we use *than*.

Asha is taller than Kamala.

b When we make a comparison of more than two persons or things we use the superlative:

Sanjay is the tallest boy in the class.

Sanjay is the tallest of all the boys in the class.

Note the difference between *the tallest boy in the class* and *the tallest of all the boys in the class*. In the second phrase *the tallest* functions as a noun phrase meaning *the tallest boy*.

c Study the way the sentences are constructed in each set below. The three sentences in each set express the same idea.

i Sanjay is the tallest boy in his class. (superlative degree)

Sanjay is taller than all the other boys in his class. (comparative degree)

No other boy in the class is so/as tall as Sanjay. (positive degree)

ii Of all the boys in the class Sarin makes the fewest mistakes. (superlative degree)

Sarin makes fewer mistakes than any other boy in the class. (comparative degree)
No other boy in the class makes as few mistakes as Sarin. (positive degree)

d Note the difference in meaning between the following pairs of sentences:

Superlative degree

Australia is *the biggest* island in the world. (No other island is equal to Australia in size). Sri Lanka is *one of the biggest* islands in the world. (There are only a few other islands in the world which are equal in size to Sri Lanka.)

Comparative degree

Australia is *bigger than all other* islands in the world.
Sri Lanka is *bigger than most other* islands in the world.

Positive degree

No other island in the world is as big as Australia. Only some (a few) islands in the world are *as big as* Sri Lanka.

e Look at this sentence:

Prema is not taller than Padma. (comparative degree)

This sentence expresses a negative comparison using the comparative degree. When we put this in the positive degree, the comparison has to be expressed as:

Padma is at least as tall as Prema.

Similarly,

Sri Lanka is not the largest island in the world.
(Negative comparison using the superlative degree)

When we put this in the positive degree, the comparison has to be expressed as:

Some islands in the world are at least as large as Sri Lanka.

When we put this in the comparative degree the comparison has to be expressed as:

Some islands in the world are bigger than Sri Lanka.

4 *Use of some Comparatives and Superlatives*

a *Elder, older*

Older is the normal comparative form used for comparing age and it is followed by *than.*

Our school is older than all the other schools in the city.

Elder cannot be followed by *than,* and is used exclusively in connection with human family relationships.

Ravi is the elder of his two sons.
He is my elder brother.
He is elder to me.
Mr Thakur's eldest son is a doctor.
Of his three sons, Ramesh is the eldest.

Note that *elder* may be used as a noun in the singular and plural.

Ram was Lakshman's elder.
Respect your elders.

(*Older* cannot be used as a noun).

b *Farther, further, farthest, furthest*

Most people prefer *further* for all meanings. *Farther* is common when distance is referred to.

I will take a decision after gathering further information. (additional)
Nampally station is farther from my house than Secunderabad station.
That is the farthest you can go in a train.

c *later, latest, latter, last*

Later means further beyond the set time: 'more late' in time (It is the normal comparative.):

I cannot wait later than Sunday.

Latest means 'last up to now':

The latest news from the war front is encouraging.

Latter: This is used in the phrase 'the latter' (of two things) and means the second in the order:

The teacher gave me two books, one by Mr Shah and another by Mr Dave. I found the latter more interesting.

Similarly, *the former*:

I didn't like the former very much.

last: This is used in the sense of *final*.

The last train leaves at 11.30 in the night.
Last week/month/year: The week, month, year before the current one.

nearest*, *next

Nearest is used to express distance:

Which is the nearest railway station from here?

Next is used to express position:

My house is next to the Town Primary School.

Exercise 2

Fill in the blanks, choosing the right word from those given in brackets:

1 I am ——— than Sridhar. (elder, older)
2 This book is of ——— use to me, so I am returning it. (a little, little)
3 Vinod is much senior ——— me. (than, to)
4 Mr Menon was the ——— speaker on the resolution. (last, latest)
5 I have said enough about the subject and I don't wish to say anything ———. (farther, further)
6 'May I ask ——— questions on the subject brought up by you?' (a few, few)
7 'Did you hear the ——— news about the strike?' (latest, last)
8 The post-office is ——— to the co-operative store. (next, nearest)

Exercise 3

Express the meaning of each of the following sentences using the degrees of comparison other than the one you find in it:

1 Bombay is one of the biggest cities of India.
2 Many people think that the mango is the best fruit.
3 Abdulla is at least as fast a swimmer as Kesav.
4 This is the most welcome news I have had this year.
5 Ooty is colder than Coonoor.
6 Very few boys in the class are as brilliant as Raghu.
7 Leela is not a better dancer than Syamala.
8 These compositions are better than the ones you wrote earlier.
9 A foolish friend can be more dangerous than a wise enemy.

D Adjectival Phrases

Look at these sentences:

The watchman *at the gate* did not let the boys in.

The milk *inside the coconut* is sweet and refreshing.

The words in italics in these sentences are phrases that function as adjectives. Each of the phrases qualifies the noun before it. These phrases are called *adjectival phrases.* They usually come after the nouns they qualify.

Each of the adjectival phrases can be expanded into an adjectival clause.

The watchman *who was at the gate* did not let the boys in.

The milk *which is found inside the coconut* is sweet and refreshing.

7 THE VERB

1 Look at these sentences:

The baby *cried.*
The baby *was* ill.
The baby *had* temperature.

The words *cried*, *was* and *had* are verbs which, together with the words that follow them, form the predicates of these sentences.

Verbs tell us what the subject *does*, *did*, *has done*, etc. or what the subject *is*, *was*, *has been*, etc. or what the subject *has*, *had*, etc. Or it may tell us what happened to the subject: The baby *was given* some milk; or what will happen to the baby: The baby *will be examined* by the doctor.

2 Look at these sentences:

Birds *fly.*
The baby *broke* the doll.

In these sentences *fly* and *broke* are verbs used without any helping verbs going before them. They are called 'main' verbs.

Look at these sentences:

Some birds *can fly* long distances.
You *may play* for some time.
The doctor *will examine* the baby today.

In these sentences each of the main verbs takes another kind of verb before it: *can*, *may*, *will*. These verbs are called *auxiliary* or *helping* verbs. Auxiliaries give a special meaning to the main verbs they go with.

The verb together with the auxiliary is called a *verb phrase.*

There are, therefore, two classes of verbs in English:

a Auxiliaries, such as *can*, *may*, *will*, *must*, *have*, etc.
b Ordinary verbs such as *fly*, *go*, *break*, *shoot*, etc.

3. **Intransitive Verbs**

a Fire *burns.*
The sun *rose.*

These verbs do not require objects. They are called **intransitive verbs.**

b This book costs *ten rupees.*
Mr Pillai weighs *seventy-six kilograms.*
He ran *six kilometres.*
The play lasted *an hour.*
The room measures *twelve by twelve.*
The forest stretched *several kilometres.*

The verbs in these sentences are also intransitive. They do not take any objects. The phrases that follow them are *complements*, that is, they are phrases which are needed to complete the meaning. These complements are called *adverbial complements* because they function somewhat like adverbs.

4 Linking Verbs

a Kamala *is* a student in the B.A. class.
The child *appears* happy.
That child *seems* restless.
This vegetable *tastes* bitter.
His excuse *sounds* strange.

In these sentences the words that follow the verbs are subject complements. The verbs act as links between their subjects and the complements. Verbs of this kind are called *linking verbs*. The verbs in the sentences above denote a certain state or steady condition. They are therefore called *stative* linking verbs. Here are some other verbs in this class:

They *feel* worried.
The books *lay* scattered.
He *looks* satisfied.
I *remain* unconvinced.
Rest assured.

Since these verbs are stative in nature, they are generally not used in the present progressive tense. Sentences such as the following are unacceptable:

I am remaining unconvinced.
Kamala is being a student in the B.A. class.

He is *becoming* weaker and weaker.
She is *growing* old.
They *got* ready for the journey.
The milk *turned* sour.

The verbs in the sentences above are linking verbs of another kind. They denote a process or a change in the person or thing mentioned in the subject. They are called *dynamic* linking verbs and they can be used in the present progressive tense.

c He is *weak*.
He grew *tired*.
He looks *disappointed*.
She appeared *helpless*.

In these sentences the subject complements are adjectives.

Look at these sentences:

He is a *student* in the P.U.C.
Dhanraj became a *brigadier* in the Army.
He looks a *gentleman*.

In these sentences the subject complements are nouns.

Exercise 1

Fill in the blanks with suitable adjective complements. Number 7 is done for you as an example.

1 The boys walked all day; they grew —— towards evening.
2 Whenever I eat in a hotel, I fall ——.
3 It is autumn and the leaves are turning ——.
4 A: Why does he look so ——?
B: He went in to bat and
5 With a small salary and a big family to support he remained —— all his life.
6 Call a rose by any other name, still it smells ——.
7 His suggestion sounds ——; let's give it a trial.
Complement: practical.

Exercise 2

Fill in the blanks with appropriate linking verbs:

1 Is something wrong with you? You don't ——— well.

2 Uncle has promised to take us to the pictures and he will be here soon. Let's ——— ready.

3 Please let me go, Mother. ——— assured I'll be back home before nine.

4 I have heard all your arguments, but I ——— as unconvinced as before.

This dish ——— very nice.

5 Transitive Verbs

a Look at these sentences:

The Principal hoisted *the flag* on Independence Day.
Professor Sharma will inaugurate *the College Union.*
Nehru liked *children* very much.
My father has written *a novel* in Hindi.

In each of these sentences the verb takes an object (given here in italics). A verb that takes an object is called a **transitive verb.** The object usually answers the question *what?* or *whom?*

b There are a number of verbs which can be used with or without objects, that is, 'transitively' or 'intransitively'.

Here are some examples:

Intransitive use	*Transitive use*
My father is reading.	He is reading the newspaper.
The cup broke.	Gita broke the cup.
Our team won.	Our team won the match.
The play ended at five.	Rain ended the play.

c Transitive verbs can be 'stative' or 'dynamic'. Look at these sentences:

He knows his subject well.
I understand your difficulties.
I see the point.
He realises his mistake.
He owns a car.

The verbs in these sentences have each an object and are transitive verbs. But they are stative in meaning, that is, they describe a certain state. They are therefore called 'stative transitive verbs'. We do not generally use these verbs in the present progressive tense.

Look at these sentences:

We are visiting the zoo tomorrow.
He drives his car himself.
The enemy attacked the fort.
The Minister for P.W.D. is inaugurating the bridge.

In these sentences the verbs express something dynamic, something in progress. They can be used in the present progressive tense.

d Look at the sentences in this table:

Subject	*Verb*	*Indirect object*	*Direct object*
Father	bought	me	a bicycle.
Mr Yadav	found	his daughter	a rich husband.
Balu	gave	the door	a kick.
	Buy	me	some paper.
He	got	us	a good house.
The college	awarded	Mohan	a scholarship.

In these sentences the noun phrases in the last column answer the question 'what'. These are called *direct objects.* The nouns or pronouns in the third column answer the question 'To whom?' or 'For whom?'. They are called *indirect objects.*

The indirect object comes immediately after the verb and the direct object comes after it. If you want to put the indirect object after the direct object, you will have to put *to* or *for* before it, and the order is changed.

Examples:

Mr Yadav found a rich husband *for* his daughter.
The college awarded a scholarship *to* Mohan.

e Look at these sentences:

The students elected Prasad captain.
We painted the doors yellow.
The judge pronounced the accused guilty.

In these sentences the verbs are transitive and take objects. But in addition to the objects they take complements (nouns or adjectives). These complements refer to the objects and are therefore called *object complements*.

f He *explained* his reasons *to* me.
He *said* nothing *to* his father.
He *described* the accident *to* the police.

The verbs in the sentences above belong to a group of transitive verbs which take the indirect object only with the preposition *to* or *for*. We cannot say, for example:

He explained me his reason.
He said his father nothing.

Exercise 3

Rewrite the following sentences putting the indirect object next to the verb, without *to* or *for*.

Examples

Give the pen to me.
Rewritten: Give me the pen.
Buy a ticket for me.
Rewritten: Buy me a ticket.

1 Can you do a favour for me?
2 Tell everything to me.
3 I have sent two parcels of books to my brother.
4 I have sent my umbrella to Radha.

5 Get a cup of coffee for the patient.
6 Could you get a job for my son in your office?

Phrasal Verbs

Look at these sentences:

The plane *took off* after repairs.

He *gave up* smoking, on the doctor's advice.

Note that each of the verbs in the sentences above has an 'adverb particle' attached to it, *off*, *up*, in the examples above. The verb and the adverb particle together form a 'phrasal verb'. Each phrasal verb forms a single meaning unit.

For example: in the sentences above 'took off' means 'left the ground and went up in the air'; 'gave up' means 'stopped'.

Phrasal verbs can be transitive or intransitive:

Examples of transitive phrasal verbs:

blow up : The soldiers blew up the bridge to stop the enemy from advancing.

bring about : The Principal brought about several changes in the college administration.

bring up : An old woman brought up the orphan child.

called off : We called off the match because of rain.

carry out : 'You must carry out my orders and not question them.'

close down : Mr Lal has closed down his business, because of heavy loss.

come across : I came across this story in a foreign magazine.

cut off : His electricity was cut off when he failed to pay his electricity bills.

draw up : The college management has drawn up plans for a new building.

find out : I could not find out what was wrong with my radio.

get back : I got back my lost umbrella.

keep up : The audience kept up the cheering for several minutes.

leave out	:	I left out two questions, because they were difficult.
let in	:	No one was let in without a ticket.
let out	:	He opened the cage and let out the bird.
look after	:	An old woman looked after the children when their mother was in hospital.
look for	:	We are looking for a good building for the new school.
look up	:	We look up the meanings of new words in a dictionary.
make out	:	I couldn't make out the writing on the stone.
make up	:	He made up a false excuse for his absence from duty.
pick out	:	The child was asked to pick out the toys he wanted.
point out	:	The teacher pointed out the mistakes in Mohan's composition.
put off	:	Don't put off till tomorrow what you can do today.
put on	:	He put on a coat, took a walking-stick and went out.
put out	:	He put out the lights and went to bed.
ring up	:	He rang up the police and told them about the burglary.
see off	:	We went to the station to see off our Principal who was going abroad.
set up	:	The athlete set up a new record in long jump at the National Games.
take down	:	The boys took down the sentences given by the teacher.
take up	:	'I shall take up the next lesson on Monday,' the teacher said.
turn down	:	The company turned down the request of the clerk for an increase in his salary.
turn on/off	:	Please turn off the fan when you leave the room. He turned on the fan and sat in his chair.

wind up	:	He wound up his business owing to heavy losses.

Examples of intransitive phrasal verbs;

back out	:	He promised to support our plan but backed out at the last moment.
break down	:	The machine broke down and the work had to be stopped.
break out	:	An epidemic of cholera broke out after the floods.
fall out	:	Mohan and Ashok have fallen out owing to a silly misunderstanding.
fall through	:	Our plans for a holiday fell through because of my brother's illness.
get away	:	The thief was chased by some persons but got away.
get on	:	He is getting on well in his business.
get up	:	I get up before five every morning.
give in	:	The soldiers inside the fort had to give in when their supplies were exhausted.
go off	:	The gun went off when it was being cleaned.
hold out	:	The soldiers inside the fort held out for many days, in spite of great odds.
look out	:	Look out! There is a child running across the road.
make off	:	The thief made off with a lot of cash.
pull up	:	A police van pulled up in front of the house.
run out	:	We have run out of provisions. We should buy some immediately.
set in	:	Summer has set in, and the days are getting warm.
set off	:	The boys set off on their excursion early in the morning.
set out	:	Mohan's parents have set out on a pilgrimage.
stand out	:	Being a six-footer he stood out in the gathering. The soldiers stood out against the enemy with great bravery.

take off : A helicopter can take off vertically.
turn out : Our fears turned out to be unnecessary.
wear out : Cheap cloth wears out soon.

There are some points to be noted about the use of phrasal verbs.

1 Look at these sentences:

The wind blew off his hat.
They called off the match.
He got back his umbrella.
Mohan left out two questions.

In these sentences the objects of the phrasal verbs are put after the adverb particle. But if instead of nouns or noun phrases we use pronouns as the objects, *the pronouns are put between the verb and the particle.*

The wind blew it off. ('The wind blew off it' is wrong.)
They called it off. ('They called off it' is wrong.)
Mohan left them out. ('Mohan left out them' is wrong.)

Similarly, when we use a self-pronoun, or *this* or *that* as object, it is put between the verb and the particle:

The thieves gave themselves up to the police. ('The thieves gave up themselves to the police' is wrong.)
He gave that up. ('He gave up that' is wrong.)

2 When the object is a noun or noun phrase it can be placed either after the particle or between the verb and the particle:

The wind blew off his hat—The wind blew his hat off.
They called off the match — They called the match off.
Mohan left out two questions — Mohan left two questions out.

But this alternative construction is not suitable for some phrasal verbs.

Examples:

The clerk carried out the instructions. (*not* 'The clerk carried the instructions out.')

He found out the solution after a long time. (*not* 'He found the solution out after a long time.')

3 When the noun phrase is not short but long, it is not put between the verb and the particle. For example, we do not say, 'The wind blew the brown hat which he had bought the day before off.'

Exercise 4

Fill in the blanks in the following sentences with the phrasal verbs given in italics, using suitable pronouns in place of the objects.

Examples:

a Can you *make out* this writing? No, I can't ——— because I don't know the script. *Answer*: (make it out)

b I *rang up* Mrs Rao yesterday. I ——— in the evening. *Answer*: (rang her up)

1 The teacher asked the boys to *take down* the new word. The boys ——— in their notebooks.

2 The dentist *pulled out* two of my teeth. He ——— without causing any pain.

3 Mr Lal's cousin *took over* Mr Lal's business after his death. He ——— last month.

4 He *will get back* the money he has deposited after a year. He ——— with interest at 6% per annum.

5 You *should make up* the time you have lost. You ——— by steady and hard work.

6 The principal has *put up* the marks-list on the notice board. He ——— an hour ago.

8 AUXILIARIES AND MODALS

Primary Auxiliaries

Study the verbs in the sentences in the two columns below:

A	B
Azeez *is* now in Madras.	He *is coming* here tomorrow.
I *have* a lot of modern novels at home.	I *have read* them all.
Do as I tell you.	*Don't disobey* me.
	Do you *know* the answer to this question?

In column A the verbs *is*, *have* and *do* are used as full verbs. In column B they are not used as full verbs, but as 'helping verbs'. They help the main verbs (*come*, *read*, *disobey*) to form certain tenses, or to make questions or commands or to make negative sentences. *Is* is used in the first sentence in column B to form the present continuous tense of the main verb *come*. (Note that *is* is a form of the verb *be*.) *Have* is used in the second sentence to form the present perfect tense of the main verb *read*. *Do* is used in the third sentence to form the negative of the main verb *disobey*. *Do* is used in the fourth sentence to form a question with the main verb *know*.

When used in these ways, the verbs *be*, *do* and *have* are called **auxiliaries** or 'helping verbs'. They are called 'primary auxiliaries.' because they help to form certain important grammatical constructions such as tenses, questions, negative sentences, passive voice, etc.

The forms of '*be*': *be, is, are, am, was, were, being, been.*

The forms of '*have*': *have, has, had, having.*

The forms of '*do*': *do, does, did, doing, done.*

The primary auxiliaries change their form according to the number and person of the subject, as can be seen from the chart below. They have also different tense forms.

	Singular	Plural
First Person :	I am/was. . .	We are/were. . .
Second Person:	You are/were. . .	You are/were. . .
Third Person :	He is/was. . . She is/was. . . It is/was. . .	They are/were. . .

First Person :	I don't/didn't. . .	We don't/didn't. . .
Second Person:	You don't/didn't. . .	You don't/didn't. . .
Third Person :	He doesn't/didn't. . . She doesn't/didn't. . . It doesn't/didn't. . .	They don't/didn't. . .

First Person :	Do/did I. . .?	Do/did we. . .?
Second Person:	Do/did you. . .?	Do/did you. . .?
Third Person :	Does/did he. . .? Does/did she. . .? Does/did it. . .?	Do/did they. . .?

First Person :	I have/had eaten. Have/had I eaten?	We have/had eaten. Have/had we eaten?
Second Person:	You have/had eaten. Have/had you eaten?	You have/had eaten. Have/had you eaten?
Third Person :	He has/had eaten. Has/had he eaten? She has/had eaten. Had/had she eaten? It has/had eaten. Has/had it eaten?	They have/had eaten. Have/had they eaten?

Uses of the Primary Auxiliaries

Be

a *To form the continuous tenses*

Examples:

I *am reading.* (present)
He *was taking* a walk. (past)
They *were making* a lot of mistakes. (past

b *To form the passive voice*

Examples:

He *was elected* President.
You *are excused*.
They *were defeated* in the match.

Do

a *To make verbs negative*

Examples:

I *do not* (don't) *smoke*.
He *does not* (doesn't) *play* tennis.
They *did not* (didn't) *go* to the meeting.

b *To make questions*

Examples:

Does he *play* tennis?
Do you often *go* to films?
Did they *attend* the meeting?

c *To make sentences emphatic*

Examples:

She *does* speak well.
He *did* say this.
They *do* need help.

Have

To form the perfect tenses

Examples:

I *have finished* the work.
You *have made* a mistake.
He *had seen* the man earlier.
We *had had* good rains the previous week.

Modal Auxiliaries

Look at the sentences in this table.

Subject	*Auxiliary*	*Main verb*	
Mohan	can	drive.	
You	may	go and play	now.
He	will	take up	the job.
We	shall	be	in Bombay tomorrow.
He	should	see	a doctor at once.
They	would	want	to attend the party.
We	could	get	to the station well in time.
The plane	might	arrive	late.
You	must	work	much harder.
You	needn't	worry	about this matter.
He	daren't	face	his father.
You	ought	to obey	the rules of the road.
He	used	to play	tennis in the evenings.

The words in the second column of the table above are also 'auxiliaries or 'helping verbs'. They are called *modal auxiliaries*. Together with the main verbs that follow, they express the 'mode' or manner of the actions denoted by the verbs. That is, they express such ideas as ability, probability, possibility, permission, obligation or duty, advisability, etc.

Example:

You may go and play now means 'You are free to go and play now.' Similarly, *Mohan can drive* means 'Mohan has the ability to drive.' *He should see a doctor at once* means 'It is advisable for him to see a doctor at once.'

Note:

1 The modal auxiliary does not change according to the number or person of the subject, as the primary auxiliaries do.

For example:

I *can* drive. You *can* drive. We *can* drive.
He *can* drive. They *can* drive.

2 The modal auxiliary does not stand alone, but always goes with a full verb.

For example: You *must work* much harder.

3 Only the base or the dictionary form of the full verb can be used after a modal auxiliary. For example, we cannot say 'He can driving', or 'He can drove', or 'He can driven'.

But if the primary auxiliary *be* or *have* is put after the modal auxiliary, the main verb can be put in its different forms. For example, we can say: 'He may be *playing*,' 'He could have *said* this.'

Uses of Modal Auxiliaries

Will

a In the sentences below *will* helps in the formation of the future tense.

My brother will leave for Bombay tomorrow.

b In the sentences below *will* expresses willingness.

I will help you as far as I can.
Will you please close the door?
Won't you sit down?

The last two sentences express polite requests.

c In the sentences below, *will* is used to express intention or promise:

I will come as soon as I am well.
I won't speak for more than half an hour.

d In the sentences below *will* expresses determination:

We will fight to the finish.
We will root out corruption.

e *Will* in the sentences below expresses prediction:

If you step on a snake it will bite you.
Water will always find its level.
He will never tell a lie.

Shall

a *Shall* is used to express the future when the subject is *I* or *we*:

I/we shall leave for Bombay this evening.

b He shall report for duty tomorrow.
They shall suffer for this.

Shall in these sentences expresses a command or threat.

c *Shall* I make a cup of coffee for you?
Shall I drop you at the college?

Shall when used in questions with *I* or *We* expresses an offer, or suggestion.

Will is used with *I* or *We* in questions to express futurity.

Will I be all right tomorrow?

Can

a He can speak four languages including French.

The doctor cannot see you now; he can see you only in the afternoon.

Can is used above to express ability, temporary or permanent. It has the meaning *be able to, know how to.*

b You can go home now.
You cannot touch the exhibits.
Can I smoke here?

In these sentences *can* expresses permission. It means *be allowed to, be permitted to.* *Can* is less formal than *may* in this sense.

Can't help is an idiom. It means *can't avoid.*

The children can't help laughing at seeing the fat man.

c Accidents can happen to anyone.
Anyone can make mistakes.

Can here expresses possibility.

May

a You may collect your notebooks.
May I borrow your car?

May here expresses permission. It is more formal than *can*.

b It may rain this evening.
He may not get a good job.

May here expresses possibility.

c May he live long!
May she have good health!

May is used here to express a wish.

Would

a Direct speech: He said, 'I will look into the matter.'

Indirect speech: He said that he *would* look into the matter.

Direct speech: 'I shall send for the doctor,' said Mr Sastri.

Indirect speech: Mr Sastri said that he would send for the doctor.

In these sentences *would* is used as the past tense of *will* or *shall* in indirect speech.

b Once every week he would go for a swim in the sea.
Every morning Gandhiji would go for a long walk.

Here *would* is used to express a habitual or characteristic activity in the past.

c Would you care for a glass of lemonade?
Would you close that door?

Would is used in this way to express a suggestion or a polite request.

d *Would* with *rather* is used to express a wish or preference:

I would rather starve than beg.

I would rather have a glass of water than coffee or tea.

e *Would* is used to express the imagined result of an imagined or supposed condition:

I would build a hospital if I won a lottery.

If I were a cosmonaut, I would take you to the moon.

f *Would like to* is used to express a wish or preference:

I would like to ask you something.
He says he would like to go with you.

Should

a He said, 'The workers shall report for duty on Monday.'

He said that the workers should report for duty on Monday.

Should is used as the past tense of 'shall' in indirect speech.

b People should not tell lies.
You should take regular exercise.

Should is used here to express obligation or advisability. *Should* does not imply compulsion like *must* or *have to*. The statement with *should* is more like advice than a command.

c They should be home by now.
Our suits should be ready by now.

Should is used here to express logical necessity or probability.

d Should I see him, I will speak to him.
Should they play well, they will win.

Should is used here to express probable condition.

e I should like to say (i.e. if you permit me) that I haven't done anything against the rules.

Should is used here to express (a request for) permission.

Might

a He said that the results might appear in the next day's papers.

Might is used here as the past tense of *may* in indirect speech.

b It might rain.
The Chief Minister might visit our town.

Here *might* expresses probability but in a lesser degree than *may*.

c Might I make a suggestion?
Might I have a word with you?

In such questions asking for permission, *might* implies more politeness than *may*.

Could

a He said he could finish the book in a day or two.

Could is used here as the past tense of *can* in indirect speech.

b I could read without glasses until six months ago.
We could buy a good meal for fifty paise twenty years ago.

Could expresses ability in the past. *Could* here means *was/were able to*.

c Could you wait for a few minutes?
Could you tell me the time?

Could is used here to express a polite request.

d If we had the money, we could buy that house.
You could get a first class if you made up your mind to work hard.

Could is here used to express contingent possibility i.e the possibility of something happening under a certain condition.

Must

a The letter must leave by today's mail.
You must see a doctor at once.

Must is used here to express obligation, compulsion necessity or emphatic advice. It means *have to*, *have got to* *be obliged to*. For the past we use *had to*: I told him that he had to finish the work the same day.

But in reported speech we may use *must* instead of *had to*
The teacher said that the boys must bring their textbooks to the class every day.

There are two negatives for *must*:

i *needn't*, or *don't have to*:
You needn't bring your certificates.
You don't have to stay.

ii *Mustn't* means *not permitted to*:
You mustn't walk on the grass.
You mustn't use my bicycle.

b If this is litmus paper, it must turn blue.
There must be a mistake somewhere.

Must is used here to express logical necessity or expectation, something that can be inferred from circumstances. *Must* this sense is not used in sentences with negative or interrogative meanings; *Can* is used instead:

There cannot be a mistake anywhere. Can this be true?

Need

a *Need* is commonly used with *not* in statements. It is used without *not* in questions. *Need not* expresses the idea that *there is no compulsion.* In this sense it is the opposite of *must.*

A: Must I leave tomorrow?
B: No, you needn't.

A: Must I pay the amount in one instalment?
B: You needn't; you can pay it in two instalments.

I need hardly tell you that you are always welcome.

The following examples show the situations in which we use *must, need not* and *must not.*

Obligation	*No Obligation*	*Prohibition*
ou must eat all of it.	You needn't eat all of it.	You mustn't eat all of it.
ou must see him today.	You needn't see him today.	You mustn't see him today.
ou must wait.	You needn't wait.	You mustn't wait.

b Need I wait any longer?
Need I tell you anything more?

Need is used here in interrogative sentences.

c *Need* can be used also in the following types o sentences:

You need answer only six questions.
There is only one thing more I need refer to.

Need as a modal does not have a past tense form. But a a full verb it takes the past tense form:

I needed a hundred rupees for my expenses, but I ha only fifty. (=had need for)

The past tense of need as a modal is expressed as *ne have* or *need not have:*

Need I have come to the party?
You need not have come.

Ought

You ought to obey your parents.
We ought not to speak ill of others.
You ought to be ashamed of yourself for suc conduct.
Ought you to go now?

Ought is used to express duty, or moral or social oblig tion. It is used nearly in the same sense as *should.*

Note that the verb that follows *ought* always takes th *to*-form.

Dare

How dare you say such a thing?
I daren't leave without permission.
Dare we interrupt him?

Dare is used to express fearlessness of any consequence. It means *be brave enough to.*

Dare can also be used as an ordinary verb and mea *have the courage* (to do something):

He did not dare to criticise the government.

The expression *I dare say* means *it seems to me probable likely.*

Used to

a He used to go for a walk every morning; now he doesn't.

He used to visit us every day; now he comes only occasionally.

'Used to' + verb expresses a habit in the past. It doesn't have a present tense form. Habit in the present can be expressed by the use of the present simple tense.

b *Used to be* expresses the existence of something in the past.

There used to be a park in this place long ago.

The negative form of 'used to':

He usedn't (or usen't) to go to films, but now he goes often.

An alternative form heard in conversation is: *didn't use to.*

He didn't use to smoke, but now he does.

'Used to' in interrogative sentences:

Used he to smoke?

Usen't (or usedn't) he to smoke cigars?

Look at these sentences:

He is used to a hard life.

You have to get used to standing in queues these days.

Used to here means 'accustomed to'. It is preceded by *be/seem/get/become*, etc.

Exercises

Fill in the blanks with modals appropriate to the meaning indicated in brackets.

1 You must be leaving now. I ——— meet you at the railway station. (future)
2 You ——— come to the party, won't you? (future)
3 I ——— walk twenty-five kilometres in five hours. (present ability)

4 You ——— leave those papers on my desk and go. (permission)
5 I am afraid the weather ——— not improve for another two or three days. (probability)
6 You ——— be able to see him if you hurried up. (slight possibility)
7 You ——— not hide from them what they should know. (moral obligation)
8 You ——— go (permission), if you ——— (compulsion).
9 If he ——— (ability) come as far as my neighbour's house why ——— (ability) he come to mine?
10 He ——— apologise or face the consequences. (command)
11 You ——— not ask for any more leave for the rest of the year. (prohibition)
12 If you ——— put in a word to the manager, I ——— be very grateful. (polite request)
13 I ——— wait (willingness) if I ———. (obligation)
14 You ——— (duty) take the initiative and do things.
15 You ——— wait (advisability) till you are asked to do something.
16 It ——— rain soon, or the crops will die. (necessity)
17 You ——— not come to see me in my office. It is enough if you give me a ring. (absence of compulsion)
18 ——— we go to Nagarjunasagar for our picnic? (suggestion)
19 He ——— tell his father the whole truth. (absence of courage)
20 Gokhale and Bose ——— sit for hours together talking and Gandhiji ——— sit and listen eagerly. (habitual action in the past)
21 We ——— not go abroad to learn English; we can learn it well right here. (absence of compulsion)
22 I ——— rather stay at home than go for a walk in this weather. (preference)

9 ADVERBS AND ADVERBIAL PHRASES

1 Formation

a Look at the table below:

Adjectives	*Adverbs*
glad	gladly
happy	happily
gay	gaily
cunning	cunningly
ironic	ironically
capable	capably
agitated	agitatedly

The adverbs in the table are formed by adding /ly/ to the corresponding adjectives.

In the case of adjectives ending in /y/, the /y/ is changed into /i/ in forming the adverbs.

In the case of adjectives ending in /c/, /ally/ is added. *Publicly* is an exception. In the case of adjectives ending in /able/ or /ible/, the final /e/ is dropped and /y/ is added. For example: capable – capably; sensible – sensibly.

b deep, early, far, fast, high, hard, late, low, little, much, near.

These words can be used both as adjectives and as adverbs.

Adjective	*Adverb*
This is a fast train.	This train runs fast.
These questions are hard.	He worked hard.
There isn't much water in the tank.	He enjoyed the food very much.

c highly, lowly, lately, deeply, hardly.

These words can be used as adverbs, but with restricted meanings.

Mr Rao was highly praised for his efficiency. (a great deal)

He has been lately indifferent. (recently)

He was deeply moved at the child's condition. (emotionally)

He hardly did any work. (negative meaning)

d *Some Adverb Formations*:

i	*Prepositional Adverbs*	*Adverbs*
	on	onward (s)
	back	backward (s)
	up	upward (s)
	down	downward (s)
ii	*Noun*	*Adverb*
	heaven	heavenward (s)
	earth	earthward (s)
	home	homeward (s)

In d(i) above the suffix *ward* or *wards* is added to prepositional adverbs. In d(ii) it is added to nouns. The suffix *ward* is added to denote direction:

He looked backward.
He looked heavenward.

The suffix *wards* denotes movements, in addition:

He walked backwards.
He went homewards.

2 Uses of Adverbs

a Look at these sentences:

He walked *briskly*.
She sang *delightfully*.

In these sentences the adverbs modify verbs. They add to the meanings of the verbs.

b The children were *unusually* quiet.
He looks *prematurely* old.
This coffee is *too* sweet.
He is *very* weak after his recent illness.

The words in italics are adverbs and they modify the adjectives that come after them.

c ‘There is a school ahead; don't drive *too* fast.’
Meena sang *so* delightfully yesterday.
He spoke *extremely* well.
He spoke *clearly* enough.

In these sentences the adverbs modify other adverbs.

But note: only some adverbs such as those above can modify other adverbs.

d *Frankly*, I don't like his attitude. (=If I am to be frank)

Obviously, you don't agree with me. (=As is obvious)

Personally, I am for your resigning. (=If I may give personal advice)

In short, they have spoilt a good case. (=If we are to put it briefly)

Strictly speaking, you cannot take a seat here. (=If we are to be strict)

The adverbs and adverb phrases above are called ‘disjuncts’. Each of them modifies the whole sentence but is grammatically not connected with it. Each one can be replaced by a clause, as shown in the brackets.

3 Kinds of Adverbs and Adverb phrases

a *Adverbs of Time*

The judge will pronounce the judgement *tomorrow*.
I have to leave *immediately*.

The words in italics are adverbs of time. They are placed at the beginning or the end of a clause, the end position being the more usual.

The words *already*, *still*, *just* and *yet* are also time adverbs. *Already* indicates an action completed in the past:

The results have already come out.
They have already sent for a taxi.

Still shows an action in progress:

The parcel is still on its way.
Raju is still in bed.

Just indicates an action completed in the immediate past:

The consignment has just arrived.

Yet can show action in progress. It means 'up to the time of speaking' and is chiefly used in negative and interrogative sentences:

Hasn't your father completed his book yet?
No, he hasn't completed it yet.

Adverb phrases of time

This week we are going on a study tour.

At the stroke of twelve the Devil appeared and dragged Faustus to hell.

The phrases in italics are adverb phrases of time. So too are *this week/month/year, last month/year, next day/week/month/year, in the year* 1980, *a year ago*, etc.

Adverbs and adverb phrases of time generally take the end position. They may however, take the front position for emphasis, contrast or continuity.

On the 16*th* we were in Bombay and *on the* 20*th* in Delhi.

b *Adverbs of frequency*

During the monsoon, trains *often* run late.

Why are those boys complaining *always*?

It doesn't *usually* rain here in December, but *sometimes* we have a few showers.

He *rarely* gets angry; but when he does, he gets really angry.

Does he *ever* tell the truth?

Sometimes he walks all the way to school.

Adverbs of frequency tell us how often an action is performed or an event happens. These adverbs may occupy the front, mid or end position as seen in the examples above.

c *Adverbs of place*

Wait *here* till I am back.
The ferryman agreed to row us *across*.
The guards walked *up* and *down*.
We returned *home* at eleven.
Leave *aside* your books and come *out*.

These adverbs indicate the place of an action or event or the direction of movement in space.

d *Adverbs of manner*

He works very *hard*, seven days a week.
The speaker spoke *frankly* about the problems that the country faced.
The statue has been *beautifully/superbly/magnificently/attractively* painted.

These adverbs indicate how an action is performed or how an event comes about.

In exclamatory and interrogative sentences beginning with *how*, the adverb of manner comes immediately after *how*:

How *well* he speaks!
How *fast* he can run!

e i *Adverbs of degree or intensity*

It gets *quite* hot in Hyderabad in May.
It is *somewhat* sticky in summer in Kerala.
The days are *rather* warm in May in Bangalore.
It is *pretty* hot in Madras for the most part of the year.
It gets *too* hot here in summer.
All of us were *very* tired.

ii *Adverbs of negation*

He made a *not* very illuminating speech.
He occupies an office of *no* mean dignity.
He *never* writes anything but bills.
I am *no more* interested in this institution.
He is *no longer* employed in that firm.

No longer implies time. Many speakers use *no more* in place of *no longer*.

Adverbs of negation usually stand before the verbs, adverbs or adjectives they modify.

iii *Semi-negative adverbs*

It is *hardly* a kilometre to the station.

I can *hardly/scarcely* see anything without my glasses.
We *seldom* see each other nowadays.
Seldom have I heard such words of wisdom from so young a speaker.

These adverbs occur before the words they modify. Note the subject verb inversion when *hardly*, *scarcely*, *never*, *seldom*, take the front position.

'Never in the annals of human endeavour was so much owed by so many to so few.'

f *Interrogative Adverbs*

Adverbs used for asking questions are called interrogative adverbs.

i *When* do you leave for the States?
How long will you be away?
How early do you get up every day?
How soon can you make these shirts for me?

These are interrogative adverbs of time.

ii *Where* do you live?
Where are they importing rice from?
Wherefrom does he get all this money?

Where and *wherefrom* are interrogative adverbs of place.

iii *How many* members are there on the Board?
How often do they meet?

These are interrogative adverbs of number or frequency.

iv *How* did the interview go off?
How is your father today?

How is an interrogative adverb of manner.

v *Why* didn't he stand for the election?

Why is an interrogative verb of reason.

g *Relative Adverbs*

This is the place *where* the Buddha preached his first sermon.

Could you tell me the reason *why* he resigned?

That was the time *when* rice sold at Rs. 10 a kg.

Where, *why*, and *when* are relative adverbs; they function as connectives that join or relate two clauses.

4 The Comparison of Adverbs

The Comparative and Superlative forms

a With adverbs of two or more syllables the comparative is formed by putting *more* before the adverbs and the superlative by putting *most*; *less* and *least* are used for negative comparisons.

Positive	*Comparative*	*Superlative*
fortunately	more fortunately	most fortunately
satisfactorily	less satisfactorily	least satisfactorily

b In single-syllable adverbs and the adverb *early* we add /er/ and /est/:

fast	faster	fastest
hard	harder	hardest
early	earlier	earliest

c Some adverbs have irregular forms for the comparative and superlative:

well	better	best
ill/badly	worse	worst
late	later	last
little	less	least
much	more	most

a For the positive degree we use *as. . .as* with an affirmative verb:

I work as hard as I can.
The woman spoke as angrily as the man.

b For the comparative degree we use *than*:

The play ended earlier *than* I had expected.
He eats more *than* anyone of us.

c For the superlative we use '*of*' + *noun/pronoun.*

He ran fastest of the six runners.

of + noun can also be implied:

He likes hockey best. (of all games)

Look at these sentences:

He acted most foolishly.
The prince fought most courageously.

Most here means *very* and is called 'the superlative of eminence'. There is no comparison involved.

5 Adverbs and Adverb phrases

Look at the sentences in the two columns below:

A	B
The soldiers fought *very courageously.*	The soldiers fought *with great courage.*
The defeated army surrendered *unconditionally.*	The defeated army surrendered *without laying any conditions.*
I wish to thank you *wholeheartedly.*	I wish to thank you *with all my heart.*
I searched for the missing umbrella *everywhere.*	I searched for the missing umbrella *in all places.*
We waited *very anxiously* outside the operation theatre.	We waited outside the operation theatre *with great anxiety*

The words in italics in the sentences in column A are adverbs. The sentences have been rewritten in column B replacing the adverbs with adverb phrases. This kind of transformation one way or the other is possible with a number of adverbs and adverb phrases.

Exercise 1

Rewrite the following sentences substituting adverb phrases for the adverbs in italics.

1 Mr Satish spoke very *confidently.*
2 He resigned his job *regretfully.*
3 Please wait here, I'll be back *soon.*
4 *Nowhere* can you get oranges so cheap.
5 Why do you look at me *suspiciously*?
6 I met him *accidentally*, at the post office.

Exercise 2

Rewrite the following sentences substituting adverbs for the adverb phrases given in italics.

1 The beggar waited at my door *with patience.*
2 He does any work given to him *with sincerity and earnestness.*
3 He spoke to us *with great indifference.*
4 The boys listened to the talk *with great attention.*
5 He acted *in a thoughtless manner.*
6 He spoke *with great eloquence.*

10 PREPOSITIONS

1 Look at this sentence:

There is a temple on that hill.

The word *on* is a preposition and *that hill* is its object. *On that hill* is a prepositional phrase.

2 Most of the prepositions in English are single-word prepositions such as *in, on, at, for,* etc. They are called 'simple' prepositions. The following is a list of simple prepositions:

aboard	about	above	across
after	against	along	alongside
amid/amidst	among	around	at
before	behind	below	beneath
beside	besides	between	beyond
but	by	despite	down
during	for	from	in
into	inside	minus	notwithstanding
of	off	on	opposite
outside	over	past	per
plus	round	since	than
through	throughout	till	to
toward(s)	under	until	underneath
up	upon	via	with
within	without		

3 The following words are used like prepositions though they look like verbs or adjectives:

except	excepting	barring	concerning
considering	following	including	granted
pending	minus	like	near
save	unlike	worth	plus

4 Complex or Phrase Prepositions

Besides the one-word simple prepositions, there are a number of phrases which are called 'complex' prepositions. Here are some examples:

Adverb + preposition: along with, apart from, as for, as to, away from, on to, out of, together with, up to, such as.

Verb/adjective/conjunction, etc. + preposition: except for, owing to, due to, but for, because of.

Preposition + noun + preposition: by means of, on account of, in comparison with, in accordance with, in view of, in spite of, instead of.

Each complex preposition is a unit that performs the work of a single preposition although it may consist of more than one word or grammatical unit, as seen above.

5 Kinds of Prepositional objects

Prepositions can take different kinds of objects.

Examples:

Spread this carpet on *the floor*. (a noun phrase)
Don't run after *pleasures*. (a noun)
Society has a duty to *the deaf* and *the blind*. (adjectives functioning as nouns)
The play was about *to begin*. (an infinitive)
I am fond of *reading* detective stories. (a gerund)
At *first* he said ' no ' to my request. (adverb functioning as a noun)
The noise comes from *inside that house*. (a prepositional phrase)
He doesn't worry about *what people might say*. (a noun clause)

Positions of Prepositions

A preposition is usually put before the noun it governs. But it is also put in other positions in some constructions.

Examples:

The teacher has a chair to sit on, a piece of chalk to write with, and a table to work at.
This is the book that I told you about.
What price did you sell your books at?
What do they want these benches for?

Notes on some prepositions

beside, besides

Beside means *by the side of*.

The Queen sat beside the King.

Besides means *in addition to*.

Besides a house in the city, he owns a house in the suburbs.

at, in (for places)

In is used for continents, countries, states, cities and large towns.

He lives in Delhi.

At is used for towns. villages, addresses,etc.

He was born at Purulia in West Bengal.
He lives at 12 Market Road, Secunderabad.

A big city can also be treated as a point, when we speak of global distances; in that case, *at* is used.

While flying to London I had a brief stopover at Paris.

on, in, at, by (for time).

At indicates a point of time.

I woke up at 5 o'clock.

In indicates a period of time.

I go for a walk in the morning.
(in summer/in January/in 1972, etc.)

On is also used with a longer period of time such as a day in the week.

He met me on Sunday.

By indicates the latest time before which an action is completed.

He returns from his office by 8 o'clock every day.

between, among

Between is used when we refer to two persons, things, etc.

Sita sits between Kamala and Lata.

Among is used when we refer to more than two persons, things, etc.

The parties quarrelled among themselves.

under, underneath

Underneath is usually used with regard or reference to things.

A sub-inspector works under an inspector.
Tuck this away underneath that box.

Exercise 1

Fill in the blanks with suitable prepositions:

1 The secret ——— success lies ——— hard work.
2 By just putting one's faith ——— fate one cannot hope to gain much.
3 He didn't give any reply ——— my question.
4 His stories are full ——— humour.
5 The Principal will be ——— leave ——— two months ——— the 15th of this month.
6 Some managements find themselves ——— the mercy ——— the trade union leaders.
7 There was an acute shortage ——— food that year ——— account ——— the failure ——— the monsoon.
8 The room was filled ——— the sweet smell of roses.
9 Man does not live ——— bread alone.
10 The municipality is planting trees ——— the main roads.
11 The twins look so exactly alike that you can't distinguish one ——— the other.
12 ——— my way back I will call ——— the hospital and see our friend.
13 Mr Roy lives ——— a house ——— Tambaram.
14 Don't worry ——— finding your way ——— my house. I will write down the instructions ——— full ——— you.
15 Since the prisoner was hard ——— hearing, questioning him ——— detail was not easy.

A number of verbs take certain specific prepositions after them, to be connected to the nouns or noun phrases that are the objects of the prepositions.

Examples:

Look *at* this picture.
He depended *on* his friend's word.

Here are some more examples of *verb+preposition* combinations. The specific objects given after the preposition are only examples.

Verb	*Preposition*	*Object of Preposition*
acquit (someone)	of	a charge, crime, etc.
accuse (someone)	of	a crime, etc.
admit (someone)	to	a course, etc.
agree	to	a plan, suggestion, etc.
aim	at	a position, object, etc.
apologise	to	someone (for a mistake, offence, etc.)
appeal	to	(someone) (for mercy, etc.)
appoint (someone)	to	a post, etc.
arrive	at	a place, a conclusion, etc.
avail (onself)	of	an opportunity, leave, etc.
believe	in	something
bestow (something)	on	someone
boast	of	something
call	on	someone
	at	a house, etc.
	for	an explanation, report etc.
care	for	someone or something
catch up	with	someone
charge (someone)	with	a theft, etc.
compare (someone,)	with	someone or something
(something)	to	someone or something
compete	with	someone
complain	of	a pain, etc.
complain	against	someone or something
comply	with	a request, order, etc.
confide	in	someone
congratulate (someone)	on	something
consent	to	a proposal, etc.
convict (someone)	of	crime, etc.
deal	in	something
depend	on	someone or something
deprive (someone)	of	something
differ	from	someone or something
dissuade (someone)	from	something

Verb	*Preposition*	*Object of Preposition*
distinguish (something)	from	something
do away	with	something
entrust (something)	to	someone
(someone)	with	something
exchange (something)	for	something
furnish (somebody)	with	something
get	through	an examination, etc.
grumble	at	something
guard	against	a danger, etc.
inform (somebody)	of	something
inquire	into	an accident, etc.
insist	on	something or something being done
interfere	in	someone's affairs, etc.
interfere	with	one's studies, etc.
invite (someone)	to	lunch, etc.
laugh	at	something, someone, etc.
live	at	a place
	in	a city
	on	fruits, etc.
	by	something, etc.
long	for	something
look	at	something or someone
look down	upon	something or someone
look forward	to	something
look out	for	something or someone
meddle	with	something, someone's affairs, etc.
object	to	something
part	from	someone
prefer (something or someone)	to	something or someone
present (someone)	with	something
preside	over	a meeting, etc.
prohibit (someone)	from	saying or doing something
put up	with	somebody or something
quarrel	over	something
recover	from	illness, etc.

Verb	*Preposition*	*Object of Preposition*
refer	to	a book, a person, etc.
rely	on	someone or something
remind (someone)	of	something
repent	of	an action
take revenge	on	someone
stand	by	someone
search	for	something
suspect (someone)	of	something
sympathise	with	someone
warn (someone)	against/of	something
yield	to	a temptation, a threat, etc.

Exercise 2

Fill in the blanks with suitable prepositions.

1 My friend reminded me ——— our appointment this evening.
2 The judge convicted the accused ——— murder.
3 The manager approved ——— my suggestion.
4 He wants to dispose ——— his house and build a new one.
5 We should not put up ——— this kind of treatment.
6 Mr Roy, our neighbour, has invited us ——— dinner tomorrow.
7 I must apologize ——— you ——— this mistake.
8 The President congratulated the
its splendid victory.
9 Very young children depend ——— their parents ——— all their needs.
10 The clerks grumbled ——— the low pay they were getting.

A number of adjectives take certain specific prepositions after them, to be connected to the nouns or noun phrases that are objects of the prepositions.

Examples:

The child was afraid *of* policemen.
He was greedy *for* money.
Line AB is parallel *to* line CD.

Here are some more examples of commonly used *adjective + preposition* combinations.

The specific objects given after the prepositions are only examples.

Adjective	*Preposition*	*Object of Preposition*
abounding	in	something
absorbed	in	work, thought, etc.
acceptable	to	someone
accomplished	in	music, etc.
accused	of	a crime, etc.
accustomed	to	something
acquainted	with	a person, a subject, etc.
acquitted	of	a charge, etc.
addicted	to	a habit, etc.
affectionate	to	children, friends, etc.
afraid	of	something
alarmed	at	the news, etc.
alien	to	a culture, one's nature, etc.
alive	to	a danger, etc.
allied	with	a country, party, etc.
	to	something
amazed	at	something
angry	with	a person
	at	something
annoyed	at	something
	with	someone
answerable	to	someone
	for	something
anxious	for	something or someone
	about	something
applicable	to	someone or something
appropriate	to	an occasion, etc.
ashamed	of	something, e.g. bad conduct, etc.
associated	with	something or someone
astonished	at	something
averse	to	something, e.g. hard work, etc.
based	on	something, e.g. evidence, etc.
bent	on	doing something
beset	with	difficulties, dangers, etc.

Adjective	*Preposition*	*Object of Preposition*
blessed	with	prosperity, health, etc.
blind	to	someone's fault, etc.
boastful	of	something, e.g. one's wealth, etc.
born	of	rich, poor, etc. parents
bound	for	a place
busy	with	something
capable	of	something, e.g. hard work, etc.
careful	about	one's health, money, etc.
	with	one's work, etc.
	of	one's health, etc.
certain	of	something, e.g. success
	about	failure, etc.
charged	with	a crime, etc.
clear	of	blame, etc.
committed	to	a course of action, a principle, etc.
common	to	everyone, etc.
comparable	to	something
concerned	about	something
	with	something or someone
confident	of	success, etc.
conscious	of	something, e.g. one's faults, position, duties, etc.
contented	with	something
contrary	to	something, e.g. a rule, an opinion, etc.
convicted	of	a crime
convinced	of	one's innocence, etc.
deaf	to	advice, pleadings, etc.
defective	in	workmanship, etc.
deficient	in	something
delighted	with	one's success, etc.
	at	the news, etc.
deprived	of	one's right, property, etc.
determined	on	some course of action, etc.
devoid	of	something, e.g. good sense, etc.
diffident	of	success, etc.
disappointed	with	someone
	at	something

Adjective	*Preposition*	*Object of Preposition*
disgusted	with	someone or something
disqualified	for	a post, etc.
doubtful	of	success, etc.
	about	what to do, etc.
endowed	with	an ability, etc.
engaged	in	something, e.g. some work
	to	someone
entitled	to	something
envious	of	someone, something
essential	to/for	happiness, etc.
exhausted	with	work, etc.
familiar	to	a person
	with	facts, etc.
famous	for	something
fascinated	by	something
favourable	to	someone
full	of	something
fond	of	something, e.g. music, etc.
foreign	to	something, one's culture, temperament
gifted	with	an ability, etc.
given	to	a habit, etc.
glad	of/about	something, some result, etc.
good	at	something, e.g. drawing, etc.
grateful	to	someone
	for	something
greedy	for	something, e.g. money, etc.
guilty	of	a crime, etc.
harmful	to	something, e.g. health, etc.
heedless	of	consequences, dangers, etc.
honoured	with	something, e.g. an award, etc.
hopeful	of	success, gain, etc.
identical	with	something
ignorant	of	something, e.g. rules, etc.
ill	with	a fever, etc.
impatient	with	someone
	at	something happening, e.g. delay, etc.
	of	something, e.g. waiting for a long time, etc.

Adjective	*Preposition*	*Object of Preposition*
inclined	to	something
indebted	to	someone
	for	something
independent	of	something
indifferent	to	something, some result, etc.
indispensable	to	some task or result, e.g. success in something
infested	with	something, e.g. rats, etc.
innocent	of	something, e.g. a crime
intimate	with	someone
irrelevant	to	something, e.g. a subject or matter in hand
jealous	of	somebody or something
liable	for	something, e.g. someone's debts
	to	a fine, illness, etc.
loyal	to	someone
mad	with	anger, pain, etc.
	about/at	something, e.g. missing the train
	for	something, i.e. wanting it very much
mistaken	for	something or someone
negligent	in	work, etc.
	of	duties, etc.
notorious	for	something bad, e.g. cheating people
obliged	to	someone
	for	something
occupied	with	some work, business, etc.
offended	with	someone
overwhelmed	with	grief, pity, gratitude, etc.
parallel	to	something
partial	to	someone
peculiar	to	someone or something
polite	to	someone
preferable	to	something else
prepared	for	something, some consequence, etc.
proficient	in	something, e.g.music, mathematics
profitable	to	someone

Adjective	*Preposition*	*Object of Preposition*
proud	of	something, e.g. one's learning or wealth
ready	for	something, e.g. an action, an occasion
reduced	to	some state or condition, e.g. poverty
regardless	of	something, e.g. some consequence
relevant	to	some matter or subject
repentant	of	one's mistakes, etc.
repugnant	to	something, e.g. one's caste or creed
respectful	to	someone superior
responsible	to	someone
	for	something
restricted	to	place, person, quantity, etc.
rich	in	something, e.g. natural resources, etc.
sacred	to	the memory of someone
satisfied	with	something, e.g. what one has got
sensitive	to	something, e.g. criticism, etc.
short	of	something needed, e.g. money
silent	about	a matter, etc.
similar	to	something
skilful	in	doing something
slow	at	something, e.g. doing sums
sorry	for	someone
	about	something
subject	to	rules, authority, etc.
sufficient	for	a purpose
suitable	for	a purpose or an occasion, e.g. a picnic, wearing in cold weather, etc.
sure	of	something, e.g. winning, etc.
suspicious	of	someone
vexed	with	someone or some state of affairs.
	at	something, e.g. failure
wanting	in	something, e.g. good manners
worthy	of	praise, etc.

Exercise 3

Fill in the blanks with suitable prepositions:

1 The police are responsible ——— the maintenance of law and order.
2 'I am quite satisfied ——— your work.'
3 The bus ran short ——— petrol and stopped.
4 Tobacco in any form is injurious ——— health.
5 'Be content ——— what you have.'
6 His life was dedicated ——— the service of the poor.
7 The tourist was not familiar ——— the customs of the country.
8 'I am grateful ——— you ——— all your kindness.'
9 He was not acquainted ———the language I spoke.
10 The judgement of the High Court was favourable ——— the government.
11 He was found guilty ——— neglect of duty and was dismissed
12 Is not learning preferable ——— wealth?

A number of nouns take certain specific prepositions after them, to be connected to the nouns or noun phrases that are objects of the prepositions.

Examples:

I have no acquaintance *with* that man.
His capacity *for* hard work seems unlimited.

Here are some examples of *noun phrase + preposition* combinations.

Noun	*Preposition*	*Object of Preposition*
access	to	some place or person
acquaintance	with	someone or something
adept	in	something, e.g. photography
advantage	over	
	of	something
advice	on	some matter
agreement	with	someone
	on	something

Noun	*Preposition*	*Object of Preposition*
alliance	with	someone
anxiety	about	something or someone
	for	something, e.g. knowledge
appetite	for	something, e.g. food
appreciation	for/of	something, e.g. help, poetry, etc.
approach	to	a place, a problem, a subject, etc.
attention	to	something
attitude	toward(s)	something, e.g. one's duty
authority	on	something, e.g. a subject
	for	something, e.g. making a statement
aversion	to	something, e.g. hard work
basis	for	something, e.g. a charge
bearing	upon	some matter
capacity	for	something, e.g. hard work
cause	for	something, e.g. worry, anxiety, etc.
	of	something, e.g. accident
chance	of	something, e.g. success; doing something, e.g. going abroad
choice	of	one thing or another
	between	two or more things, courses of action
collision	with	something, e.g. a transport vehicle, an opposing party, etc.
command	of	army, situation, subject, etc.
comparison	with	something
	between	two things
	of	something *to* something
concern	about	a matter
	for	someone or something
	in	a business, etc.
confidence	in	someone
consequence	of	something, e.g. an error of judgement
contempt	for	someone, something

Noun	*Preposition*	*Object of Preposition*
contrast	between	two things, persons, etc.
control	of	something
	over	someone, or a situation, etc.
craving	for	something, e.g. sweets
cure	for	a disease, etc.
danger	of	something happening
demand	for	something, e.g. higher wages, etc.
descendant	of	someone, an ancestor, a family, etc.
desire	for	something, e.g. food, wealth, etc.
difference	between	two or more things
difficulty	in	doing something
disagreement	with	someone
	on or over	something
discussion	on/about	some subject
disgust	at	something happening, a policy, etc.
distaste	for	something, e.g. film music
distrust	of	someone
doubt	about	something, e.g. the pronunciation of a word, someone's honesty, etc.
duty	to	someone, e.g. one's parents
enmity	to/toward(s)	someone
	with	someone, in the phrase *at enmity with*
esteem	for	someone, e.g. one's teacher
exception	to	a rule, a principle, etc.
excuse	for	doing or having done something
experience	in	something, e.g. nursing
expert	in	something, e.g. foreign affairs, economics, repairing of clocks, etc.
exposure	to	something, e.g. cold, light, etc.
expression	of	some thought, feeling, etc.
	to	something, in the phrase *give expression to.*

Noun	Preposition	Object of Preposition
extent	of	something
facility	for	something, e.g. writing stories, making speeches, etc.
faith	in	a person, a belief, a principle
(in) favour	of	someone
fear	of	something, e.g. snakes, losing money
feeling	toward(s)	someone
	about	some matter
fondness	for	something, e.g. sweets
grasp	of	something, e.g. a subject, a topic, etc.
gratitude	to	someone
	for	something
hope	of	something, e.g. finding something lost
hunger	for	something, e.g. adventure
impression	on	someone, in the phrase *make an impression on*
improvement	of	something or someone
	in	something, e.g. one's spelling
	on	some other thing
influence	on/over	someone
information	about/on	something
interest	in	something, e.g. the fine arts
interference	with	something
invitation	to	a wedding, a dinner, etc.
judge	of	something, e.g. people
knack	for	something, e.g. saying the right things
	of	doing something
knowledge	of	something, e.g. some language
lack	of	something, e.g. money
likeness	to	something or someone
liking	for	something
limit	to	something, e.g. one's tolerance
love	for	something, e.g. music
match	for	something or someone in some skill, etc.

Noun	*Preposition*	*Object of Preposition*
method	of	doing something
motive	for	some action
necessity	for	something
need	of	something, e.g. advice, etc. in the phrase *in need of*
	for	something, e.g. anxiety, a plan, a book
objection	to	something
opinion	on/about	something, e.g. the government's policy
payment	for	something, e.g. a new car
penalty	for	an offence, etc.
pity	for	someone
	on	someone, in the phrase *take pity on*
preference	for	something or someone
prejudice	against	something, or someone, e.g. a new idea, a person, etc.
preparation	for	something, e.g. a journey
prevention	against	something, e.g. a disease
proficiency	in	something, e.g. Sanskrit
progress	in	something, e.g. studies
proof	of	something, e.g. someone's guilt
provision	for	something, e.g. the education of one's children
punishment	for	a crime, etc.
pursuit	of	something, e.g. knowledge
reaction	to	something, e.g. some proposal
recovery	from	an illness, etc.
regard	for	someone
relief	from	some trouble, etc.
relish	for	something, e.g. food, active life, etc.
remedy	for	an illness, etc.
reply	to	some question, a letter, etc. in the phrase *in reply to.*
request	for	something, e.g. leave
resemblance	to	something or someone
	between	two things or persons

Noun	Preposition	Object of Preposition
response	to	something, e.g. an appeal
result	of	something that has taken place
revenge	on/upon	someone, in the phrase *take revenge on*
	for	something done, e.g. an insult
reward	for	something, e.g. an act of honesty
sequel	to	something, e.g. a story, a happening
skill	in	something, e.g. car-driving
stranger	to	a place, or thing, e.g. Secunderabad
substitute	for	something else
suggestion	for	some course of action
superiority	over	someone
surprise	at	something, in the phrase *show/express surprise at*
sympathy	for	someone, some cause, etc.
talent	for	something, e.g. singing
taste	for	something, e.g. painting
	of	something
thankful	to	someone
	for	something
thirst	for	something, e.g. knowledge
tolerance	for	something, e.g. others' opinions
triumph	over	an opponent, a difficulty, etc.
use	of	something
	for	something, e.g. in phrases such as *find a use for, have no use for*
victim	of	circumstances, a trick, etc.
witness	to	something that happens
zeal	for	something, e.g. social service
zest	for	something, e.g. sports

Exercise 4

Fill in the blanks with suitable prepositions:

1 The Minister expressed his concern ——— the people affected by the floods.
2 Our connection ——— that business was severed many years ago.
3 He has no capacity ——— sustained work.
4 'Please pay attention ——— what I am going to say.'
5 'There is an exception ——— every rule.'
6 Fifty members voted ——— favour ——— the resolution.
7 We have no hope ——— finding our lost dog.
8 Raghu is no match ——— Sunil in table-tennis.
9 'Have you any objection ——— my coming in dhoti and shirt?'
10 The clerk made a request ——— a month's leave.

11 CONJUNCTIONS AND CONNECTORS

A Kinds of Conjunctions

1 *Co-ordinating Conjunctions*

Look at the italicized conjunction in these sentences:

a Men *and* women had gathered in large numbers at the meeting.
b He spoke loudly *and* clearly.
c She wore black *and* white beads.

In Sentence (a) the conjunction *and* joins two nouns, 'men' and 'women'; in Sentence (b) it joins two adverbs, 'loudly' and 'clearly'; in Sentence (c) it joins two adjectives, 'black' and 'white'.

Conjunctions like *and* are called *Co-ordinating conjunctions*. Co-ordinating conjunctions join two grammatical units of the same kind — that is, noun and noun, adjective and adjective, adverb and adverb, etc.

Here are some more examples of grammatical units that a co-ordinating conjunction can join:

The frog can live *in water* and *on land.* (two adverbial phrases)

He learnt *to drive* and *to repair* cars. (two verbs)

Boys *who don't attend the test* and *who don't send in a proper leave-letter* will be fined. (two subordinate clauses)

He opened the basket and *out came a big cobra.* (two main or principal clauses)

Here is a list of some other co-ordinating conjunctions and sentences to illustrate their use:

or : Give me a pen or a pencil.
He must obey my order or be prepared for dismissal.

for : I want to see the principal, for I have something to tell him urgently.

but : I wrote to him, but he didn't reply.

still : He worked very hard, still he couldn't get a first class.

yet : He is rich, yet he is unhappy.

so : The patient's condition became bad, so we took him to hospital.

otherwise : You should go by taxi, otherwise you may miss the train.

nor : He has not come to see me, nor has he sent me a message.

neither : He has not come to see me, neither has he given me a ring.

as well as: Ram as well as his brother is studying medicine.

('As well as' is a phrase conjunction.)

2 *Correlative Conjunctions*

Look at these sentences:

I can *neither* read *nor* speak Urdu.

I can't say *whether* he will come *or* not.

He spoke *so* loudly *that* everyone in the hall heard him clearly.

Mr Das's elder son is not *so* clever *as* his younger son.

There was *such* a long queue at the theatre *that* I came away without buying a ticket.

The old man was *both* blind *and* deaf.

Though he is rich, *yet* he is unhappy.

The pairs of conjunctions (in italics) in each of the sentences above are related to each other and are called *Correlative Conjunctions*.

Here are a few more correlative conjunctions with sentences to illustrate their use. Some of these are phrases:

He is *not only* bright *but also* hardworking.

No sooner did the match begin *than* the rain started.

3 *Subordinating Conjunctions*

Look at these sentences:

I didn't think *that* he would come.

Tell me *where* you have put my watch.

He was not told *why* he was arrested.

The boy wanted to know *how* birds fly.

We were shocked *when* we heard the news.

The words in italics in the sentences above are conjunctions which help to connect subordinate clauses to main clauses. They are therefore called *Subordinating Conjunctions.*

Here is a list of other subordinating conjunctions, with sentences to illustrate their use. Some of these are single words and some, phrases:

though/
although : Though/although we invited him personally, he didn't come.

since : Since he was suffering from a fever, he couldn't take the examination.

after : The train started after the engine was repaired.

till/until : No one left the hall until/till the singing of the national anthem was over.

as : Do as I tell you.

because : The match was postponed, because the ground was covered with water.

before : We reached the station before the train arrived.

than : He writes better than he speaks.

if : If you drop it, it will break.

unless : I won't go to the wedding unless I am invited.

while : While the lawyer was arguing, the judge stopped him to ask a question.

whether : Do you know whether there is a flight to Delhi in the morning?

lest : 'Don't go out in the rain, lest you should catch a cold.'

in case : 'Take some more money with you, in case you need it.'

so that : 'I am working hard, so that I may make up for lost time.'

as if : It looks as if it is going to rain.

as long as : 'You can stay in this house as long as you stay in this town.'

as soon as : As soon as the match began, it started raining.

Note that subordinating conjunctions are sometimes put at the beginning of the sentence (as in some of the examples above), that is, when the clauses they introduce are put at the beginning.

Exercise 1

Fill in the blanks with the conjunctions given. You may have to use some of them more than once:

and, yet, but, nor, or, as well as, so, otherwise, for.

1 I am very tired. Give me a cup of coffee ——— tea.

2 There are sixty boys ——— twenty girls in this class.
3 Mohan is tall, ——— his brother is short.
4 We need to have rains very soon, ——— the crops may wither up.
5 His uncle gave him a good education ——— money to start a business.
6 We should be kind to all living creatures; ——— they are all the creations of God.
7 He has never told a lie, ——— will he ever do it.
8 We bought this car only last month, ——— it has started giving trouble already.
9 He didn't send in a leave-letter, ——— he was marked absent.

Exercise 2

Fill in the blank in each sentence below, with the conjunction (single-word or phrase) that pairs with the one italicized:

1 '*Neither* a lender ——— a borrower be.'
2 He says he can't decide *whether* to marry ——— not.
3 The coffee was *so* hot ——— it scalded my tongue.
4 'Nothing is *so* irritating ——— a good example,' said Mark Twain.
5 There was *such* a heavy downpour in the morning ——— the entire playground was covered with knee-deep water.
6 *Both* Mr Das ——— his wife have been abroad.
7 The robbers *not only* robbed the travellers ——— beat them up.
8 *No sooner* did the teacher enter the class ——— the boys stood up.
9 The food in the hostel was ——— very good *nor* very bad.
10 'I'm going to marry this girl, ——— you like it *or* not,' said the young man to his elder brother.
11 'These mangoes are not ——— nice *as* the ones we bought yesterday.'

12 'I have never eaten ——— nice mangoes *as* these.'

13 'I have known ——— Ramu *and* his brother since their boyhood.'

14 He ——— got a first class in his M.A. examination *but also* stood first in the university.

15 ——— had the speaker begun his speech, *than* a man stood up to ask a question.

12 THE TENSES: FORM AND USE

A The verb in a sentence expresses an action or event or state. It also expresses the time to which these belong. That is to say, it tells us whether an action or event took place sometime ago (i.e. in the *past*), or whether it takes place now (i.e. in the *present*) or, again, whether it will take place sometime from now (i.e. in the *future*). The verb shows the time by certain forms it takes. These forms are called the **tense** forms of the verb.

There are four tense forms which English verbs take:

1 The *dictionary or base form*: This is the form which the verb takes in the **present simple** tense. (It is also called the 'bare infinitive' form.)

Examples:

I *walk* five miles a day.
You *speak* too loudly.
They *keep* watch at night.

This form of the verb, however, takes an /s/ after it when the subject of the verb is in the third person singular.

Examples:

He *walks* five miles a day.
She *speaks* English very well.

2 The **simple past** form:

Examples:

He *walked* five miles.
She *spoke* very well.

3 The **present participle** (or -ing form): This is the form the verb takes when it combines with the auxiliary *be* to form the **present continuous** or **past continuous** tense.

Examples:

The children are *playing* in the garden.
Father is *reading* the newspaper.
He was *practising* at the bar.
They were *making* a lot of noise.

4 The **past participle** form: This is the form the verb takes when it combines with the auxiliary *have* to form the *present perfect* or the *past perfect* tense.

Examples:

He has *posted* the letter.
They have *broken* the rules.
We had *seen* the film before.

B Formation of the Simple Past and Past Participle forms

In the case of most verbs in English the past tense and past participle forms are formed by the addition of /d/ or /ed/ to the dictionary (or simple present) form, with a change in spelling in some cases. Such verbs are called ' regular ' verbs.

Here are some examples:

Simple Present	*Simple Past*	*Past Participle*
act	acted	acted
defy	defied	defied ('y' is changed into 'i')
earn	earned	earned
hurry	hurried	hurried
manage	managed	managed
rebel	rebelled	rebelled (consonant doubled)

A large number of verbs form their past tense and past participle forms in other ways. Such verbs are called 'irregular' verbs. There are no rules to guide the learner in finding these forms. He can only learn them by familiarity.

Here are some examples:

Present Tense (Plain form)	*Past Tense* (-ed form)	*Past Participle* (-en form)
arise	arose	arisen
awake	awoke/awaked	awoke/awaked
bear	bore	borne/born
beat	beat	beaten
become	became	become
befall	befell	befallen
begin	began	begun
behold	beheld	beheld
bend	bent	bent
bereave	bereaved/bereft	bereaved/bereft
bet	bet/betted	bet/betted
bid	bade/bid	bidden/bid
bind	bound	bound
bite	bit	bitten
bleed	bled	bled
blow	blew	blown
break	broke	broken
breed	bred	bred
bring	brought	brought
broadcast	broadcast	broadcast
build	built	built
burn	burned/burnt	burned/burnt
burst	burst	burst
buy	bought	bought
cast	cast	cast
catch	caught	caught
chide	chided/chid	chided/chid
choose	chose	chosen
cleave	clove/cleft	cloven/cleft
cling	clung	clung
come	came	come
cost	cost	cost
creep	crept	crept
cut	cut	cut

Present Tense (Plain form)	*Pase Tense* (-ed form)	*Past Participle* (-en form)
deal	dealt	dealt
dig	dug	dug
do	did	done
draw	drew	drawn
dream	dreamed/dreamt	dreamed/dreamt
drink	drank	drunk
drive	drove	driven
dwell	dwelt	dwelt
eat	ate	eaten
fall	fell	fallen
feed	fed	fed
feel	felt	felt
fight	fought	fought
find	found	found
flee	fled	fled
fling	flung	flung
fly	flew	flown
forbear	forbore	forborne
forbid	forbade	forbidden
forget	forgot	forgotten
forgive	forgave	forgiven
forsake	forsook	forsaken
freeze	froze	frozen
get	got	got
give	gave	given
go	went	gone
grind	ground	ground
grow	grew	grown
hang	hanged/hung	hanged/hung
have	had	had
hear	heard	heard
hide	hid	hid/hidden
hit	hit	hit
hold	held	held
hurt	hurt	hurt
keep	kept	kept
kneel	knelt	knelt

Present Tense (Plain form)	*Past Tense* (-ed form)	*Past Participle* (-en form)
knit	knit/knitted	knit
know	knew	known
lay	laid	laid
lead	led	led
lean	leaned/leant	leaned/leant
leap	leapt	leapt
learn	learned/learnt	learned/learnt
leave	left	left
lend	lent	lent
let	let	let
lie	lay	lain
lie (speak a falsehood)	lied	lied
light	lighted/lit	lighted/lit
lose	lost	lost
make	made	made
mean	meant	meant
meet	met	met
mislead	misled	misled
mistake	mistook	mistaken
put	put	put
quit	quitted/quit	quitted/quit
read	read	read
rid	rid	rid
ride	rode	ridden
ring	rang	rung
rise	rose	risen
run	ran	run
saw	sawed	sawn
say	said	said
see	saw	seen
seek	sought	sought
sell	sold	sold
send	sent	sent
set	set	set
sew	sewed	sewn

Present Tense (Plain form)	*Past Tense* (-ed form)	*Past Participle* (-en form)
shake	shook	shaken
shave	shaved	shaved/shaven
shed	shed	shed
shine	shone	shone
shoot	shot	shot
show	showed	shown
shrink	shrank	shrunk
shut	shut	shut
sing	sang	sung
sink	sank	sunk
sit	sat	sat
slay	slew	slain
sleep	slept	slept
slide	slid	slid
sling	slung	slung
slink	slunk	slunk
smell	smelied/smelt	smelled/smelt
sow	sowed	sown
speak	spoke	spoken
speed	speeded/sped	speeded/sped
spell	spelled/spelt	spelled/spelt
spend	spent	spent
spill	spilled/spilt	spilled/spilt
spin	spun/span	spun
spit	spat	spat
split	split	split
spoil	spoiled/spoilt	spoiled/spoilt
spread	spread	spread
spring	sprang	sprung
stand	stood	stood
steal	stole	stolen
stick	stuck	stuck
sting	stung	stung
stink	stank/stunk	stunk
strew	strewed	strewn
strike	struck	struck/stricken
string	strung	strung
strive	strove	striven
swear	swore	sworn

Present Tense (Plain form)	*Past Tense* (-ed form)	*Past Participle* (-en form)
sweep	swept	swept
swell	swelled	swelled/swollen
swim	swam	swum
swing	swung	swung
take	took	taken
teach	taught	taught
tear	tore	torn
tell	told	told
think	thought	thought
thrive	thrived/throve	thrived/thriven
throw	threw	thrown
thrust	thrust	thrust
tread	trod	trod/trodden
understand	understood	understood
wake	woke/waked	waken/woke
wear	wore	worn
weave	wove	woven
weep	wept	wept
win	won	won
wind	wound	wound
withdraw	withdrew	withdrawn
withhold	withheld	withheld
withstand	withstood	withstood
work	worked	worked/wrought
wring	wrung	wrung
write	wrote	written

Present Simple Tense: Uses

a Roger *gets up* at five in the morning.
He *goes* to church every Sunday.
College *begins* at ten o'clock.

In these sentences the *simple present* tense expresses habitual action. This is the main use of this tense. But the tense does not necessarily tell us whether or not the action is being performed at the moment of speaking.

b The sun *rises* in the east.
Water *boils* at 100°C.
Calcutta *stands* on the banks of the Hoogli.

In these sentences the tense expresses permanent or verifiable truths or facts.

c A platform ticket *costs* 50 paise.
The sun *sets* a little after six these days.

In these sentences the present tense expresses a fact that is true at the time of speaking.

d Ashok *passes* the ball to Ravi and Ravi *throws* it right on the stumps and Mohan *is* out!

Here the tense describes events as they are actually going on. This tense is often used in running commentaries during sports events.

e We *leave* Hyderabad at 8-30 p.m. next Tuesday and *arrive* in New Delhi at 11 a.m. on Thursday. We *spend* a day in Delhi and *leave* again at 12 noon on Friday. We *arrive* in Calcutta at 3 p.m. on Sunday.

The simple present tense is used in these sentences to express a planned future action, or a series of such planned actions.

f Portia made a moving speech before the judge. She appealed to Shylock to accept the money that Antonio was ready to give. But Shylock rejected her pleas.

Now Shylock *comes* forward with a pair of scales in one hand and a knife in the other. He *moves* towards Antony. Just then Portia *tells* him, 'Tarry, Jew,' and the Jew *stops*.

The present tense in the last three sentences describes a past event in a vivid or dramatic manner. When used in this way the tense is called the *historic present*.

The Present Continuous Tense: Uses

My father *is taking* his bath.

Hassaman and Sainabee *are doing* their homework.

I *am doing* my homework too.

In these sentences the verb is in the *present progressive* or the *present continuous tense.* The form of the verb is:

$$\left.\begin{array}{l}\text{am}\\\text{is}\\\text{are}\end{array}\right\} +\text{verb}+\text{ing}$$

a Father *is reading* the newspaper.
The children *are playing* in the garden.

Here, the present continuous tense is used to describe an action that is in progress, the attention being drawn to the continuity of the action.

b My father *is writing* a book.
The college authorities *are building* a new hostel.

Here the present continuous tense is used to describe an action that is in progress and will be continued, but not necessarily going on at the moment of speaking.

c I *am meeting* the Chief Minister tomorrow morning.
He *is visiting* the town tomorrow.

Here the present continuous tense expresses an action that has been arranged to take place in the near future. One usually uses this tense to express one's immediate plans.

Note that the time of the action must be generally mentioned, otherwise there may be confusion between the present and the future meanings.

d The boys are always complaining about the food.
My brother is always watching television.

When the present continuous tense is used with *always*, *constantly*, *repeatedly*, *regularly*, it carries a suggestion of disapproval of the action. For example, the first sentence implies that the boys are making complaints too often. The second implies that the boy is spending too much time in front of the TV.

e There are a number of verbs which are not normally used in the present continuous tense. These are:
   i verbs of perception: see, hear, smell, notice.
   ii verbs used to express feelings or states of mind: want, desire, wish, refuse, forgive, care, hate, adore, like, dislike, admire.

iii verbs involving the process of thinking:
think (when no opinion is expressed), feel (=think), know, mean, suppose, remember, realize, recollect, forget, recall, mind.

iv verbs denoting possession:
examples: have, own, owe, belong, possess.

v verbs such as contain, consist, keep, cost, seem.

When some of the verbs listed above are used in the present continuous tense, their meanings change.

I see a temple on that hill.	I am seeing the principal at 3 p.m. (visiting)
We hear several rumours about the missing M.P.	The judge is hearing the case tomorrow. (conducting the trial)
I think the committee will reject his appeal.	He is thinking seriously of resigning. (considering)

Exercise 1

Fill in the blanks with the simple present or the present continuous forms of the verbs given in the brackets. Choose the form for each verb according to the meaning of the sentence:

1 The boys generally —— to their uncle's house for the holidays, but this year they —— there. (go, not go)
2 My nephews —— here tomorrow. They usually —— their vacation here. (arrive, spend)
3 I —— some light literature, such as novels and short stories during my vacations. (read)
4 He generally —— a gray suit, but today he —— a white one. (wear, wear)
5 He rarely —— an umbrella, but he —— one now. (carry, carry)

6 Ravi ——— his homework still. His brother who always ——— quicker has finished his and ——— in the garden. (do, work, play)
7 I ——— you ——— a copy of *Airport*. How do you like the book? (notice, have)
8 'Ask the man what he ———.' (want)
9 You ——— to enjoy this film; I don't really. (seem)
10 I usually ——— to college. But today I ——— in my brother's car. (walk, go)

Exercise 2

Fill in the blanks with the correct forms (present simple or present progressive) of the verbs given in brackets:

1 Ice ——— at 0° centigrade. (melt)
2 'Silence please. The students ——— their examination in the next room.' (write)
3 What ——— an apple fall? (make)
4 I ——— a continuous noise in the next room. What ——— there?
5 Hurry up, the taxi ———. (wait)
6 The car ——— servicing. I ——— it to the garage tomorrow. (need, send)
7 It ——— hard. I am afraid the match will have to be cancelled. (rain)
8 My sister ——— lessons in Western music. She ——— on the piano every day. (take, practise)
9 He ——— that he ——— now. (say, not leave)
10 The boys ——— a play for College Day. (rehearse)

The Simple Past Tense: Uses

Look at these sentences:

An accident *happened* in front of my house yesterday.
A car *knocked* down a boy riding a bicycle.
Luckily the boy *escaped* with minor injuries.

The verbs in these sentences are said to be in the *simple past tense.*

Each of the verbs describes an event that took place and was completed in the past with reference to the time of speaking.

a Look at these sentences:

Every day he *read* a few chapters of the Gita.
His mother *gave* him some pocket money every day.

The simple past here expresses a habitual or regular action in the past. The verb is often accompanied by an adverbial like *every day.*

b He *lived* in Delhi for ten years.
(He does not live there now).
He *served* in this college for twenty years.
(He is no longer working here).

In these sentences the simple past tense expresses an action which occupied a period of time in the past, which is now ended.

c My father *left* for Delhi *yesterday.*
I *bought* this watch *in Bombay.*
A strong wind *blew last night* and *knocked* down a number of trees in our garden.
The old man *walked* very *slowly.*
They *put up* a fence *around the garden.*
The police *caught* the thief *at the railway station.*

In these sentences the simple past tense is used to express events that occurred at a particular point in the past. When used in this way, there is usually a word or phrase indicating time, an adverbial phrase, or, in the case of transitive verbs, an object.

However, in a narrative sequence, an adverbial of time may not be necessary:

The car knocked down a cyclist. Luckily he escaped with minor injuries. He came home tired and shaken. He told his mother about the accident. She made some tea for him. He drank the tea and felt refreshed. He then went and lay down in bed.

The adverbial, similarly, is not needed when a sentence in the simple past is spoken in answer to a question:

Who broke this glass?
Anil did.
How did he go to school?
He walked.

The Present Perfect Tense: Uses

Look at these sentences:

I *have written* a new novel. (Read it and tell me how you like it.)

I *have spoken* to the manager. (He will see you tomorrow.)

The children *have eaten* all the sweets. (So, there are no more sweets left.)

The old tenant *has vacated* the house. (I must now look out for another tenant.)

The Principal *has gone* to Delhi. (He is not here now.)

I *have seen* the film once. (I don't want to see it again.)

In the sentences above the verbs are said to be in the *present perfect tense*. The form of the verb in the present perfect tense is '*has/have + the past participle*. For example: *has gone, have eaten*.

In the examples above, the present perfect tense express actions or events that were completed in the past. But what is said in each sentence has 'current relevance,' that is, son link with what is said or done or thought of now. The sentence in brackets given after each example above is to show you the nature of this link.

a I *have seen* the Taj Mahal.
I *have eaten* Chinese food.
They *have been* to Delhi several times.

In the above sentences, the present perfect tense expresses an experience in the past.

b He has lived in this house for twenty years. (He still lives here.)
He has been in the army for five years.
They have been here since six o'clock.

The present perfect here expresses an action which began in the past and is still continuing.

Note that *for* and *since* are commonly used with the present perfect tense when the tense is used as shown above. 'For' here shows a *length* of time upto now; 'since' shows some *point* of time in the past as being the starting point of the action or event:

Examples:

We have waited for our friend for an hour.
They have walked for three hours and are tired.
It has not rained in this town since last September.
I have not slept since one o'clock in the morning.

c The train has left *already*.
Our people have not arrived *yet*.
The plane has *just* landed.
Haven't you found a job *yet*?

The words in italics in the sentences above are examples of adverbs which are often used with the present perfect tense.

d Mr Kapoor lived in Delhi for fifteen years.
Mr Kapoor has lived in Delhi for fifteen years.

In the first sentence, the simple past tense indicates that the period of Mr Kapoor's residence in Delhi ended at some time in the past. In the second sentence, the present perfect indicates that Mr Kapoor still lives in Delhi at the time of speaking.

Compare also the following sentences:

For generations, Nepal *has provided* some of the world's finest soldiers. (It continues to provide them.)
For generations Sparta *produced* Greece's greatest soldiers. (Now this is no longer the case.)
My mother has been an invalid all her life.
(My mother is still alive.)
My mother was an invalid all her life.
(She is now dead.)

Here are some time expressions which go with the simple past and some that go with the present perfect:

Simple Past Tense	*Present Perfect*
yesterday	so far
a week ago	since
last Tuesday	
at 8 o'clock	
in the morning	hitherto
	upto now
	lately
	recently

Exercise 3

Fill in the blanks with the correct forms (the past tense or the present perfect form) of the verbs given:

lay	lie	bind	bleed
sting	throw	buy	meet
rob	have	shrink	bid

1 The robbers ——— the traveller of all his money, ——— his hands and legs with a rope and ——— him into a ditch.
2 I ——— this pen yesterday at the super bazaar.
3 He was badly wounded, and ——— profusely.
4 My friend, Mr Thapar ——— with an accident and is in hospital.
5 Look how this shirt ——— after the very first wash.
6 A scorpion ——— my brother. Do you know of any first aid?
7 Before he left for the U.S.A. he ——— farewell to his friends.
8 This heap of rubbish ——— here for a week. Remove it.
9 Our hen ——— two eggs yesterday and just now it ——— another.
10 I have ——— a motor cycle for many years now.

Exercise 4

Fill in the blanks in each item below with the correct forms (the past tense or the present perfect form) of the verb given in brackets:

1 I —— this book; I —— it last month. (read)
2 I —— its author; I —— him at a conference in Madras. (see)
3 My father —— several books. He —— his eighth novel last month. (write, finish)
4 A: Where is Ganesh?
B: I —— (not see) him after he left home in the morning.
He —— (tell) his mother this morning that he would be in for lunch.
5 Shopkeeper: Do you know that lady who —— (just leave) the shop?
Customer: Yes, that is Miss Thorat. Why?
Shopkeeper: She —— (be) here several times but she never —— (buy) anything.
6 An hour ago someone —— (ring) up the airport and —— (say) that there —— (be) a time bomb in the Jumbo jet. The police and the crew of the plane are searching for it but so far they —— (not find) anything. This is the third time they —— (have) a scare like this.
7 I —— my lunch. I —— it half an hour ago. (have, have)
8 All the guests ——. They —— half an hour ago. (leave, leave)
9 I —— to bring my English textbook. I —— to bring it yesterday too. (forget, forget)
10 I —— all my life in this village and at 84 I don't want to leave it and go to a city. (live)

Exercise 5

Complete the following sentences with each of the two endings given, using *since* or *for*, whichever is right, in the blanks:

Example: We have had a severe drought in our State ———.

a a year now
b January last

Ans: a We have had a severe drought in our State for a year now.
b We have had a severe drought in our State since January last.

1 They have lived in this town ———
a quite a long time.
b 1900.

2 I haven't smoked a cigarette ———
a the day my teacher advised me against smoking.
b the last 15 years.

3 My brother hasn't sent us any money ———
a the beginning of the year.
b ten months now.

4 I haven't eaten anything ———
a last night
b a whole day.

5 We haven't written to each other ———
a nearly one year.
b last January.

6 He has worn the same suit ———
a two weeks.
b the beginning of this month.

Past Progressive Tense: Form and Use

Look at these sentences:

Once a hunter *was walking* through a forest.
I *was ironing* my shirt when the electricity failed.
The boys *were playing* in the garden when it started to rain.

In each of these sentences the verb is in the *past progressive* or *past continuous tense*. The form of the verb is:

'was'/'were' + verb + *-ing*

While the present continuous tense expresses an action in progress in the present, the past continuous tense expresses an action in progress in the past.

a At 7 a.m. this morning I *was reading* the newspaper.
At 8-30 a.m. I *was having* my breakfast.
At 9 a.m. I *was getting* ready for office and the children *were getting* ready for school.

In these sentences the past continuous tense expresses an action that was in progress at a point of time in the past, having begun before that point and probably continuing after it.

b The boys *were listening* to the cricket commentary the whole of yesterday.
A: What *were* you *doing* yesterday evening?
B: I *was writing* letters.

The past continuous tense here expresses an action continuing over a period of time in the past.

c The train *was passing* on the bridge when the bridge gave way.
I *was reading* the newspaper when the telegraph peon knocked at the door.

Here, the past progressive tense expresses a continuing action at some point in the past, when another event took place.

d While some boys *were reading* in the library the others *were playing* in the playground.
While Rome *was burning* Nero *was fiddling.*
Sita *was playing* the sitar, Radha *was singing* and Mohan *was playing* the tabla.

The past continuous tense here describes two or more actions going on at the same time; often the conjunction *while* is used to connect the clauses.

e Some adverbs used with the past progressive tense are:

always, continually, constantly, for ever.

She was *always* scolding her children.
He was *continually* asking for money.
The children were *constantly* asking for sweets.

The sage was *for ever* praying for the welfare of humanity.

Note the position of the adverbial (in italics above) in sentences of this type.

Exercise 6

Fill in the blanks with the simple past tense or past continuous tense forms of the verbs given, so as to make meaningful sentences:

1 Ravi ——— some letters, when I ——— to see him. (write, go)
2 He ——— across the road when a bicycle ——— him. (walk, hit)
3 She ——— her finger while she ——— potatoes. (cut, cut)
4 The lights ——— while we ——— at dinner. (go off, be)
5 As he ——— the bus, it ——— with a jerk. (get off, start)
6 Mother ——— into the kitchen and ——— that the milk ——— over. (go, find, boil)
7 While the priest ——— the sermon, some people ——— out of the window. (preach, look)
8 He ——— his pen while he ——— yesterday evening. (lose, play)

Past Perfect Tense: Form and Use

Look at these sentences:

On reaching the school I found that I *had forgotten* to bring my English textbook.

When we reached the theatre, the play *had begun* already.

I had to borrow some money from a friend of mine, since I *had lost* my purse.

The verb in italics in each of these sentences is in the *past perfect tense.*

The form of the tense is: 'had' + past participle. In each of these sentences there are two actions or events both taking place in the past, but one taking place earlier than the other. The two are in some way related to each other, that is, the earlier action has some link with the later action. The earlier action or event in such cases is expressed in the past perfect tense and the later action in the simple past.

For instance, in the first sentence, 'I had forgotten' is the earlier action. 'On reaching the school I found' is the later action.

This tense is used when we wish to emphasise the sequence of the two actions in the past, and when that earlier action has some relation to the later action or situation.

It is often possible to bring out the earlierness of either action without the use of the past perfect tense but with the help of conjunctions like *before* or *after*.

The train left before I reached the station.
I reached the station after the train left.

But these sentences are mere factual statements. They only express the time sequence of the two actions described and do not necessarily carry any other significance.

a The train *had left* when I reached the station.
By the time he got the telegram, his father *had died*.
By the time the police arrived on the scene, the rioters *had fled*.

The past perfect tense here expresses an action in the past which was completed before another action, also in the past. The tense expresses the past of past or the 'before' past.

b In general the past perfect tense is used when from a point of time in the past, we look backward at an event that happened earlier in the past. That point of time may be expressed

i merely as a time phrase; for example, *at* 8 *o'clock*, *by evening*, *by the year* 1900, *at* 18 *years of age* etc; or ii by a clause that refers to an action that took place at a point of time in the past; for example, *when he wrote to me, by the time we called in the firemen,* etc.

Examples:

At nine o'clock the plane had left.

By 3 o'clock in the afternoon 6000 voters had cast their votes.

At 18 years of age he had already travelled a lot.

When he wrote to me about his success in the IAS examination, I had already known the result from the newspapers.

c I did not know the man because I had not seen him before.

The doctor found the patient restless because he had not had any sleep the night before.

In these sentences the past perfect tense is used to express actions or events in the past which denote causes or reasons for later actions, also in the past.

d I wish I had accepted the job. (But I did not accept it and I am sorry.)

I wish I hadn't written that letter. (I wrote it and I feel sorry now.)

I would rather you had not gone there. (But you did.)

If only the letter had arrived in time! (But it did not.)

Here the past perfect tense expresses an unfulfilled wish in the past.

e If he *had worked* hard he would have passed. (He didn't work hard so he failed.)

If he *had gone* in a taxi, he would have caught the train. (He did not go in a taxi and he missed the train.)

The past perfect tense is used here to express an unfulfilled condition in the past.

f When he had made his speech he sat down.
When he had eaten his lunch he got up.

The past perfect is used in these sentences when two simple past tenses might give the impression that the two actions happened at the same time. Example: *When he made his speech he sat down* may give the impression that during his speech he sat down.

Exercise 7

Fill in the blanks with the simple past or the past perfect forms of the verbs given in brackets, to make the sentences meaningful:

1 By the time the doctor ——— the patient ———. (arrive, die)
2 The teacher ——— they could go home when they ——— the work assigned to them. (say, complete)
3 We ——— the poem after the teacher ——— it to us. (understand, explain)
4 Several hours before the match ——— the spectators ——— the stadium. (begin, pack)
5 I wish you ——— your application by the due date. (submit)
6 Jain ——— to get a first class. He ——— only a second class and was naturally disappointed. (hope, get)
7 They ——— hungry because they ——— nothing to eat since the previous evening. (be, have)
8 I ——— my friend for many years, and he ——— a lot; so when I ——— him last week I ——— him at first. (not see, change, meet, not recognize)

Exercise 8

Combine each of the following pairs of sentences using the past perfect tense to express the earlier action or event:

Examples:

a The film began at 9-30 p.m.
We reached the cinema hall at 10 p.m.
When we reached the cinema hall, the film had already begun.

b He joined his father's business.
He was then nearing twenty years of age.
By twenty he had joined his father's business.

c I did not see him for many years.
I did not recognise him at once.
I did not recognise him at once because I had not seen him for many years.

1 The train left at 8.
We reached the station at 8-15.

2 I went to bed.
The telephone bell rang a minute later.

3 The fire burnt down all the huts.
The fire engine arrived later.

4 Mother made the coffee.
We woke up a little later.

5 The bell rang.
Soon after, the teacher entered the classroom. (use 'just')

6 The sun rose.
The traveller woke up sometime later.

7 He took his M.A. degree.
He was then nearing 18 years of age.

8 The typist typed eight letters.
A little later it was 11 o'clock.

The Present Perfect Continuous: Form and Use

Look at these sentences:

Mr George has been teaching in this college for ten years.

I have been having a pain in my back ever since the accident.

The verbs in these sentences are in the *present perfect continuous tense*.. The form of the verb in this tense is:

'has'/'have' + 'been' + verb +-ing

Look at these sentences:

a I have been living in this house since 1940.

That stone has been lying there for weeks.

He has been fishing for two hours, but hasn't caught anything yet.

How long have you been waiting for the bus?

In these sentences the present perfect continuous tense is used to express an action or event that began some time ago, has continued till now and is still going on.

b I am cold because I have been swimming for an hour.

I have been running round the town all day and need a rest.

He has been drinking a lot. He hasn't yet got up from bed.

In these sentences the present perfect continuous tense expresses an action which was going on till a very recent point of time and whose effect or result is still present.

Note that we can use the present perfect tense in place of the present perfect continuous tense in several of these sentences, especially in the case of verbs which themselves carry the sense of a continuous action. We generally use *for* or *since* in such sentences.

I have lived in this house *for five years*.
I have been living in this house *for five years*.
I have taught in this college *since 1960*.
I have been teaching in this college *since 1960*.

<u>Exercise 9</u>

Fill in the blanks with the correct forms (present perfect or present perfect continuous) of the verbs given in brackets:

1 I —— to him again and again but —— from him yet. (write, not hear)

2 I ——— you for a long time. What ——— all these days? (not see, do)
3 That lime tree ——— near our house ever since I was a boy. I'm glad no one ——— it down yet. (stand, cut)
4 These boys ——— English for three years now. (learn)
5 They ——— the house and ———. (lock up, go away)
6 The boys ——— ten kilometres and are now resting. (walk)
7 'You ——— a lot lately. You ought to do something about it.' (cough)
8 The workers ——— for a rise in their wages for the last one year, but they ——— to go on strike on this account. (agitate, not dare)

The Past Perfect Continuous: Form and Use

i Look at these sentences:

The telephone *had been ringing* for five minutes but there was no one to attend to it.

I met Balu at the bus stop. He *had been waiting* for his bus for half an hour, he said.

The italicized verbs in these sentences are in the *past perfect continuous tense.* The form of the verb is:

had been + verb + -ing

Look at these sentences:

Our football team *had been winning* the annual tournament until last year.

He *had been teaching* vocal music for fifteen years when he lost his voice and had to retire.

In these sentences the past perfect continuous tense expresses an action or event that had begun and was going on upto a given point of time in the past. This tense bears the same relation to the past perfect that the present perfect continuous bears to the present perfect.

Exercise 10

Make sentences from the table below to match the clues. The clues are given in the same order as the sentences to be made from the table. The first one is done for you as an example:

Clues

1 The bus came at last. (Matching sentence: We had been waiting for it for an hour.) (3)
2 The workers decided to go on strike yesterday.
3 Mohana showed me a sweater.
4 Mr Jain was transferred from Bombay to Calcutta.
5 Fatima got the first rank in the examination.

1 We 2 They 3 She 4 He 5 She	had been	knitting it for two months. working in Bombay for five years. waiting for it for an hour. working hard for this success. demanding a rise in their wages.

Exercise 11

Fill in the blanks with the right tense forms of the verbs given in brackets, making use of what you have learnt so far about the uses of the various tense forms:

1 Rajesh ——— out of the bank when a policeman ——— him. (just come, catch)
2 I ——— down to my work when I was transferred again. (hardly, settle)
3 The man in the story ——— the goose that ——— a golden egg every day. (kill, lay)
4 This quarrel ———— on far too long. It must stop now. (go)
5 The man who ——— now is our candidate for the Assembly constituency. (speak)
6 We ——— heavy rains in this place for the last two weeks. (have)

7 Mr Sami ——— for his glasses for nearly ten minutes when he found he ——— them all the time. (look, wear)

8 My son ——— coarse rice. He ——— any rice for a week now because our ration shop ——— short of fine rice. (not like, not eat, run)

9 I ——— some trouble with my eyes for a week now. I ——— not able to read anything. (have, be)

10 Rangan ——— his breakfast when the taxi arrived. The taxi had to wait. (not have)

The Future: Form and Use

English has verb forms for the present and past tenses, and for the perfect and progressive tenses, but not for expressing future time. Instead, there are several ways of expressing future time in English. One of these ways is to use *shall* or *will* with the bare forms of the verb: shall come, will go, etc. These phrases ('shall' or 'will' + verb) are commonly referred to as the *future tense*. But there are other ways of expressing the future which are more common.

a Our cricket team *leaves* for Bombay this evening. They *play* two matches in Bombay. They *play* one at Poona. They *return* next Monday.

In these sentences the present simple tense is used to express a series of intended or planned actions in the future.

b The Director of Collegiate Education *is visiting* the college tomorrow.
The college team *is playing* a football match with the town team next Sunday.

The present continuous tense is used in these sentences to express a future event. Usually the time is mentioned (tomorrow, next Sunday, etc.) and it is in the near future. This way of expressing the future is very common in English.

The verb *go* and *come*, however, can be used without any time expression.

We are going for a walk.
Are you coming with me?

c I am going to buy a bicycle.
If he doesn't apologise, I am not going to excuse him.

The structure '*am*'/'*is*'/'*are*' + '*going to*' + *verb* is used to express the subject's intention to perform a future action.

Note that the verbs *go* and *come* are not usually used with *going to*. We don't say, for instance, *He is going to come here tomorrow*. We say, *He is coming here tomorrow*. We don't say, *He is going to go to Bombay tomorrow*. We say, *He is going to Bombay tomorrow*.

Going to + *verb* is also used to express the speaker's certainty about an event in the near future. This certainty is based on some present indication.

Examples:

Look at these dark clouds. It is going to rain.
That boy has eaten a lot; he is going to be sick, I'm afraid.
Mrs Ram is going to have a baby.

d I shall return your notebooks on Monday.
We shall begin a new lesson tomorrow.
You will know your result in a day or two.
Our team will win the match, everybody thinks.
Men will land on Mars some day.

The future is expressed in all these sentences with '*shall*' or '*will*' + *the bare form of the verb*. *Shall* is used with the first person (*I* and *We*) and *will* with the second and third persons. Note, however, that in current usage *will* is also widely used with the first person to express the simple future.

Examples:

I will return this book tomorrow.
We will miss the 8 o'clock train.

e Will I get my papers back tomorrow?
Will you be here tomorrow morning?
Will the bookshops be open tomorrow?

In interrogative sentences *will* can be used with all the three persons to express the future.

We can however say: *Shall I help you* when an offer of help is to be expressed.

f The train *is about to leave.*
The Chief Minister *is about to speak.*

This construction *be about to* + *verb* expresses events whose happening is imminent, that is, which are likely to happen in a very short while.

g I am to be at a meeting at 5 o'clock.
There is to be an enquiry into the railway accident.
He is to preside over this year's College Day.

In these sentences the form '*be*' + '*to*' + *the bare form of the verb* is used to express a duty or necessity or planned course of action, in the future.

Exercise 12

Fill in the blanks in the sentences given below, using the verbs in brackets, in one of the ways that express the future:
'*shall*' or '*will*' + *verb*, '*be going to*' + *verb*; *present continuous*; *present simple.*

1 I find an extra plate on the table. Who ——— to dinner? (come)
2 We have telephoned to the police.
They ——— here any moment. (be)
3 I ——— at home next week. I ——— for Delhi tonight. (not be, leave)
4 There are dark clouds in the sky. I think it ———. (rain)
5 'The roof has caught fire. I'm afraid it ———. Stand back.' ' (fall)
6 My programme:
I ——— office in the forenoon.
I ——— for Madras by the 2-30 plane.
I ——— my business in Madras in an hour and ——— the 6-30 plane back to Hyderabad. (attend, leave, finish, take)

7 Mr Ahmed ——— present at the meeting next week. He ——— abroad. (not be, go)

8 The rule says that in the absence of the Chairman, the Vice-Chairman ——— the chair. (take)

9 'Isn't it too hot inside?'
'I ——— the windows if you like.' (open)

10 Did you see the notice on the notice-board? The annual examinations ——— on the 15th. They ——— on 31st March and college ——— the same day for the summer vacation. College ——— on 15th June. (begin, end, close, reopen)

The Future Continuous: Form and Use

Look at these sentences:

A: Please have lunch with me.

B: I'm sorry. Mr Gopal has asked me to lunch and he *will be waiting* for me.

The verb in italics is in the *future continuous tense*. The form is: '*shall*'/'*will*' + '*be*' + *verb* + *ing*.

a My brother *will be taking* his I.A.S. selection examination next month.

A fresh stock of saris *will be arriving* next week.

The future continuous tense is used here to express an event that is expected to take place in the normal course. It is less definite than the present continuous. For example:

We are seeing the Chief Minister tomorrow.

We will be seeing the Chief Minister tomorrow. (less definite)

The first sentence implies some deliberate arrangement on the part of the speakers. The second suggests no such arrangement. It suggests something that is expected to happen.

Similarly:

We will ask Dr James to examine Mother.

We will be asking Dr James to examine Mother.

The first sentence expresses a deliberate intention. The second is a mere statement of what will happen as a matter of routine.

b When I reach Simla it *will be snowing* there.
At this time tomorrow you *will be flying* across the Atlantic.

In these sentences the future continuous expresses actions that will be in progress at a given point of time in the future.

The Future Perfect: Form and Use

Look at this sentence:

I *shall have typed* all the letters by 6 o'clock.

The verb is in the *future perfect tense.* The form of the verb is: '*shall*'/'*will*' + '*have*' + *past participle of the verb*.

a I *shall have finished* this book by the middle of next month.
The train *will have left* by the time you reach the station.

The verb in italics in each of these sentences expresses an action which is expected to be completed by a certain time in the future.

b 'You will have read about the Wright Brothers who invented the aeroplane,' said the teacher.
'You will have heard about our plans for the Diamond Jubilee of our college,' said the lecturer.

Note that *the future perfect* is used in such sentences to express not the future but the speaker's belief that something *has* taken place; for example, that the students *have* read about the Wright Brothers (in the first sentence above) and that the students *have* heard about the plans for the Diamond Jubilee (in the second sentence).

Exercise 13

Make sentences from table B to match the sentences under A. The first one is done for you as an example.

A

1 The half-yearly examination will be held in December. (Sentence: *The class will have completed ten lessons by then.*)
2 Come at 8 o'clock for your dinner.
3 The fire engines will take at least half an hour to get here.
4 You can reach the railway station before ten.
5 How can you expect the tailor to give you your suit next Monday?
6 How can I hope to buy a house after retirement?
7 We no doubt have some debts.

B

1 The class 2 I 3 The fire 4 The train 5 He 6 I 7 But we	will/shall have will/shall not have	destroyed all the huts by then. made it by then. saved enough money for a house. completed ten lessons by then. cooked the dinner by then. paid them off by the end of the year. left by that time.

13 CONCORD: SUBJECT-VERB

1 Look at the sentences under A and B.

A	B
The *book is* on the table.	The *books are* on the table.
A *child likes* sweets.	*Children like* sweets.
The *boy has* left.	The *boys have* left.

The subjects in the sentences under A are singular and so the verbs are singular. The subjects in the sentences under B are plural and so too the verbs. This subject-verb agreement in number is called grammatical concord .

2 a Look at these sentences:

A	B
The public consists of all kinds of people	The public are tired of agitations and strikes.
A new Board has been constituted for the college.	The Board have revised the rules of admission.
The audience on College Day was huge.	The audience were getting bored and restive.
This family is descended from Shri Thyagaraja.	My neighbour's family often quarrel among themselves.
The Committee was unanimous on the choice of the President.	The Committee were divided on the choice of the Secretary.
The Government has made a grant of land to the college.	The Government are determined to put down smuggling.

In the sentences under A there is grammatical concord because the group of people in each case is considered as one undivided body and therefore the verbs are singular in number. In the sentences under B, there is no grammatical concord and the singular subject is followed by a plural verb. The plural form of the verb is used because the subject is thought of as individuals forming a group. For example, 'the Board' stands for the members who form the Board. Agreement or concord of this kind is called 'notional concord' and it is often preferred to grammatical concord.

b Look at these sentences:

A	B
Twenty-five years is a long time.	Twenty-five years have passed since we were married.
The hammer and sickle is flying over the Communist Party Office.	The hammer and the sickle together form the symbol of the Communist Party.
Bread and butter is the main concern of the common man.	Bread and butter have gone up in price.
The cow and calf is the emblem of the Congress party.	The cow and the calf that we bought are both black.

The subject in each of the sentences under A is plural, but it takes a singular verb and this again is a result of notional concord because the two things mentioned in the subject are regarded as forming one unit. In the sentences under B each subject consists of more than one unit, each considered separately, and is therefore followed by a plural verb.

c A large number of people have applied for the job.

The majority of the students are boys.

More than a thousand members have signed the petition.

In the sentences above the head word of the subject is singular (*number*, *majority*, *more*) but the verb is plural because the noun phrase as a whole expresses a plural idea. (*people*, *students*, *members*)

3 Either your sister or your brothers *are* to answer for this.

Either your brothers or your sister *is* to answer for this.

Nobody, not even the members, *were* present.

In each of these sentences the verb takes the number of the noun in the subject which is nearest to it. This concord arises out of the principle of 'proximity' or nearness.

There are, therefore, three principles in concord:

a The principle of grammatical concord. This is the safest, though it is not strictly followed by speakers, and sometimes even writers.

b The principle of notional concord. This is natural in colloquial English, that is, speech.

c The principle of proximity.

4 Look at the sentences given below and study the subject-verb concord in them.

a Mr John *or* Mr Samuel is to move the resolution. (The singular subjects are connected by *or* and the verb has to be in the singular.)

b *Either* Ravi *or* Raju has damaged this lock. (The singular subjects are connected by *either. . . . or* and the verb has to be in the singular.)

c *Neither* the boy scouts *nor* the girl guides are participating in the rally. (The subjects joined by *nor* are both plural and so the verb has to be plural.)

d *Either* those children *or* my own son has picked all the flowers. (The verb is singular since out of the two subjects connected by *or* (the first plural, the second singular) the singular subject is nearer the verb.)

e *Either* my son *or* those children have done this. (The plural subject is nearer the verb, hence *have*.)

f *Good and bad behaviour* are inculcated by example. (The subject is *good behaviour and bad behaviour*. Hence the verb is plural.)

g *None of them* are right.
(The plural verb is preferred because of notional concord as well as the principle of proximity.)

h Nobody, *not even the teachers*, were present.
(The verb is plural because of the proximity of *teachers* to the verb.)

i Either you *or* I am mistaken.
(*I* is nearer to the verb. Hence *am*.)

j A boy *with his sister and brother* is standing at the gate.
(The subject is *boy* and hence *is*.)

k The Chairman, *as well as* the members, is to blame for this misfortune.
(When *as well as* connects two subjects, the verb takes the number of the first subject.)

l Mohan, *rather than/more than the others*, is guilty.
(When *rather than/more than* connects two subjects, the verb takes the number of the first subject.)

m *What we now need* is good government.
(When the subject is a clause, it always takes a singular verb.)

n *What I say and do* are none of your concern.
(The subject has two clauses; what I say, what I do. Hence *are*.)

o *One* of the boys in the camp has fallen ill.
(The head word *one* in the subject is singular and hence takes a singular verb.)

p *Most* of the members were late for the meeting.
(Notional concord operates here. But when *most* refers to an uncountable noun, or part of a whole, it takes a singular verb. Examples: Most of the money *has* been spent. Most of the talk *was* inaudible.)

q *Billiards* is a rich man's game.
(*Billiards* is the name of a game and is singular.)

r *Politics* is a dirty game, someone has said. (*Politics* is usually treated as singular.)

s The *news* from the war front is very encouraging. (*News* is singular.)

t At *Every boy* and *Every girl* in our village goes to school. (Noun phrases with *each* and *every* take singular Verbs.)

Exercise 1

Fill in the blanks with the correct form, singular or plural of the verbs given in the brackets. Use the verbs in the tenses indicated.

1 The names of the boys ——— called and one of the boys ——— absent. (be, be) (simple past)
2 Fifty years ——— half a century. (be) (present simple)
3 Iddli and sambar ——— the breakfast in many homes in the South. (make) (present simple)
4 I wanted five books and none of them ——— available in the shops. (be) (past simple)
5 Either you or your brother ——— to come with me. (be) (present simple)
6 Of the forty boys thirty ——— small pox. (have) (present perfect)
7 Neither the men in the car nor the driver ——— hurt in the accident. (be) (simple past)
8 The Committee ——— divided on the question of revision of the memb ship fee. (be) (simple past)
9 Father, as well as the others in the family ——— to move into a new house. (want) (present simple)
10 Father, with Mother and the children, ——— on a long tour to the South. (go) (present progressive)
11 Each of the drawers ——— a separate key. (have) (present simple)
12 I have read the book; most of it ——— to be borrowed matter. (seem) (present simple)
13 Five times ten ——— fifty. (be) (present simple)
14 There ——— a typewriter and a telephone on Mr Madhav's desk. (be) (present simple)
15 Every man, woman and child in the town ——— vaccinated. (be) (present perfect)

14. NEGATIVE AND INTERROGATIVE SENTENCES

Negative Sentences

1 Look at the sentences in A and B.

A	B
Father is at home.	Father is not at home.
Those boys were tired.	Those boys were not tired.
Those people are tourists.	Those people are not tourists.
He was interested in politics.	He was not interested in politics.

The sentences in A are affirmative sentences. In the sentences in B the negating word *not* is added after the verbs to make them negative sentences. The verbs in the sentences in both A and B are forms of *be*. Sentences with *be* as full verb are turned into negative ones my merely adding *not* after the verb.

2 Look at the sentences in A and B:

A	B
Mr Jha is going to Delhi. His wife and children are going.	Mr Jha is not going to Delhi. His wife and children are not going.
Balu has finished his examinations.	Balu has not finished his examinations.
The schools have been closed.	The schools have not been closed.
They will pass the examination.	They will not pass the examination.

The sentences in A are affirmative and those in B are negative. The negative sentences in B are formed by adding *not* to the auxiliary *is*, *are*, *has*, *have* or *will*. Note that *not* comes between the auxiliary and the main verb.

3 Father isn't at home.
The boys weren't tired.
Those people aren't tourists.
He wasn't interested in politics.

In these sentences we see the contracted or abbreviated forms of the negative *not* used and the contracted form is linked to the auxiliary. These contracted forms are very common in informal and spoken English.

4 Look at this conversation:

Ravi: Tomorrow is a holiday, Raju.
Raju: No, tomorrow is not a holiday. I asked the Professor this morning.

The speaker uses the full form *is not* instead of the short form *isn't*, to express strong contradiction, or to give added force to his statement.

5 They're not tourists.
Father's not at home.
They've not closed the schools.

In these sentences the auxiliary is contracted and linked to the subject. In such cases the negative *not* is not contracted.

6 He comes here every day.
We buy our milk from a milkman.
Mr David went to Bombay yesterday.

In these sentences the verb is present simple or past simple and hasn't got any auxiliary. The negative sentences are formed in these cases by introducing the auxiliary *do* and adding *not* to it.

Comes is split up into *does come* and the negative is added to *does*: He comes every day—He *does come* every day — He *does not come* every day.

Buy is split up into *do buy* and the negative is added to *do*: We buy our milk from a milkman — We *do buy* our milk from a milkman — we *do not buy* our milk from a milkman.

Went is split up into *did go* and the negative is added to *did*: Mr David went. . . . . — Mr David *did go*. . . . . — Mr David *did not go*. . . . .

So we have the following sentences:

He does not (doesn't) come here every day.
We do not (don't) buy our milk from a milkman.
Mr David did not (didn't) go to Bombay yesterday.

Note the contracted forms given in brackets.

7 Look at these sentences in A and B.

A	B
Do it again.	Don't do it again.
Come here tomorrow.	Don't come here tomorrow.
Take away your books.	Don't take away your books.

The sentences here are imperative sentences. When these are put in the negative form, the auxiliary *do* is used and the negating word *not* or, more often, the contracted form /n't/ is added to the auxiliary.

8 He hadn't any money.
He hasn't any money.

In these sentences the verb *have* is used as a full verb. It is made negative by adding the contracted form /n't/ to it. Some speakers use the auxiliary *do* to form the negative of *have*: He doesn't have any money. He didn't have any money.

There is no difference in meaning between these two ways of making the negative of *have*. Here are some more examples:

She doesn't have any children.
She hasn't any children.
They don't have a car.
They haven't a car.

Exercise 1

Turn the following sentences into negative sentences:

1 I am quite well.
2 He came here a second time.
3 Hari is honest.
4 My father was asleep.
5 These answers are wrong.
6 He did it again.
7 They were present here yesterday.
8 Open the door.
9 It is/was raining heavily.
10 Our Professor is retiring next month.
11 My children speak Urdu well.
12 Please wait for me.
13 He needs your help.
14 He has a daughter to be married off.

Exercise 2

Complete the following sentences with the verbs given in brackets putting them in the appropriate tense form and in the negative.

Examples:

a Ravi has borrowed a book from the library, but he ——— reading it. (start)
Ravi has borrowed a book from the library, but he hasn't started reading it.

b He sat for the examination, but he ——— it. (pass)
He sat for the examination, but he didn't pass it.

1 He has done four years' research, but he ——— his degree yet. (got)
2 If you ——— a taxi, you will miss your train. (catch)
3 In spite of his earnest request they ——— the question of his promotion. (reopen)
4 The lady looked at dozens of saris, but ——— any. (buy)

5 'I ——— anywhere. I just came here to see a friend off.' (go)
6 'If the weather ——— with you there, you may come back.' (agree)
7 'Your face is familiar, but I ——— your name.' (remember)
8 Although he ——— in the house, he pays the rent regularly. (live)
9 I used to play cricket regularly, but I ——— for the last five years. (play)
10 She has been dieting for the last six months, but ——— much weight. (lose)

9 Look at these sentences:

I *seldom* go to the pictures.
He *rarely* speaks in public.
He has *little* knowledge of the subject.
He is a shy type of man and has *few* friends.
He was *barely* sixteen when he took his B.A. degree.
There is *scarcely* any milk in the house.
There is *hardly* any logic in his arguments.

The words in italics are negative in meaning, though not in form. They are followed by the non-assertive words such as *any*, *anything*, *anywhere*, rather than the assertive words such as *some*, *something*, *somewhere*.

I seldom eat any non-vegetarian food.
He has hardly any excuse for his action.
I scarcely go out anywhere.

Note: *Little* means *not much.*
Few means *not many.*

10 Seldom have I discussed the subject with him.
Rarely/scarcely do I go to the pictures.
Little does he care about his children.
Barely can he read and write.

The examples above will show that when a sentence begins with one of the words that have negative meaning, the subject is put before the auxiliary.

Interrogative Sentences

Yes-or-No Questions

a Look at these sentences:

A *Statements*	B *Questions*
This is the road to the University.	Is this the road to the University?
All the rooms are vacant.	Are all the rooms vacant?
They have a car.	Have they a car?
There is a canteen in the college.	Is there a canteen in the college?

The sentences in A are statements. Each sentence has a subject and the subject precedes the verb.

The sentences in B are questions. The verb (*is*, *are*, *have*), comes first and the subject is put after it. In other words, there is an inversion of subject and verb. This inversion is a common feature of questions in English.

[*Note*: Questions with *have* can also be made with the auxiliary *do*: Do they have a car?]

b Look at these sentences:

A *Statements*	B *Questions*
Mr Mathur is writing a book.	Is Mr Mathur writing a book?
The doctor has arrived.	Has the doctor arrived?
The owner will get the house painted.	Will the owner get the house painted?
They haven't gone to the match.	Haven't they gone to the match?

The sentences in B are questions. In these sentences too, the auxiliary (*is*, *has*, *will*, *haven't*) comes before the subject.

When we use modal auxiliaries too, such as *can*, *could*, *should*, etc. with verbs, the auxiliaries are put before the subjects.

Can you get these letters typed?
Should we send for the plumber?
Oughtn't we to see him?

c Look at these sentences:

A *Statements*	B *Questions*
The train arrived on time.	Did the train arrive on time?
He works in the Corporation office.	Does he work in the Corporation office?
They go to the park every evening.	Do they go to the park every evening?

As we saw in the case of negation, in the questions in B the auxiliary *do* or a form of it is provided in questions and it is put before the subject.

The answer to any of the questions in B in a, b and c above is either 'yes' or 'no'. Questions of this type are therefore called 'yes-or-no' questions.

d Is anyone absent today?
Did you see my brother anywhere here?
Have you ever travelled in an aeroplane?
Do you have anything to say on the proposal?
Has the train left yet?

Note that in these yes-or-no questions, non-assertive forms, *anyone*, *anywhere*, *yet*, *ever*, etc. are used. This is a characteristic of yes-or-no questions.

e Is someone absent today?
Did you see my brother somewhere here?
Has the train left already?

Note that in these sentences assertive forms such as *someone*, *somewhere*, *already*, etc. are used. These questions show that the speaker has reason to believe that the answer is 'yes,' and he merely asks the question for confirmation of his assumption. These are positive-oriented questions. Hence the use of the assertive forms.

f i Can't you tell the truth?
(I had thought you would, but it seems you won't.)

ii Aren't you ashamed of your conduct?
(You ought to be, but it appears you are not.)

iii Hasn't he any sense?
(I thought he had, but it appears he hasn't.)

iv Don't you see my point?
(I thought you would, but you don't seem to.)

These questions for which the answer is negative are negative-oriented questions. They begin with an auxiliary in the negative.

Exercise 3

The following is the report of a conversation between a lawyer and a witness during the trial of a case. Only the witness's answers are given and you have to frame the questions the lawyer may have asked to get the answers given. The witness gives only short answers, the rest being unsaid or understood. The understood or unsaid portions are in the brackets and they will help you to make the lawyer's questions.

Example:

Lawyer: ....?
Witness: No, I'm not. (a weaver)
Answer: Are you a weaver?

Lawyer: ....?
Witness: No, I'm not (related to Mr Shah)
Lawyer: ....?
Witness: No, he isn't. (a friend of mine)

Lawyer: ....?
Witness: Yes, I do. (know him)
Lawyer: ....?
Witness: No, he hasn't. (lent me money)
Lawyer: ....?
Witness: Yes, he does. (charges high interest)
Lawyer: ....?
Witness: Yes, he did. (lend money to the prisoner)
Lawyer: ....?
Witness: Yes, I was. (at the prisoner's shop on 30th September)
Lawyer: ....?
Witness: Yes, he (Mr Shah) was. (there at that time)
Lawyer: ....?
Witness: Yes, he (prisoner) did. (stab Mr Shah)
Lawyer: ....?
Witness: Yes, I did. (see the stabbing)
Lawyer: ....?
Witness: Yes, he did. (use a knife)
Lawyer: ....?
Witness: Yes, it is. (the knife I saw)
Lawyer: ....?
Witness: Yes, I am. (quite sure)

Tag Questions

Look at these sentences:

Mr Keskar is at home, isn't he?
They are coming to visit us, aren't they?
It rained yesterday, didn't it?
Mr Keskar isn't at home, is he?
They aren't coming to visit us, are they?
It didn't rain yesterday, did it?
The train hasn't left, has it?

Each of these sentences consists of a statement and a short question separated by a comma. The short question is called a tag question or question tag. Question tags are generally confined to spoken English and informal writing. Although they nominally ask the opinion of the person to whom they are addressed, they do not really do so. They take his agreement for granted.

Note these points about the formation of tag questions.

a The tag question consists of an auxiliary and a subject.

b The auxiliary is the same as the auxiliary of the verb in the statement. If there is no auxiliary in the statement, *do* is made the auxiliary.

c If a personal pronoun is the subject of the statement, it is repeated as the subject of the tag. *There* is also similarly repeated. If a noun or a pronoun other than a personal pronoun is the subject of the statement, the subject of the tag is the pronoun that can stand for the noun, i.e. *he*, *she*, *it*, etc. as the case may be. The pronoun *one* is followed by *one.*

He is all right after his recent illness, isn't he?
Kamala has passed her B.A., hasn't she?
One has to be careful in dealing with him, hasn't one?

d An affirmative statement takes a negative tag, and a negative statement takes an affirmative tag.

He is coming to the show, isn't he?
He is not coming to the show, is he?
We had expected this difficulty, hadn't we?
We hadn't expected this difficulty, had we?

Exercise 4

Rewrite the following sentences, adding appropriate tag questions. Remember to separate the tag by a comma.

1 We are travelling by train.
2 Mr Jacob has invited us to dinner.

3 Kashmir summers are wonderful.
4 A large number of tourists are expected this year.
5 You haven't booked our tickets.
6 You hope to get tickets for all of us.
7 You don't want me to come with you.
8 Mr Prasad is giving us a talk on Electronics this evening.
9 Our team hasn't won a single match.
10 None of the girls liked the entertainment.

Question-Word Questions or Information Questions

a Look at these questions:

Why is this a difficult problem?
Where are you working now?
When did Mr Rao return from Madras?
How did the prisoner escape?

These questions are called question-word questions or information questions. They begin with question-words such as *when*, *why*, *where*, *how*, *who*, *what*, etc. These questions ask for some information in every case and you cannot answer them with just 'yes' or 'no'.

Note how question-word questions are formed:

Statement	*Yes-or-no form*	*Question-word form*
You are working now.	Are you working now?	Where are you working now?
This is a difficult problem.	Is this a difficult problem?	Why is this a difficult problem?
Mr Rao returned from Madras.	Did Mr Rao return from Madras?	When did Mr Rao return from Madras?
The prisoner escaped.	Did the prisoner escape?	Where/how did the prisoner escape?

We first form a yes-or-no question and then put the appropriate question-word before it.

b He ate *a mango*.
Mr Rao returned from Madras *last Monday*.
The prisoner escaped *by scaling the wall*.

To get the information, italicized in each statement above, we make these questions:

What did he eat?

When did Mr Rao return from Madras?

How did the prisoner escape?

c Study these information questions, made with phrases formed by the question-word *how* joined to an adjective or adverb.

Statements	*Questions*
The prison wall was *twenty feet high.*	*How high* was the prison wall?
There are *two* colleges in the district.	*How many* colleges are there in the district?
The postman comes here *three times a day.*	*How often* does the postman come here?
This car can run at *a hundred kilometres an hour.*	*How fast* can this car run?
This book costs *ten rupees.*	*How much* does this book cost?
The train is *half an hour late.*	*How late* is the train?

d Question-word questions with *who*, *which* and *what*, when these words stand for the objects in the sentences, are made as shown below.

i The maid *broke* the plates.
The maid *did break* the plates.
Did the maid *break* the plates? (what)
What did the maid break?

ii They *invited* the judge.
They *did invite* the judge.
Did they *invite* the judge? (whom/who)
Who/whom did they invite?

iii She *chose* the red sari.
She *did choose* the red sari.
Did she *choose* the red sari? (which sari)
Which sari did she choose?

iv That is Sekhar's house.
Is that Sekhar's house? (whose house)
Whose house is that?

e The maid broke the plates. Who broke the plates?
The black book is mine. Which book is yours?
This happened in Bombay. What happened in Bombay?

In these sentences the question-word replaces the subject and becomes the subject. In such cases there is no subject-verb inversion.

If the question-word replaces the object, inversion takes place.

He was talking to his neighbour.	Who/whom was he talking to?
He left out the last question.	Which question did he leave out?
He wants ice-cream.	What does he want?

A question-word can replace

i a subject:
That tall lady is the school doctor.
Who is the school doctor?

ii the object:
She is buying *bananas*.
What is she buying?

iii the verb:
She *is buying* bananas.
What is she doing?

iv the determiner and adjective:
That tall boy won the prize.
Which boy won the prize?

v the adverbial:
He lives *in Varanasi*.
Where does he live?

He paid five rupees *for this pen*.
How much did he pay for this pen?

f Look at these statements/answers and questions.

Statements/Answers	*Questions*
I want a knife *for mending the pencil.*	What do you want a knife *for*?
I signed the cheque *with a ball-point pen.*	What did you sign the cheque *with*?
I dipped it *in milk.*	What did you dip it *in* ?
I am buying this *for my son.*	Who are you buying this *for*?
I gave it *to my neighbour.*	Who did you give it *to*?

In questions like those above, the preposition that goes with the question-word is placed at the end of the sentence. But we can also put the prepositions before the question-word, but this makes the sentence too formal:

With what did you sign the cheque?
On what did you base your conclusions?
To whom did you give it?

g *Alternative questions*

Look at these sentences:

Questions	*Answers*
Would you like to come with me or stay here?	Stay here/come with you.
Shall we go to the pictures or go for a walk?	Pictures/for a walk.
Is your friend coming today or tomorrow?	tomorrow/today.

These questions are called 'alternative questions'. The answer to each has to be one of the choices offered, and not 'yes' or 'no'.

A yes-or-no question can be changed into an alternative question by adding *or not.*

Are you eating or not?
Is he happy or not?

h *Rhetorical questions*

Look at these questions:

Who can predict the future? (No one can.)

Who will do this dirty work? (No one will.)

Is that a good reason for not going to school? (That is not a good reason.)

Do you think no one is going to marry me? (Someone will, surely.)

These are neither yes-or-no questions nor information questions. They only make forceful statements in the form of questions. They are called 'rhetorical' questions. A positive rhetorical question is a strong negative assertion and a negative rhetorical question is a strong positive assertion, as the statements in brackets show.

Exercise 5

The conversation between the lawyer and the witness is continued below. This time the questions of the lawyer are question-word questions. The question-words with which his questions begin are given. Make the questions.

Lawyer: Where..........................?
Witness: I saw it on the counter in the prisoner's shop.
Lawyer: When ....?
Witness: I saw it on 29th September.
Lawyer: Why ....?
Witness: I went (to the shop) to buy some meat.
Lawyer: How ....?
Witness: (I know this was the knife) because it has the same kind of handle.
Lawyer: What kind ....?
Witness: It was a kitchen knife.

i *Short Responses with Auxiliaries*

Look at the conversation below:

Ali: Has David come to the class?
Ravi: Yes, he *has*.
Ali: Does he know we have a test today?
Ravi: Yes, he *does*.

Ali: Do you know tomorrow is a working day?
Ravi: Yes, I *do*.
Ali: Was Rajan absent yesterday?
Ravi: No, he *wasn't*.

Look at Ravi's answers. He used auxiliaries. He uses

has in place of *has come*,
does in place of *knows*,
do in place of *know*,
wasn't in place of *wasn't absent*.

These short responses are used to avoid the repetition of verbs, especially in spoken English and in short replies. The subject and the verb follow in the normal order.

Responses with 'so' and 'nor'

Look at the following statements and the responses that follow.

A: Mr Sharma owns a scooter.
B: So does Mr Rao.
A: He is going home.
B: So am I.
A: I don't agree with him on some points.
B: Nor do I.
A: I like chess.
B: So does my room-mate.
A: My wife doesn't like onions.
B: Nor does my wife.

In these short responses *so* is used when what is stated in the statement is true with regard to another person; *nor* is used when the response is to a negative statement.

Notice that in these responses there is subject-auxiliary inversion.

15 THE PASSIVE VOICE

Look at these sentences:

1 A Committee of lecturers *prepared* the College Annual Report.

2 They *got* it printed.

3 It *was read* by the Principal on College Day.

Sentences 1 and 2 above say what the Committee did: they prepared the report; they got it printed. The Committee is the subject of the two sentences and the verbs express the actions performed by them. They are transitive verbs and their object is the noun *report*. The verbs are said to be in the **active voice.**

In sentence 3 above, the subject is the report, but the verb, *was read*, does not express any action done by *the subject*, but only what was done *to it*. The verb expresses the action that the report ' received ' or ' suffered '. The form, *was read*, is used to express this idea. Verbs in this form are said to be in the **passive voice.**

So while verbs in the active voice express actions performed by a ' doer ' or ' agent,' verbs in the passive voice express what the *objects* of those actions ' suffered ' or ' received'. In other words, the passive voice form of verb is used when the object of an action is made the subject of a sentence. Hence we say: *The report was read.*

When to use the Passive Voice

1 Look at these two sentences:

The Principal read the report.

The report was read by the Principal.

There is practically no difference in the meaning or idea expressed by the two sentences.

But this is not always so. Often the active voice and the passive voice express a difference in emphasis. Look at these two sentences:

> The Panchayat dug a well to provide water to the village.
>
> A well was dug to provide water to the village.

Here we would prefer to use the second rather than the first sentence, because what we want to refer to is not the action of the Panchayat but the result of the action, namely, a well being provided in order to supply water to the village. Who dug the well is not the main idea in our minds. In other words, we are interested in the particular happening, not in anyone's action. So we would use the passive voice here.

Here are some more examples of contexts in which the passive voice is preferred.

> A bridge was built across the river.
> (Who built it is not important.)
>
> A mistake was made in totalling the marks.
> (Who made the mistake is not our concern here, but only the occurrence of the mistake.)
>
> Term fees should be paid before the 15th of this month. (This is an order expressed *impersonally*. Compare this with: 'You should pay your term fees before the 15th of this month!')

Since the passive voice sounds impersonal it is used in preference to the active voice, in describing scientific or technical processes. For example: Common salt *is got* from the sea. Sea water *is collected* in salt pans. It *is allowed* to evaporate in the sun. As a result, salt crystals *are formed* at the bottom. They *are removed and dried* in the sun.

2 The results were published *last week.*
The new books were placed *on a separate shelf.*
Rice is grown *in many parts of the world.*

You will notice that the italicized adverbials in the sentences above are necessary to complete the meaning of the sentences.

Now look at these sentences:

> The electric bulb was invented *by Edison.*
> *Hamlet* was written *by Shakespeare.*
> The tiger was killed *by a shepherd boy.*

You will notice that the *by + noun* (*agent*) phrase in the sentences above are necessary to complete the meaning of the sentences. Hence they are used in these sentences. If the *by + agent* phrase is not needed for completing the meaning, it is not used. For example, we say: 'The house was sold for Rs. 35,000.' We don't have to say: 'The house was sold for Rs. 35,000 by its owner.'

3 *The form of the passive*

Look at the sentences in the two columns below.

	Active		*Passive*
a	Mr Dinesh sells radios.	a	Radios are sold by Mr Dinesh.
b	They grow rice.	b	Rice is grown by them.
c	The servant washes our clothes	c	Our clothes are washed by the servant.
d	He teaches me.	d	I am taught by him.

Note the changes we make when we transform sentences from the active voice to the passive. These are illustrated in the two columns above.

a We put the object of the active verb in the subject position. For example 'radios,' the object in the sentence 1 above under 'Active,' is made the subject in sentence 1 under 'Passive'.

b The number of the verb is changed according to the number of the subject. For example Mr Dinesh is the subject of sentence (a) under 'active'. So the verb is singular: *sells.* We have changed this sentence into the passive in sentence (a) under 'Passive,' and 'radios' has become the subject. So the verb is plural: *are* sold.

c The form of the verb is changed in the passive: *sells* becomes *are sold*; in sentence (b) *grow* becomes *is grown*.

4 The verbs in the active sentences in 3 above are in the present simple tense. The form of the verb in the passive is: *a form of 'be' (am, is, are)* + the past participle, namely, *are sold, is grown, are washed, am taught.*

The form of the verb in the passive varies according to the tense of the verb in the active. In order to be able to make sentences in the passive voice, the forms which verbs take when put in this voice have to be learnt. Here is a chart giving the passive voice forms of verbs in the various tenses, together with examples. (The letters 'p.p.' used in the chart stand for 'past participle'.)

Tense	*Form*	*Example*
Present Simple	am + p.p.	I *am helped* by him.
	is + p.p.	Rice *is grown* there.
	are + p.p.	Lamps *are lighted* on that day.
Past Simple	was + p.p.	The book *was sold out.*
	were + p.p.	The trees *were cut.*
Present Continuous	am + being + p.p.	I *am being trained* for teaching.
	is + being + p.p.	He *is being trained* as a mechanic.
	are + being + p.p.	Houses *are being built* for Harijans.
Past Continuous	was + being + p.p.	A meeting *was being held.*
	were + being + p.p.	The papers *were being corrected.*
Present Perfect	has + been + p.p.	The house *has been white-washed.*
	have + been + p.p.	The rooms *have been locked.*

Tense	*Form*	*Example*
Past Perfect	had + been + p.p.	The questions *had been leaked* out.
Future	will/shall + be + p.p.	Lamps *will be lighted* on that day. We *shall be informed* of the result.
Future Perfect	will/shall + have + been + p.p.	The boys *will have been admitted.* We *shall have been told.*

The passive forms of Present Perfect Continuous, Past Perfect Continuous and Future Perfect Continuous are not given above, because these are rarely used.

Here is a chart showing some examples of passive voice forms of verbs when combined with modal auxiliaries.

Active	*Passive*
He can win the prize.	The prize *can be won* by him.
We may drive the car through the tunnel.	The car *may be driven* through the tunnel.
Our team could win the match.	The match *could be won* by our team.
You must send a reply.	A reply *must be sent.*
A doctor should see him.	He *should be seen* by a doctor.
We ought to show respect to our elders.	Our elders *ought to be shown* respect.
Ants must have eaten the cakes.	The cakes *must have been eaten* by ants.
The child may have broken the mirror.	The mirror *may have been broken* by the child.

Exercise 1

Rewrite the following sentences in the passive voice. Use the *by + agent* phrase only where it is found necessary.

1 Alexander cut the Gordian knot.

2 A Committee makes the selection of students.
3 The lecturer marks the attendance every period.
4 The auditors are checking the accounts.
5 The police are investigating the murder.
6 The Reception Committee has made all the arrangements.
7 Mother has cooked the dinner.
8 The cat drank all the milk.
9 The enemy bombed the city last night.
10 The chairman was ringing the bell.
11 The students were decorating the college hall.
12 The General Body had passed two of the resolutions.
13 The municipality had sanctioned the construction of the theatre.
14 The Principal will interview the students in the afternoon.
15 A high court judge will conduct the enquiry.
16 He will have completed it by the end of next month.
17 They will have announced the results by the beginning of June.
18 We have posted most of the invitations.
19 Alexander Fleming discovered penicillin.
20 They have added two hundred books to the library.

5 *Passive of Commands*

Look at these sentences:

Put up this picture on that wall.
Send these letters by registered post.
Inform the police of the accident.

Commands such as these are put in the passive as follows:

Let this picture *be put up* on that wall.
Let these letters *be sent* by registered post.
Let the police *be informed.*

The form of the verb is *let* + *be* + *past participle*, and the subject is put between *let* and *be* + *past participle.*

6 *Passive of questions*

A Look at these sentences:

Do they speak Tamil?

Can we send this big parcel by air?
Must we cut this tree?
Will they hold the elections?
Has he invited you?

Yes-or-no questions such as these are put in the passive voice as follows:

Is Tamil spoken by them?
Can this big parcel be sent by air?
Must this tree be cut?
Will the elections be held?
Have you been invited by him?

The form of the verb in the passive voice question is:

a a form of *be* + *past participle*, if the question in the active voice begins with *do*, *does* or *did*.

Example: Is Tamil spoken by them?

b *Modal auxiliary* + *be* + *past participle*, if the question in the active voice begins with a modal auxiliary.

Example: Can this big parcel be sent by air?

c *Has/have/had* + *be* + *past participle*, if the question in the active voice is in the present or past perfect tense.

Example: Have you been invited by him?

Note that in all yes-or-no questions in the passive voice the subject is put between the auxiliary and the main verb.

B Look at these question-word questions:

Where did you buy this pen?
Why did they pull down the building?
When do they deliver the mail?
Where will they send these prisoners?
What did they buy in the shop?
Who wrote *Hamlet*?

These information questions are put in the passive, as follows:

Where was the pen bought by you?
Why was the building pulled down?
When is the mail delivered?
Where will these prisoners be sent?
What was bought by them in the shop?
Who was *Hamlet* written by? *or*
By whom was *Hamlet* written?

The form of the verb is: a form of *be + the past participle*, or, if a modal auxiliary is used in the active voice: *Modal auxiliary + a form of be + past participle.* Example: Why *should* these trees *be cut*?

7 *Passive of Negative Sentences*

Look at these negative sentences:

Some members did not attend the meeting.
The Assembly will not pass this bill.
We should not raise this question now.
They don't teach English in the lower classes.

These sentences are put in the passive as shown below:

The meeting was not attended by some members.
This bill will not be passed by the Assembly.
This question should not be raised now.
English is not taught in the lower classes.

You will notice in the examples above that the passive is formed in the same way as in the case of affirmative sentences, but with the negative word *not* put between the auxiliary and the past participle.

Exercise 2

Put the following sentences into the passive voice. Use the *by + agent* phrase only where necessary.

1 Type these letters before 4 o'clock.
2 Deposit this money in the bank.

3 Send invitations to all the parents.
4 Do you take colour photos?
5 Did they hire a bus?
6 Is the doctor examining the patient?
7 Where do they play the match?
8 Why did they raise this question?
9 Where can you get good silk saris?
10 When do they clear the mail?
11 Who broke the news?
12 What did they discuss at the meeting?
13 We can't take up this work now.
14 Some persons don't eat onions.
15 The tourists didn't visit this place.

8 Look at these sentences:

The police gave him a reward of Rs. 1,000.
Mr Kumar taught us English.

Each of these sentences has two objects, the indirect object *him/us*, and the direct object *a reward of Rs. 1,000/ English*. The sentences can be rewritten in the passive voice making either the direct or the indirect object the subject and retaining the other object.

a He was given a reward of Rs.1,000 by the police.
b A reward of Rs. 1,000 was given him by the police.
c A reward of Rs. 1,000 was given to him by the police.

a We were taught English by Mr. Kumar.
b English was taught us by Mr. Kumar.
c English was taught to us by Mr. Kumar.

Sentences marked (*a*) above read more natural and hence they are more commonly used. That is, it is more common to make the indirect object (*him, us* in the two sentences above) the subject of the sentence in the passive voice.

9 The teacher was satisfied *with* Balu's progress.
Mathur is interested *in* gardening.
I am disgusted *with* his behaviour.
We were surprised *at* the news.

Verbs such as the ones in these sentences take other prepositions such as *with*, *in* and *at*, instead of *by*.

Exercise 3

Put each of the sentences below into the passive voice, in the three ways shown in the examples.

Examples:

a Active voice:

Mr Kumar teaches us English.

Passive voice:

We are taught English by Mr Kumar.
English is taught us by Mr Kumar.
English is taught to us by Mr Kumar.

b Active voice:

They gave the child an injection.

Passive voice:

The child was given an injection.
An injection was given the child.
An injection was given to the child.

1 The manager refused the clerk leave.
2 Someone showed me the photograph.
3 Why did they give him so much money?
4 My uncle gave me a good education.
5 You should teach the man a lesson.

Exercise 4

Put the sentences below into the passive voice as shown in the examples.

Examples:

a Active voice:

The members elected Mr Das Chairman.

Passive voice:

Mr Das was elected Chairman.

b Active voice:

The accident left the man a cripple.

Passive voice:

The man was left a cripple by the accident.

1 Woollen clothes keep us warm.
2 The children called Nehru 'Chacha'.
3 We have painted the house green.
4 They named the child Dinesh.
5 The judge found the prisoner not guilty.

Exercise 5

Put the sentences below into the passive voice as shown in the examples.

Examples:

a Active voice:

The teacher permitted the boys to go and play.

Passive voice:

The boys were permitted to go and play.

b Active voice:

The teacher made the boys stay back.

Passive voice:

The boys were made to stay back.

c Active voice:

He taught me how to sing.

Passive voice:

I was taught by him how to sing.

1 The principal asked the boy to wait.
2 The doctor advised the young man to give up smoking.

3 You can help me to solve this problem.
4 The constable noticed a man throw a stone.
5 He taught me how to face an interview.

Exercise 6

Put the sentences below into the passive voice, as shown in the examples.

Examples:

a Active voice:
The boys laughed at the mad man.
Passive voice:
The mad man was laughed at by the boys.

b Active voice:
The discovery surprised the researcher.
Passive voice:
The researcher was surprised at the discovery.

1 We have talked to the workers.
2 The agreement satisfied the workers.
3 Social work interests Mrs Das very much.
4 The news surprised everyone.
5 The admission work engaged the principal the whole day.

16. NON-FINITES

Look at these sentences:

1 He wants *to buy* a new house.
2 *Buying* a new house needs money.
3 I found him *looking for* a new house.
4 *Shaken* by the experience he was ill for a few days.
5 I heard his name *called* twice.

The words *to buy*, in sentence (1), *buying* in sentence (2), *looking for* in sentence (3), *shaken* and *called* in sentences (4) and (5) are forms of verb called *non-finites*. They have none of the tenses, have no number and take no modals.

To buy is called an *infinitive*;
the form of the infinitive is *to* + the *bare verb*.

Buying is called a *gerund*;
the form of a gerund is *verb* + *ing*.

Looking for is a *present participle*;
the form of a present participle is *verb* + *ing*.
Shaken and *called* are *past participles*.

There are, therefore, four non-finites: the infinitive, the gerund, the present participle and the past participle.

The Infinitives

1 Look at the forms of the infinitive in the following sentences:

a Jaya wanted *to learn* photography.
b She is reported *to be learning* it.
c She is reported *to have learnt* painting already.
d She is known *to have been learning* music for the last five years.

In these sentences you see four forms of the infinitive. Those in sentences (b), (c) and (d) are formed with the help of the auxiliaries *be* and *have*. The auxiliary does not undergo any change. It is the main verb *learn* that undergoes the necessary changes.

Sentence (b): to be + verb –ing
Sentence (c): to have + past participle
Sentence (d): to have + past participle of be + verb –ing

Some of these forms have the corresponding passive voice.

to learn — to be learnt
There is a great deal to be learnt in photography.
to have asked — to have been asked
He was happy to have been asked to deliver the convocation address.

2 The infinitives shown above have the word *to* before them.

But look at these sentences:

The mother made the child *drink* the medicine.
Then she let the child *go* out and *play*.
She saw the child *run* out into the garden.

The words in italics are really infinitives but *to* is omitted. This omission takes place after certain verbs:

The following are some of the important ones:
make, let, see, hear, watch, have, bid.

3 Look at the sentences in A and B.

A	B
We saw him leave.	He was seen to leave.
I heard the postman knock at the door.	The postman was heard to knock at the door.
We made them work all night.	They were made to work all night.
I helped the old woman climb the steps.	The old woman was helped to climb the steps.

Note that in A the verbs are in the active voice and take the bare infinitive. When the verbs are put in the passive voice B the infinitives take *to* before them.

The verbs that are used after the modal auxiliaries, *will*, *shall*, *can*, *dare*, *need*, etc. are said to be infinitives without *to*.

He dare not *climb* that tree.
You need not *wait* here.
I will *see* you tomorrow.
He shall *feel* sorry for this.

4 *The uses of the infinitive*

a The infinitive can function like a noun.
To drive a car needs a licence. (subject of verb)

Jaya wants to learn photography. (object of verb)
His aim in life is to be a pilot. (subject complement)
It is easy to advise others. (Here *it* is a dummy subject which anticipates *to advise*.)

b The infinitive can function as an adjunct (or an adjective) to a noun or pronoun:

His *decision to resign* is final.
He wants *somebody to talk to.*
He was *the first to come* and *the last to go.*
The *subject to be discussed* is known to you.
Give me *something to eat.*

c The infinitive can function as an adverbial modifying a verb which goes before it:

He *got up to ask* a question.
I *went to see* the minister.
We do not *live to eat*; but we *eat to live.*

This infinitive is often called the *infinitive of purpose.*

5 Look at these sentences:

He is too young to go to school.
It is now too late to do anything.
He is too inexperienced to be of any use to me.
He spoke too fast to be followed.

In these sentences the infinitive is used with *too* + *adjective/adverb*. The sentences can be transformed into complex sentences using *so........that.*

He is so young that he cannot go to school.
It is now so late that we cannot do anything.
He is so inexperienced that he is not of any use to me.
He spoke so fast that he could not be followed.

Look at these sentences:

This table is too heavy to lift.
This coffee is too hot to drink.

The infinitives in these sentences have a passive meaning though they are active in form.

This table is so heavy that it *cannot be lifted.*
This coffee is so hot that it *cannot be drunk.*

Exercise 1

Rewrite the following sentences using *to*, wherever necessary, before the infinitives given in brackets.

1 Mrs Bose asked her son ——— home before 8 o'clock. (come)
2 If you have planned ——— the airport before five, you had better ——— at once. (reach, start)
3 He wouldn't let anyone ——— his bicycle. (use)
4 We wanted ——— the house where Mahatma Gandhi was born. (see)
5 Did you really see him ——— your brother? (beat)
6 We were not permitted ——— the hospital. (enter)
7 He would rather ——— than ——— a lie. (die, tell)
8 He made us ——— for an hour. (wait)
9 I would have him ——— again for this purpose. (come)
10 You needn't ——— all the questions. (answer)

Exercise 2

Combine each of the following pairs of sentences using *too* followed by an infinitive.

Example:

The grapes were very sour.
We couldn't eat them.
The grapes were too sour to eat.
or
The grapes were too sour for us to eat.

1 He was very weak.
He could not walk.
2 You are very young.
You cannot be admitted to college.
3 He was very proud.
He wouldn't talk to us.
4 This lesson is very long.
It cannot be finished today.

5 He is very honest.
He could not have told a lie.

6 This news is too good.
It cannot be true.

The Gerund

The gerund and the present participle have the same form, *verb + ing*: swimming, walking, cutting, etc.

1 *Uses of the gerund*

a *Swimming* is a good exercise.
Speaking is easier than writing.
Looking after children needs a lot of patience.
Smoking in the auditorium is prohibited.

In each of these sentences the gerund is the subject of a verb.

b He likes *reading* detective novels.
Would you mind *waiting* for a few minutes?
I hate *waiting* at bus stops.

In each of these sentences the gerund is the object of a verb.

c He inaugurated the school *by lighting* a lamp.
He was fined *for being* drunk while driving.
He is thinking *of resigning* his job.
They resumed their journey *after resting* an hour.

The gerunds in these sentences are objects of the prepositions before them.

d Talking to him is *wasting* time.
Seeing is *believing*.

The gerunds in these sentences are subject complements.

e Look at the *-ing* form in these sentences:

He has a collection of *walking* sticks.
He bought a new *dining table*.
She wastes hours before her *looking* glass.
The dancing floor was paved with marble.
The village has a free *reading* room.

The *verb -ing* in each of these sentences is a gerund and functions like an adjective qualifying the noun that follows it. Note the meaning of the gerund in this use.

> A *walking stick* means not a stick that walks, but a stick for walking.

Similarly,

> dining table: a table for dining
> looking glass: a glass for looking in
> dancing floor: a floor for dancing
> reading room: a room for reading

2 We have seen that both the infinitive and the gerund can be objects of verbs. But some verbs usually take the infinitive after them, some take the gerund and some others take both the infinitive and the gerund. Below are some examples of verbs which usually take the infinitive:

> He *agreed to wait.*
> He *asked to see* the manager.
> They *attempted to scale* the mountain.
> He *chose to stay* at home.
> He *claims to represent* all the students.
> She *consented to marry* the man.
> We *decided to start* work.
> He *deserves to be* promoted.
> They *determined to attack.*
> He *expects to be appointed.*
> She *hopes to succeed.*
> She is *learning to drive.*
> I *long to go* back home.
> I *managed to pass.*
> He *meant to cheat.*
> He *offered to step down.*
> The boy *pretended to feel sorry.*

Here are some examples of verbs which usually take gerunds :

> He *acknowledged making* a mistake.
> He *admitted* (*to*) *telling* a lie.
> She *avoided seeing* the principal.

I *considered approaching* the minister.
He *denied using* force.
He *dislikes seeing* films.
He *enjoys playing* with children.
He *favoured closing* down the business.
They *finished counting* the votes at four.
He cannot *help drinking*.
They *kept* (*on*) *discussing* the subject.
I don't *mind waiting* an hour.
I *missed seeing* that play.
He *postponed* his *going* to Delhi.
He *practised dancing* every day.
He *stopped advising* others.
I *suggest going* for a walk.

The verbs listed below can take either the gerund or the infinitive, though with some the infinitive is more frequent and with the others the gerund.

can't bear, begin, cease, continue, dislike, dread, fear, forget, hate, intend, like, love, mean, neglect, prefer, propose, recollect, regret, remember, start, try.

Exercise 3

Fill in each blank with the correct form (either gerund or infinitive) of the verb given in brackets.

1 I hope ——— this time. (pass)
2 He managed ——— the station in time. (reach)
3 Don't forget ——— the lights before ——— to bed. (switch off, go)
4 Would you mind ——— a little? (move)
5 Please stop ———; you are disturbing the others in the library. (talk)
6 Please finish ———; I don't mind ———. (eat, wait)
7 I tried my best ——— the great man, but missed ——— him. (interview, see)
8 If we don't have all the facts, I suggest ——— our decision. (postpone)

9 I never meant ——— his order. (disobey)
10 I don't think he is ill, he is only pretending ——— ill. (be)

Exercise 4

Combine each of the following pairs of sentences into one sentence turning the sentence in italics into a phrase with a preposition followed by a gerund.

Example:

They say their prayers.
Then they go to bed.
They say their prayers before going to bed.

1 *He sells vegetables.*
He earns his living that way.
2 *She painted the best picture.*
She won a prize for it.
3 *He washed his hands.*
Then he sat down for his meal.
4 He was punished.
He was late for school.
5 *I don't argue with him.*
I don't see any good in it.
6 *The child saw the policeman.*
He began to cry.

Participles

The present participle or *active participle*

Look at the words in italics in these sentences:

The *crying* child gets milk.
We found a child *crying* for its mother.
Calling the child to us, we gave it some sweets.

The words in italics are *present participles*. The form is *verb + ing*. We have seen that the gerund has also the same form.

1· *The uses of the present participle*

a A *drowning man* catches at a straw.
An astrologer professes to predict *coming events.*
A *rolling stone* gathers no moss.
This is an *interesting book.*

In these sentences the participle does the work of an adjective, modifying the noun following it. In the sentences below the participles do the work of adjectives in the subject-complement position.

His behaviour is irritating.
His speech was illuminating.
His lectures were interesting.
The results were encouraging.

b Seeing the policemen, the crowd dispersed.
He entered, closing the door behind him.
Taking his walking stick, he went out.

In these sentences two actions by the same subject are referred to, one following the other. The earlier action is expressed by a present participle.

c He went into the bathroom singing.
He ran away whistling.
Placing his hand on the Bible, he swore he had not told a lie.

In these sentences the two actions referred to occur simultaneously and one of them is expressed by the present participle.

d Look at these sentences:

We found him watering the plants in his garden.
The doctor found the patient sitting up in bed.

The participles function as object complements in these sentences.

e The weather being fine, we decided to go for a walk.
The dinner being over, the guests started leaving.

In each of these sentences the participle and the verb of the main clause have different subjects. In cases like this the participle must follow the noun/pronoun which is its subject. Participle phrases used in this way are said to be used 'absolutely'.

2 Having seen my brother off, I came home.
Having done his homework, Anand went out to play.

In these sentences *having + the past participle of the verb* is called a 'perfect participle'. The perfect participle is used to show that the action expressed by it is completed before the second action starts.

3 Having been duped once, he did not fall into the trap again.
Having been defeated several times, the army finally surrendered.

In these sentences the perfect participle is used in the passive voice. The form is: *having* + past participle of *be* + past participle of verb.

Unrelated or misrelated participles

Look at this sentence:

*Walking on the road, a car hit him.

The word *car* is the subject of the main clause, but *walking* does not relate to it. Such a participle is called an unrelated participle. The sentence is wrong. The word to which the participle relates must be the same as the subject of the verb. The sentence can be corrected as follows.

Walking on the road, the man was hit by a car. *Or* While walking on the road, the man was hit by a car.

In this case, *walking* will relate to *the man*, the subject of the verb.

The past participle

Look at the words in italics in these sentences. They are all verbs in the past participle form and have a passive meaning. They have the same uses as the present participles.

a His *spoken* English is much better than his *written* English. (adjective)

b The Chief Minister arrived, *accompanied* by the Minister for Education.

Shot by an arrow, the bird fell to the ground.

In each of the two sentences above two actions are expressed and one of them is expressed with the past participle.

c They became *tired.*
We felt *bored.*
Don't be *disappointed.*

The past participles are subject complements in these sentences.

d We found all the chairs *damaged.*
I got a new shirt *made.*
He had his hair *cut.*

The past participle is used as object complement in these sentences.

Exercise 5

Combine each of the following pairs of sentences using either a present participle or a perfect participle. Make the **italicized** sentence in each pair into a participle phrase.

Examples:

a *They left the car on the road.*
They walked into the jungle.
Leaving the car on the road, they walked into the jungle.

b *She fed the cow.*
Then she milked her.
Having fed the cow, she milked her.

1 *I felt pity for the beggar.*
I gave him some money.

2 *Bhima raised his club.*
He struck a heavy blow.

3 *I had seen the play once.*
I had no desire to see it a second time.

4 *She fed the children.*
Then she sat down to her own lunch.

5 The lion jumped into the well.
He mistook his own image for another lion.

6 *He had already told a lie.*
He had to tell several more lies in support of it.

7 *They had taken a decision.*
They wanted to stick to it.

8 *We have decided to fight.*
Let us fight.

17. DIRECT AND INDIRECT (REPORTED) SPEECH

1 Look at the sentences given below:

> 'How have you done your English paper?' John asked Raju. 'I have done it quite well,' said Raju.

In these two sentences you have one of the two ways in which we report other people's words. Here, the words spoken are repeated exactly as they were spoken, and quotation marks enclose the words. This form of reporting is called **direct speech**.

Now look at the following sentences in which we have another way of reporting the same conversation:

> John asked Raju *how he had done his English paper.*
> Raju said *that he had done it quite well.*

Here, what is said is reported not exactly as it is spoken, but with some changes in grammatical construction. The modifications or changes are made in the verb, pronoun, etc. and are made from the point of view of the person reporting and the time and place of reporting. This form of reporting is called **indirect speech** or **reported speech**.

2 The verb *said* in the reported speech is called the 'reporting' verb. The words actually used by the speaker may be statements, commands/requests, questions or exclamations. The reporting verb we use in indirect speech depends on the kind of sentence reported. For example:

Direct speech: 'Please give me five paise,' the beggar *said* to the passer-by.

Indirect speech: The beggar *begged* the passer-by to give him five paise.

Here, *said* in direct speech is appropriately changed into *begged* in indirect speech.

Here are some verbs which can be used in reporting different types of sentences.

a *statements, affirmative and negative*

say, tell, affirm, assert, declare, state, allege, propose, maintain, set forth, depose, pronounce, represent, put forward, swear, assure, protest, announce, etc.

When something that is said in continuation is reported, we use the verbs: add, go on, continue.

If something is said in reply to a remark or question, we use the verbs:

answer, respond, reply, deny, contradict, refute, contend, disclaim, etc.

b *Commands and requests*

command, order, tell, ask, request, beg, pray, etc.

c *Questions*

ask, enquire, question, query, etc.

d *Exclamation*

exclaim, scream, cry, shout, etc.

3 Here are some examples of how the four types of sentences can be put into indirect speech:

a *Statements*

Direct speech: Raju said, 'I have bought a new bicycle.'

Indirect speech: Raju said (*that*) *he had bought a new bicycle.*

Direct speech: Ravi said, 'The English lecturer will be on leave for a week.'

Indirect speech: Ravi said (*that*) *the English lecturer would be on leave for a week.*

Direct speech: 'The annual examinations will begin on 15th March,' the principal said.

Indirect speech: The principal announced *that the annual examinations would begin on 15th March.*

The statement is changed into a *that*-clause, also called a noun clause. Quite often, especially in the spoken form, the conjunction *that* can be omitted in these sentences.

b *Commands and requests*

i *Positive*

Direct speech: The teacher said to the boys, 'Take back your books.'

Indirect speech: The teacher *asked* the boys *to take back* their books.

Direct speech: The General said to the squadron leader, 'Bomb the enemy's ammunition factories.'

Indirect speech: The General *ordered* the squadron leader *to bomb* the enemy's ammunition factories.

Direct speech: 'Please grant me leave for a day,' the clerk said to the manager.

Indirect speech: The clerk *requested* the manager *to grant* him leave for a day.

Commands and requests are reduced to phrases by changing their verbs (in the imperative) to infinitives with *to*. An appropriate reporting verb is used.

ii *Negative*

Direct speech: 'Please don't touch the exhibits,' the guide said to the students.

Indirect speech: The guide *requested* (*asked*) the students *not to touch* the exhibits.

Direct speech: 'Don't let anybody in,' said the master to the chowkidar.

Indirect speech: The master *ordered* (*told*) the chowkidar *not to let* anybody in.

Note that the negating word *not* is used before the infinitive.

c *Questions*

i '*yes-no*' *questions*

Direct speech: 'Do you wish to open an account?' the accountant said to the man.

Indirect speech: The accountant *asked* the man *whether/if he wished to open an account.*

Direct speech: The man asked, 'Can I withdraw money whenever I need it?'

Indirect speech: The man *enquired if he could withdraw money whenever he needed it.*

Direct speech: 'Didn't I tell you to take the patient's temperature every hour?' the doctor asked the nurse.

Indirect speech: The doctor *asked the nurse whether he hadn't told her to take the patient's temperature every hour.*

'Yes-no' questions are changed into noun clauses beginning with *if* or *whether.*

ii *Question-word questions*

Direct speech: 'What did you eat for breakfast today?' the doctor asked the patient.

Indirect speech: The doctor *asked* the patient *what he ate (had eaten) for breakfast that day.*

Direct speech: 'Whose portrait are you painting?' Mr Joshi asked me.

Indirect speech: Mr Joshi *asked* me *whose portrait I was painting.*

Question-word questions are reported by turning the questions into noun clauses beginning with the question-word. The subject and the verb are put back in the normal statement order.

d *Exclamations*

Direct speech: 'What a splendid building!' the tourist said when he saw the Taj.

Indirect speech: The tourist *exclaimed* when he saw the Taj, *that it was a very splendid building.*

Direct speech: 'What an idea!' said David.

Indirect speech: David *said it was an extraordinary idea.*

Exclamations are often changed into statements in reported speech. Note the use of *very* to bring out the desired emphasis or intensity of the exclamation.

4 *Sequence of tense in reported speech*

In reported speech the reports are most often concerned with what was said in the past. By the time we make our report, the events we talk about are over. The reporting verbs are therefore usually in the past tense: Mohan *said* that.......; Mohan *asked*....... Note the changes in the tenses that take place in indirect speech when the reporting verb is in the past tense.

a Direct speech: 'I don't eat meat,' my guest said.
Indirect speech: My guest said that *he did not eat* meat.

The *simple present* 'don't eat' becomes *the simple past*, 'did not eat'.

b Direct speech: 'Are you taking back all your money?' the clerk asked the man.
Indirect speech: The clerk asked the man whether he *was taking* back all his money.

The *present continuous* 'are taking' becomes the *past continuous* 'was taking'.

c Direct speech: 'You have spoken a lie,' Mr Das said to his servant.
Indirect speech: Mr Das said to his servant that he *had spoken* a lie.

Present perfect 'have spoken' becomes *past perfect* 'had spoken'.

d Direct speech: 'The visitor has been waiting for an hour to see you, sir,' the peon told the Manager.
Indirect speech: The peon told the Manager that the visitor *had been waiting* for an hour to see him.

The *present perfect continuous* 'has been waiting' becomes the *past perfect continuous* 'had been waiting'.

e Direct speech: 'The Manager will call you **after** an hour,' the peon said to the visitor.
Indirect speech: The peon said to the visitor that the Manager *would call* him **after** an hour.

The future 'will call' becomes 'would call'.

f Direct speech: 'I shall return from Delhi on Monday,' my neighbour said.
Indirect speech: My neighbour said that he *would return* from Delhi on Monday.

Note that 'I shall' becomes 'he would'. (When *I* is changed to *he*, here, *shall* is changed to *would*.)

g

Direct Speech	Indirect Speech
The teacher said to the boys, 'You may go home.'	The teacher said to the boys that they *might go* home.
'Can you ride a bicycle?' I asked Gita.	I asked Gita whether she *could ride* a bicycle.
'You must eat all the cakes,' the mother told her son.	The mother told her son that he *had to eat* all the cakes.

Note that in indirect speech the modals are changed into the corresponding past tense forms. Note that the past tense of *must* is expressed by *had to*.

h i Direct speech: Ravi said, 'I posted the letter.'
Indirect speech: Ravi said that he *had posted* the letter.
Direct speech: 'I took my lunch with me,' said Kannan.
Indirect speech: Kannan said that he *had taken* his lunch with him.

The past tense in direct speech (*posted*, *took*) usually becomes the *past perfect tense* in indirect speech (*had posted*, *had taken*). This is to make clear which action took place earlier.

ii a Direct speech: The teacher said, 'Our country became independent in 1947.'
Indirect speech: The teacher said that our country became independent in 1947.

b Direct speech: He said, 'If Ravi approached me, I would certainly help him.'
Indirect speech: He said that if Ravi approached him he would certainly help him.

c Direct speech: He said, 'When the principal walked in, the teacher was not in the class.'
Indirect speech: He said that when the principal walked in, the teacher was not in the class.

In (a) the speaker refers to a historical event.

In (b) an imagined condition is expressed.

In (c) two actions occurring at about the same time are expressed.

In such cases the past tense remains unchanged in the indirect form.

i Direct speech: He said, 'God is everywhere.'
Indirect speech: He said that God is everywhere.
Direct speech: He said, 'I go for a walk every morning.'
Indirect speech: He said he goes for a walk every morning.
Direct speech: Mr Patil said this morning, 'I am going to buy a car soon.'
Indirect speech: Mr Patil said this morning that he is going to buy a car soon.

The present tense in direct speech is not changed into past tense if the sentence spoken expresses a universal truth, a habitual action, or a fact that is true at the time of reporting. The future tense, similarly, is not changed into the past form, if what is said refers to the future at the time of reporting. See the last example above.

5 Now look at the following sentences.

Direct speech: Ravi says, 'I met Mr Rao at the railway station.'
Indirect speech: Ravi says that he met Mr Rao at the railway station.
Direct speech: 'I was at home all day yesterday,' says my neighbour.
Indirect speech: My neighbour says he was at home all day yesterday.
Direct speech: Mohan will say, 'I want two persons to assist me.'
Indirect speech: Mohan will say that he wants two persons to assist him.

When the reporting verb is in the present tense or future tense the verbs undergo no change in indirect speech.

6 *Reported speech*: *Change of person*

Direct speech: The doctor asked the patient, 'Did *you* eat anything this morning?'

Indirect speech: The doctor asked the patient whether *he* had eaten anything that morning.

Direct speech: '*I* ate bread and a few biscuits,' replied the patient.

Indirect speech: The patient replied that *he* had eaten bread and a few biscuits.

In these examples, you will notice that the pronouns are changed from the point of view of the person reporting. For him *I* and *you* in the spoken sentences are third persons; so they become *he*. When the person reporting is neither the speaker nor the man spoken to, *I*, *we*, *my*, *our*, *you*, *your*, etc. are changed to *he*, *him*, *his*, *her*, *they*, *them*, *their*, etc.

Now look at these examples.

Direct speech: I asked the policeman, 'Can you tell *me* the way to the station?'

Indirect speech: I asked the policeman whether (if) *he* could tell *me* the way to the station.

Here, the person is reporting his own words. So *me* is not changed to any other pronoun. In all these cases the pronouns are changed in reported speech from the reporter's 'point of view,' that is, according to who the reporting person is. The other changes indicated below also follow the same principle, that is, they depend on who the reporting person is, what the time of reporting is and where the reporting takes place.

7 *Other changes*

Demonstratives and ***adverbials***

Reported speech is usually about events which took place earlier than the time of reporting and away from the place of reporting. When this is the case, words denoting nearness in time and place are changed into words denoting distance. Here is a chart that shows the changes made.

Direct Speech	*Indirect Speech*	*Direct Speech*	*Indirect Speech*
this	that	tomorrow	the next day
these	those	yesterday	the day before
here	there	henceforward	thenceforward
now	then	thus	in that way
today	that day	ago	before, earlier
tonight	that night	next week	the following week
last week	the previous week		

Examples:

Direct Speech	*Indirect Speech*
Mohan: I must go to the library today and return this book.	Mohan said he had to go to the library *that day* and return *that* book.
Ashok: Can't you return it tomorrow?	Ashok asked Mohan whether he couldn't return it the *next day.*
Mohan: No, I can't, because yesterday was the last day for keeping the book.	Mohan replied that he couldn't, because *the day before* was the last day for keeping the book.
Ashok: Why should you go right now? Can't you go this evening?	Ashok asked Mohan why he should go right *then.* Couldn't he go *that evening.*
Mohan: I have to be back here this evening. A friend of mine is coming to see me.	Mohan said he had to be back *there that evening.* A friend of *his* was coming to see him.

Study these further examples:

	Direct Speech	*Indirect Speech*
i	Gita: Are you coming with me for a swim, Rita? Rita: Yes.	Gita asked Rita whether she was going with her for a swim. Rita replied that she was.
ii	He said, 'Let's stop here and rest for a while.'	He suggested stopping there and resting for a while.
iii	He said, 'Let's not do anything to discourage the boys.'	He suggested not doing anything to discourage the boys.
iv	'Let's punish that boy,' said I. 'Let's not,' said my friend.	I suggested punishing the boy. My friend was against it.
v	He said, 'Thank you very much for your help.'	He thanked me/him very much for my/his help.
vi	He said, 'Good morning.'	He wished me good morning.
vii	He said, 'Congratulations!'	He congratulated me.
viii	He said, 'If the fire spreads, we must telephone to the fire service.'	He said that if the fire spread, they would have to telephone to the fire service.
ix	He said, 'You needn't wait.'	He said that I needn't wait *or* He said I wouldn't have to wait.
x	'What fun I had!' said Mohan. 'It was a wonderful party.'	Mohan exclaimed he had had great fun indeed. It had been a wonderful party.
xi	'Have you any money, James?' Martin asked. 'Can I borrow a hundred rupees and return it after a month?'	Martin asked James whether he had any money. Could he borrow a hundred rupees and return it after a month?

Exercise 1

Rewrite the following statements in indirect speech.

1 'We are moving into a new house,' my neighbour said.
2 'If it rains we will have to cancel the match,' the captain said.
3 'We shall go to the zoo,' Ashok said to his friend.
4 Hassan said to me, 'I will see you tomorrow'. 'I am not free tomorrow,' I said to Hassan.
5 'Those who have written the essay can go home,' the teacher said.
6 All my friends tell me, 'You will be a great man one day.'
7 'I have been waiting for an hour,' complained Ashok.
8 My friend said, 'You may take my bicycle if you like. I shan't be needing it for two days.'
9 'Your husband will soon be well. Let him be in bed for a week,' Dr. Sapru told Mrs Rao.
10 'I am going to Delhi on the 10th. The interview is on the 14th,' Kassim said.

Exercise 2

Rewrite the following in indirect speech.

Example:

Arun said to Ravi, 'Please lend me your dictionary.'
Arun asked (requested) Ravi to lend him his dictionary.

1 Mr Rao said to his wife, 'I may be late for dinner. Don't wait for me.'
2 'Raju,' said Raju's mother, 'don't tell lies. Tell me the truth.'
3 The captain said to the soldiers, 'Don't fall back. Keep firing and advancing.'
4 The Gita says, 'Do your duty. Don't worry about the results of your actions.'
5 'Don't argue with your father,' Mrs Das said to her son.

6 'Grow a beard and no one will know who you are,' my friend advised me.
7 'Taste a little of this. Tell me if I have added too much salt,' she said to her daughter.
8 'Don't talk loudly. You will disturb the baby,' my aunt said.
9 'Be careful. The steps are slippery,' my friend said.
10 'Get me some paper and a pen,' my father said to me.

Exercise 3

Rewrite the following in indirect speech.

Example:

Doctor to patient: Do you have a headache now?
The doctor asked the patient if he had a headache then.

1 Shop-keeper to lady: Do you want the red sari or the green one?
2 I to policeman: Can you tell me the way to the hospital?
3 Parent to teacher: Will my daughter pass or fail?
4 My neighbour to me: Are you going to Delhi next week?
5 Ravi to Raju: Shall we plan a picnic for next Sunday?
6 Father to son: Hasn't the postman come yet?
7 Mother to me: Have you watered the plants?
8 Secretary to visitor: Whom do you want to see?
9 Mr Munshi to me: Whose portrait are you painting?
10 Uncle to me: When does the postman come every day?
11 Mrs Das to Mr Das: How many people are coming to dinner?
12 Inspector to prisoner: Where did you get these counterfeit notes from?

Exercise 4

Rewrite the following in indirect speech.

1 'What a pleasant evening! Shall we go for a walk?' said Ravi to his friends.

2 'How stuffy it's here! Let's go out and sit in the garden,' Prema said to her friends.
3 'How nice of you to have come!' my friend said to me.
4 'How persuasively your lawyer argued the case!' my friend said to me.
5 'What a pity you did not come to the party!' my friend said to me.
6 'What a lazy girl you are! How shabbily you have done your work!' the teacher said to Judy.
7 'May God bless you!' said the old man to the boy.
8 'Alas! what shall I do now?' cried the traveller. 'Who will show me the way in this jungle?'

18 SIMPLE SENTENCES

A Look at these sentences:

1 Sekhar worked hard.
2 He passed in the first division.
3 He won a scholarship.
4 He became an Engineer.

Each of these sentences has a subject and *one verb* in the predicate part. Such sentences are called **simple sentences**.

The main parts of a simple sentence are:

1 The subject. The subject may have more than one noun or noun phrase in it.
e.g. Ram and Gopal are brothers.

2 The verb. The verb is a finite verb, that is, a verb that can form the predicate of a sentence, unlike forms like *can*, *should*, *flying*, *to go*, etc.

3 An object, if the verb is transitive.
e.g. He won a *scholarship*.

In addition, the simple sentence may have the following:

a Modifiers of the nouns in the sentence, which may be adjectives or adjectival phrases (but not adjectival clauses)

Examples: The *blue* book is mine.
This is a book *of poems*.

b A subject complement

Examples: He became *an engineer*. (noun)
This book is very *interesting*. (adjective)

c An adverbial modifying the verb (but not an adverbial clause)

Examples: He sang *beautifully*.
He passed *in the first division*.

d An object complement

Examples: They made him *captain*. (noun)
The news made him *sad*. (adjective)

[*Note*: The subject is usually a noun or noun phrase or **a** pronoun. But it may also be of other kinds.]

Examples:

a *It* is very cold.
It is easy to say that.
('It' is a dummy subject.)

b *There* are sixty students in this group.
There came a severe famine in the country.
('There' is a dummy subject.)

c *To say* that is easy.
'*To fly* is to swim in the air.'
(Infinitive as subject.)

d *Walking* is a good exercise.
Solving this problem is not going to be easy.
(Gerund as subject.)

B Simple sentences fall into a number of patterns or **structures.** Here, in the tables below, are some of the main patterns of the simple sentence. Note the different parts of the sentences given in each table, and their functions.

Under each table is given an exercise which can give you practice in making sentences of the same pattern as those in the table. In each item of an exercise a group of words or phrases is given in a jumbled order. The words or phrases marked off by commas form separate units. Put these units together in the right order and make sentences like those in the table.

Pattern 1

Subject	*Verb*
Birds	fly.
The sun	set.
The stars	were shining.
The children	were playing.

Exercise

i burns, fire.
ii was sinking, the boat.
iii is crying, the baby.
iv rose, the moon.

Pattern 2

Subject	*Verb* to be	*Complement* (*noun*)
He	is	a doctor.
These	are	cheetahs.
They	are	rogues.
I	was	a teacher.

Exercise

i is, a teacher, she.
ii tourists, they, are.
iii must be, that, the postman.
iv are, these applicants, graduates.

Pattern 3

Subject	*Verb* to be	*Complement* (*adjective*)
These apples	are	good.
The meal	is	tasty.
I	am	ready to start.
They	were	panicky.

Exercise

i deaf, that girl, is.
ii are, difficult, these sums.
iii splendid, was, the scenery.
iv was, bright, the sun.

Pattern 4

Subject	*Verb* to be	*Complement* (*adverbial*)
God	is	everywhere.
Your umbrella	is	here.
Your books	are	on the table.
My wife	was	in the kitchen.

Exercise

i are, the children, in the playground.
ii is, my father, away.
iii were, here, your sons.
iv isn't, the headmaster, in his room.

Pattern 5

Subject	*Intransitive Verb*	*Complement* (*noun*)
He	became	the Chief Minister.
He	looks	a genius.
He	turned	atheist.
He	proved	an efficient administrator.
I	remained	a teacher.

Exercise

i the Manager of the company, became, she.
ii a strict disciplinarian, looks, he.
iii proved, she, a capable administrator.
iv remains, a clerk, he.

Pattern 6

Subject	*Intransitive Verb*	*Complement (adjective)*
The teacher	grew	angry.
We	became	tired.
He	appears	reasonable.
This	looks	strange.
That	sounds	funny.

Exercise

i quite reasonable, sounds, this explanation.
ii fantastic, the project, appears.
iii feel, I, very sleepy.
iv has turned, the milk, sour.
v proved, useless, our efforts.

Pattern 7

Subject	*Intransitive Verb*	*Complement (adverbial)*
The thief	ran	fast.
My brother	has gone	abroad.
He	behaved	in an indecent manner.
You	have come	at the right time.
We	walked	briskly.

Exercise

i she, eloquently, spoke.
ii miserably, failed, he.
iii rapidly, is recovering, the patient.
iv attacked, suddenly, the army.
v in no time, dispersed, the crowd.

Pattern 8

Subject	*Transitive Verb*	*Object*
Edison	invented	the electric bulb.
I	am selling	my old bicycle.
My mother	bought	a pressure cooker.
My neighbour	may sell	his house.
My grandfather	built	this house.

Exercise

i can speak, my brother, French.
ii penicillin, discovered, Alexander Fleming.
iii the meeting, postponed, they.
iv Mr Rao, a car, doesn't own.
v need, I, some money.

Pattern 9

Subject	*Transitive Verb*	*Particle*	*Object*
They	put	off	the meeting.
Father	called	in	the doctor.
He	disposed	of	his old car.
The government	put	down	the rebellion.
I	saw	through	his game.

Exercise

i out, the soldier, the orders, carried.
ii the train, the robbers, up, held.
iii to, the disappointed man, drinking, took.
iv my umbrella, I, back, got.
v out, a leaflet, the speaker, handed.

Pattern 10

Subject	*Transitive Verb*	*Object*	*Particle*
He	called	the doctor	in.
She	put	her new gown	on.
We	saw	him	off.
Raju	switched	the lights	on.
I	put	the book	aside.

Exercise

i I, off, switched, the lights.
ii the match, called, off, they.
iii drew, the lease, up, the solicitor.
iv in, handed, this, someone.
v out, left, him, they.

Pattern 11

Subject	*Transitive Verb*	*Indirect Object*	*Direct Object*
Hari	gave	me	a pen.
Gita	threw	her	the ball.
My neighbour	lent	me	his bicycle.
The thief	dealt	the traveller	a blow.
My grandmother	told	me	a story.

Exercise

i the police, a reward, him, gave.
ii a wrist-watch, promised, me, father.
iii all his properties, Mr Jain, his brother, willed.
iv me, some Kashmir apples, my friend, brought.
v a ten paise coin, gave, the beggar, he.

Pattern 12

Subject	*Transitive Verb*	*Direct Object*	*To + Indirect Object*
He	gave	the book	to me.
Gita	threw	the ball	to Kamala.
Mr Jain	willed	all his property	to his brother.
He	wrote	an angry letter	to his wife.
I	promised	a reward	to him.

Exercise

i willed, Mr Prasad, fifty thousand rupees, to his old school.
ii Uncle, a birthday present, to me, sent.
iii the message, Mr Roy, to me, telephoned.
iv have not sent, to him, I, any reply.

Pattern 13

Subject	*Transitive Verb*	*Indirect Object*	*Direct Object*
Mother	ordered	herself	a new sari.
She	found	her daughter	a good husband.
Uncle	bought	me	a bicycle.
Mother	**prepared**	**us**	**a nice dinner**
She	made	herself	a new dress.

Exercise

i he, a huge estate, his son, left.
ii the manager, sweets, his clerks, ordered.
iii a cup of coffee, prepared, she, me.
iv us, did, a great favour, they.

Pattern 14

Subject	*Transitive Verb*	*Direct Object*	*For + Indirect Object*
She	found	a good husband	for her daughter.
Father	bought	a bicycle	for me.
The secretary	wrote	a speech	for the Manager.
She	made	a new dress	for herself.
She	cooked	a meal	for us.

Exercise

i got, four tickets, I, for the family.
ii for his wife, bought, he, a gold ring.
iii cashed, for us, he, the cheque.
iv for Mr Rao, we, a new house, are looking for.

Pattern 15

Subject	*Transitive Verb*	*First Object*	*Second Object*
The teacher	forgave	the boy	his misbehaviour.
I	struck	him	a blow.
She	asked	me	a question.
We	envied	her	her luck.
They	saved	me	a lot of trouble.

[*Note*: This pattern, unlike patterns 11 and 13, cannot be rewritten either with *to* or *for*.]

Exercise

i us, God, will forgive, our sins.
ii a lot of time, us, saves, the sewing machine.
iii I, your fine garden, you, envy.
iv a heavy blow, struck, the thief, Mr Raju.

Pattern 16

Subject	*Transitive Verb*	*Object*	*Object Complement* **(noun)**
They	elected	him	Chairman.
The Board	appointed	me	Principal.
They	chose	Mr Singh	Chairman.
The boys	made	Henry	their leader.
He	called	me	a coward.

Exercise

i emperor, himself, crowned, Napoleon.
ii our dog, we, Sonny, call.
iii their son, they, Arun Kumar, named.
iv Mr Tandon, elected, President, the party.
v a liar, he, me, called.

Pattern 17

Subject	*Transitive Verb*	*Object*	*Complement (adjective)*
We	found	the servant	honest.
They	painted	the gate	yellow.
The noise	drove	him	mad.
The book	made	him	famous.
She	set	the bird	free.

Exercise

i the box, empty, found, we.
ii pronounced, the murderer, the doctor, sane.
iii litmus paper, blue, turns, acid.
iv warm, this coat, you, will keep.
v will make, this medicine, you, all right.

Pattern 18

Subject	*Transitive Verb*	*Infinitive (Object)*
He	wants	to go.
She	agreed	to marry me.
They	decided	to organize an exhibition.
She	is learning	to drive.
I	am trying	to help you.

Exercise

i to sleep, the child, wanted.
ii tried, to climb the wall, the boy.
iii forgot, he, to post the letter.
iv to see me, he, wanted.
v to consider my application, refused, he.

Pattern 19

Subject	*Transitive Verb*	*Object*	*Infinitive*
The teacher	asked	the boy	to go.
He	wanted	me	to spcak.
I	told	the servant	to open the window.
Your teacher	expects	you	to work hard.
He	liked	us	to stay on.

Exercise

i our team, we, to win, expected.
ii him, his boss, to take leave, allowed.
iii me, not to be late, Mother, warned.
iv to be rude, him, never expected, I.
v Raju, told, to clean the blackboard, the teacher.

Pattern 20

Subject	*Transitive Verb*	*Gerund*
He	avoided	seeing me.
He	likes	reading novels.
She	enjoys	playing badminton.
I	hate	talking to that fellow.
He	has stopped	talking to me.

Exercise

i staying a little longer, don't mind, I.
ii remember, I, seeing this film before.
iii has given up, gambling, he.
iv smoking, has left off, the old man.
v laughing, couldn't help, she.

Pattern 21

Subject	*Transitive Verb*	*Object*	*Present Participle*
I	found	her	cooking in the kitchen.
They	kept	us	waiting.
We	saw	them	playing.
I	heard	you	speaking.
We	watched	them	enjoying the story.

Exercise

i burning, something, smelt, we.
ii shaking, felt, we, the house.
iii we, the huts, burning, saw.
iv taking off, watched, we, the plane.
v an apple, falling to the ground, saw, Newton.

Pattern 22

Subject	*Transitive Verb*	*Object*	*Bare Infinitive*
The mother	watched	the baby	drink the milk.
We	saw	the old man	cross the road.
I	heard	her	sing this song.
We	will have	them	complete **the** work.
She	made	him	wash her clothes.

Exercise

i shake, felt, we, the ground.
ii carry the box, him, saw, I.
iii the girls, let, play, we.
iv King Bruce, the spider, succeed at last, watched.
v work so hard, have never seen, I, him.

Pattern 23

Subject	*Transitive Verb*	*Object*	*To be + Comp. (noun)*
They	considered	him	to be their guru.
We	found	the manager	to be a nice person.
They	took	me	to be an inspector.
We	believed	him	to be a spy.
Mohan's father	wanted	him	to be an engineer.

Exercise

i to be their leader, him, wanted, they.
ii I, to be a policeman, him, believed.
iii to be their slave, wanted, they, me.
iv him, to be a merchant, everyone, took.

Pattern 24

Subject	*Verb*	*Object*	*To be + Complement (adj.)*
I	knew	him	to be efficient.
The teacher	wanted	us	to be punctual.
I	understood	her	to be sincere.
We	expected	them	to be honest.
He	warned	us	to be careful.

Exercise

i He, you, to be prompt, expects.
ii to be innocent, supposed, I, him.
iii knew, her, I, to be eager.
iv you, to be straightforward, want, I.
v him, to be honest, believed, we.

Pattern 25

Subject	*Transitive Verb*	*it*	*Complement*	*Phrase with Infinitive*
We	consider	it	a privilege	to welcome you.
They	deemed	it	an honour	to have him for their leader.
We	thought	it	dangerous	to proceed further.
I	found	it	impossible	to convince him.
He	thought	it	easy	to win the prize.

Exercise

i useless, think, we, it, to pursue the matter.
ii to attend the lectures, they, useful, found, it.
iii to serve that great man, an honour, it, considered, they.
iv a privilege, deem, to welcome you, it, we.
v it, fit, thought, we, to see the secretary first.

Pattern 26

Subject	*Transitive Verb*	*Object*	*Past Participle*
I	must get	a few shirts	made.
He	got	his portrait	painted.
You	must get	your hair	cut.
She	had	her watch	repaired.
He	got	his son	trained as a pilot.

Exercise

i the house, got, whitewashed, they.
ii I, a table, made, got.
iii we, designed by an architect, got, our house.
iv pressed, my shirts, I, had.
v retyped, the letter, had, I.

Pattern 27

Subject	*Transitive Verb*	*Wh + Infinitive (direct object)*
I	don't know	what to say.
I	know	where to find it.
He	has been told	when to start.
She	doesn't know	how to operate it.
We	know	what to look for.

Exercise

i didn't know, what to do, we.
ii forgot, what to say, I.
iii didn't know, he, how to reach the place.
iv knows, when to attack, a good commander.
v where to look for it, know, I.

Pattern 28

Subject	*Transitive Verb*	*Indirect Object*	*Wh + Infinitive (direct object)*
He	told	me	how to get there.
These patterns	show	you	how to make sentences.
I	advised	him	where to go for the holidays.
No one	taught	him	how to read and write.
I	will instruct	you	when to resume the treatment.

Exercise

i will tell, where to find the book, I, you.
ii he, me, how to get here, instructed.
iii he, us, how to write letters, taught.
iv you, will show, she, how to make the pickle.
v you, these records, will teach, how to pronounce English.

Pattern 29

Subject	*Transitive Verb*	*Object*	*Adverbial*
I	saw	him	this morning.
He	promised	to come	tomorrow.
I	will return	the money	next week.
They	stopped	playing	an hour ago.
We	paid	the arrears	yesterday.

Exercise

i the money, put, he, into his bank account.
ii from 1960, claimed, I, arrears of pay.
iii these hardships, for years, have put up with, we.
iv since 1960, have not seen, him, I.
v the doctor, daily, has promised, to come.

Pattern 30

Subject	*Transitive Verb*	*Object*	*Preposition*	*Gerund*
He	earns	his living	by	selling ready-made garments
He	left	the meeting	without	saying anything.
I	used	red ink	for	marking the mistakes.
He	married	Leela	after	getting a job.

Exercise

i entertains, he, mimicking great men, you, by.
ii the party, thanking the host, she, left, without.
iii the knot, undid, by, he, cutting it.
iv the egg, knocking off its end, stood, he, by.
v her throat, she, cleared, starting to sing, before.

Pattern 31

Subject (it)	*Intransitive Verb*	*Complement* (*adjective*)	*Infinitive*
It	is	easy	to advise others.
It	was	impossible	to go across the river.
It	was	exciting	to watch the match.
It	is	difficult	to understand his motive
It	is	dangerous	to swim here.

Exercise

i pleasant, is, it, to go for a walk now.
ii would be, to predict the results, it, premature.
iii to talk to him, foolish, is, it.
iv it, to stay here, safe, isn't.
v to consult an expert, advisable, is, it.

Pattern 32

Subject (it)	*Intransitive Verb*	*Complement* (*adjective*)	*For + Object*	*Infinitive*
It	is	safe	for us	to stay here.
It	is	advisable	for you	to see a doctor.
It	is	difficult	for us	to climb that hill.
It	is	easy	for you	to answer this question.
It	is	necessary	for us	to win the match.

Exercise

i for us, to live in that house, is, insecure, it.
ii to attack the enemy, is not, for us, it, opportune.

iii for you, unnecessary, is, it, to wait.
iv is, it, for you, to learn English, useful.
v to take warm clothing with you, for you, is, it, necessary.

Pattern 33

It	*Intransitive Verb*	*Complement*	*Gerund*
It	is	no use	waiting here.
It	is	no good	seeing the Minister.
It	is	fun	playing with children.
It	is	a job	persuading him to come.
It	is	a big task	starting a college.

Exercise

i no use, is, it, consulting that doctor.
ii hurrying now, is, it, no good.
iii seeing him act, sheer joy, it, is.
iv getting an interview with her, a job, is, it.
v asking him to be chairman, a good idea, is, it.

Pattern 34

Subject	*Intransitive Verb*	*Complement (adverbial)*
This box	weighs	ten kilograms.
This pen	costs	twenty rupees.
Rajan	ran	two kilometres.
The thermometer	went up	five degrees.
The rain	lasted	all day.

Exercise

i walked, ten kilometres, we.
ii several kilometres, the jungles, stretched.
iii waited, an hour, they.
iv cost, twenty thousand rupees, this house.
v ninety-four years, lived, he.

Pattern 35

There	*Verb*	*Subject*
There	is	a college in this town.
There	are	two views on the matter.
There	have been	several thefts in this area.
There	were	few accidents last year.

Exercise

i are, five high schools in this town, there.
ii no going back on my word, is, there.
iii some reason for his behaviour, must be, there.
iv there, many accidents on that road, have been.

Pattern 36

There	*Verb*	*Subject*
There	comes	a tide in the affairs of men.
There	arose	a dispute between the brothers.
There	fell	a silence on the crowd.
There	grew	a friendship between us.

Exercise

i a quarrel between the boys, developed, there.
ii a sage in my dream, there, appeared.
iii arose, a controversy over the subject, there.
iv comes, an opportunity for every person, there.

Pattern 37

Subject	*Verb*	*Infinitive Purpose*
He	came	to see me.
We	stopped	to have a rest.
He	has gone	to bring the doctor.
We	should eat	to live.

Exercise

i to eat, we, should not live.
ii got up, to ask a question, he.
iii has gone, to fetch a taxi, Mohan.
iv is working, he, to get a first class.

Pattern 38

Subject	*Verb*	*Infinitive* (*result*)
He	lived	to be ninety-four.
He	rose	to be the Manager.
I	came	to know of his death this morning
I	got	to know her at a party.

Exercise

i to be the Principal, rose, he.
ii lived, he, to see his great grandson.
iii came, I, to know the truth of the matter.
iv to lose in this **bargain**, I, stand.

Pattern 39

Subject	*Verb*	*Object Adverbial*
Who	helped	you with money?
Who	knows	the answer?
Who	can swim	across this river?
What	happened	in my absence?
What	will happen	to him?

Exercise

i the highest mark, scored, who.
ii broke, this chair, who.
iii coffee, asked for, who.
iv to your leg, happened, what.

Pattern 40

Question Word	*Auxiliary*	*Subject*	*Verb*	*Object/ Adverbial*
What	does	he	say	to this?
Where	can	I	find	him?
When	did	she	leave	home?
Why	should	I	see	her?
How	will	he	**get**	here?

Exercise

i where, get, can, this, I.
ii this question, answer, how, I, can.
iii home, you, reach, do, when.
iv himself, did, absent, he, why.
v from us, what, does, expect, he.

Pattern 41

Auxiliary	*Subject*	*Verb*	*Object/Adverbial*
Have	you	read	this book?
Does	he	want	to see me?
Is	she	making	the tea?
Can	you	ride	a bicycle?
Should	I	help	him?

Exercise

i pay, he, the money, did.
ii he, a house, has, secured.
iii pass, he, will, this year.
iv to the market, you, going, are.
v need, do, my help, you.

Pattern 42

Auxiliary + negative	*Subject*	*Verb*	*Object/ Adverbial*
Haven't	you	read	this book?
Doesn't	he	need	my help?
Isn't	she	making	the tea?
Can't	you	ride	a bicycle?
Shouldn't	I	help	him?

Exercise

i know, she, doesn't, how to cook.
ii bought, he, his textbook, hasn't.
iii speak, Hindi, he, can't.
iv a little, wait, you, couldn't.
v apply, he, for the post, didn't.

Pattern 43

Exclamation Word	*(Article+) Adjective*	*Noun*
What	a beautiful	view!
What	a glorious	evening!
What	fine	stories!
What		nonsense!

Exercise

i tricks, wonderful, what.
ii a nasty, what, accident.
iii folly, what.
iv boy, what, a clever.

Pattern 44

Exclamation Word	*(Article+) Adjective*	*Noun*	*Subject+Verb/ Complement*
What	a nice	dinner	we had!
What	a stupid	thing	to say!
What	interesting	stories	he told us!
What		luck	they have!

Exercise

i to meet with, what, a misfortune.
ii time, a nice, we had, what.
iii jokes, he made, what, witty.
iv he gave, what, performance, a fine.

Pattern 45

Exclamation Word	*Adjective*	*Subject and Verb*
How	difficult	it is!
How	kind	you are!
How	easy	to solve it!
How	smooth	it feels!

Exercise

i stiff, how, the climb is.
ii nice, it tastes, how.

iii this train is, slow, how.
iv beautiful, how, the Taj is.

Pattern 46

Exclamation Word	*Adverb*	*Subject + verb*
How	well	he played!
How	eloquently	he spoke!
How	fast	it runs!
How	hard	it rained!

Exercise

i she speaks, beautifully, how.
ii how, it runs, smoothly.
iii it happened, how, suddenly.
iv high, it went up, how.

Pattern 47

Subject	*Intransitive Verb*	*Too + Adjective*	*Infinitive*
He	was	too tired	to walk.
The news	is	too good	to be true.
She	is	too weak	to sit up.
This writing	is	too illegible	for me to read.
His language	is	too difficult	for children to follow.

Exercise

i too excited, is, he, to say anything.
ii for me. to drink, is, too hot, this milk.
iii to learn, too old, is, he.
iv is, he, to understand all this, too young.
v this box, to carry, is, too heavy.

Pattern 48

Subject	*Intransitive Verb/ Transitive Verb*	*Adj/Adv/ Noun+enough*	*Infinitive*
He	is	strong enough	to carry this box.
He	ran	fast enough	to catch the thief.
We	have	time enough	to catch the train.
He	is	intelligent enough	to follow the argument.
She	is	old enough	to marry.

Exercise

i smart enough, is, he, to succeed.
ii to buy a car, are, they, rich enough.
iii to get a first class, hard enough, didn't work, he.
iv have, room enough, they, to accommodate all the party.
v is, beautiful enough, this picture, to adorn any drawing room.

Pattern 49

Subject	*Intransitive Verb*	*Infinitive*
I	am	to give a talk at the Lions Club tomorrow.
She	is	to be married in January.
They	are	to come here this evening.
You	are	to stand here till I am back.
Ravi	is	to marry my cousin.

Exercise

i is, the principal, to go to Delhi tomorrow.
ii He, to address a meeting, is.
iii is, he, to return on Wednesday.
iv to report at the police station, is, he.
v are, they, to be married next winter.

Pattern 50

Subject	*Verb*	*Infinitive* (*of result*)
He	hurried	only to find the train leaving.
He	has gone	never to return.
I	got in	to find all the seats occupied.
He	woke up	to find all his things stolen.

[*Note*: This pattern, unlike pattern 38, can be rewritten as a compound sentence. e.g. ' I got in to find all the seats occupied ' can be written as: ' I got in and found all the seats occupied '.]

Exercise

i to find the house on fire, woke up, they.
ii opened the box, I, only to find it empty.
iii only to find the factory burnt down, arrived, the fire-engines.
iv is going away, he, never to come back.

19 COMPOUND SENTENCES

1 Look at these sentences:

a Sekhar worked hard and passed in the first division.
b Vinod worked hard too, but he did not pass in the first division.

Each of these sentences has two different clauses of the same grammatical class linked together. The clauses in sentence (a) are:

Sekhar worked hard.
He passed in the first division.

These two clauses are linked by the conjunction *and.* They are called ***principal clauses*** .

The principal clauses in sentence (b) are:

Vinod worked hard too.
He did not pass in the first division.

The clauses are linked by the conjunction *but.*

The principal clause is also called 'chief clause' or 'main clause' or 'independent clause'. Principal clauses joined together are called 'co-ordinate clauses'.

The conjunctions used to link main clauses are called 'co-ordinating conjunctions' or 'co-ordinators'.

Sentences in which two or more main clauses are linked by co-ordinating conjunctions are called *compound sentences.*

[*Note*: Co-ordinating conjunctions link not only clauses, but also words and phrases.]

2 Here is a list of co-ordinating conjunctions with examples of the compound sentences they form:

or: You may go home or read in the library.
Eat moderately or you will fall sick.

The conjunction is similar to *and. And* shows that the clauses are added on one to another; *or* shows that they are taken one at a time.

Either....or : You may either stay in the hostel or stay with your relatives.

Neither....nor: The old woman could neither read nor write.
My father has not flown in an aeroplane, nor does he want to.

[Note how *nor* can be used without *neither.* Note also that when *nor* is used there is inversion of the subject and the auxiliary.]

but : I went to his house several times, but I was unable to meet him.

yet : He is very rich, yet he is not happy.

still : The best doctors are attending on him, still he is not out of danger.

for	:	I am very tired, for I have been working all day.
so	:	There was no quorum, so the meeting was adjourned.
not only. . . . but also	:	The enemy not only captured the city, but also destroyed several factories and buildings.
therefore	:	He was absent without leave for several days, therefore his name was removed from the rolls.
nevertheless	:	He had a high first class, nevertheless he was unable to get admission to the medical course.

3 Here are some examples of compound sentences with two or more independent clauses:

I reached Delhi at seven, finished my business by six in the evening and returned the same day.

The doctor was very competent and did his best, but the patient's condition got worse day by day.

The food had been cooked well, but we didn't eat much, for we didn't feel hungry and had no appetite.

Exercise 1

Combine each of the following groups of sentences into compound sentences using one or more of the co-ordinating conjunctions:

1 He is honest. He is faithful.
2 He knocked. No one came to open the door.
3 He gave us a long passage. He asked us to write a precis of it.
4 He gave us a fine dinner. He also drove us back home.
5 I lost my way. I asked a policeman to help me. He could not, being new to the place himself.

6 The guide took us round the fort. He gave us a lot of information. We didn't have the time to see everything.
7 His marks were not high. He managed to get admission in a college.
8 The time was short. He completed the work.

Exercise 2

Change the following simple sentences into compound sentences:

Examples:

a Simple sentence: To his great disappointment he failed in the examination.
Compound sentence: He failed in the examination and he was greatly disappointed.

b Simple sentence: He must work very hard in order to pass.
Compound sentence: He must work very hard or he will fail.

c Simple sentence: In spite of his high marks he did not get admission.
Compound sentence: He had high marks, still he did not get admission.

1 Owing to the failure of the monsoon, there was a severe drought.
2 On account of mismanagement the company suffered a great loss.
3 **Threatening the traveller with a knife, the thief robbed him of all his money.**
4 Being thoroughly prepared, he answered all the questions very well.
5 You have the choice of coming with me to Bombay or going to your uncle's place in Madras.
6 Standing on the top of a hill, the captain watched the fighting of his men.
7 We had not completed our work by sunset.
8 In spite of being supplied with the best weapons the army could not win the battle.

20 COMPLEX SENTENCES

Look at these sentences and the clauses in A and B.

A	B
I'll help you with the money	*you need.*
It started raining	*as soon as the match began.*
Did you hear	*that the P.M. is visiting our town?*

Each of the sentences above has two clauses. The clause in A is an independent or main clause. The clause is B is a dependent clause. It is so called because it cannot stand by itself. It is dependent on or subordinate to the main clause. The subordinate clause in the first sentence is an *adjectival clause*, that in the second an *adverbial clause* and that in the third a *noun clause.*

Sentences of the kind above, that is, sentences which have a main clause and a subordinate clause are called *complex sentences* . A complex sentence can have more subordinate clauses than one, but it has only *one* main clause.

Examples:

As soon as the meeting began a member said *that he wanted to raise a point of order.* (One main clause and two subordinate clauses.)

If you have flown a kite, you will know *that it goes up in the air when you pull it against the wind.* (One main clause and three subordinate clauses.)

There are three kinds of subordinate clauses: (1) the adjectival clause, (2) the adverbial clause and (3) the noun clause.

Adjectival Clauses

Look at these sentences:

The young man *who was here a little while ago* is the President of the Students' Union.

His eye caught a heap of letters *which were lying on the table.*

I have finished reading the book *(that) you gave me.*
That is the man *who taught me this mantra.*

The clause in italics in each of these sentences does the work of an adjective and is called an *adjectival clause.* Each clause defines or 'qualifies' the noun before it. It answers the question: 'Which person or thing?' Adjectival clauses are also called **relative clauses.**

The words *who, which,* and *that* introducing the relative clauses are called *relative pronouns. Who* is used to refer to persons, *which* to things, animals, etc. and *that* to persons as well as things. The noun or noun phrase which a relative pronoun refers to is called its *antecedent.*

In the last sentence given as an example above, *that* can be omitted because it is the object of the verb in the relative clause. When it is the subject, it cannot be omitted.

Subject: It was the car that belonged to Mr Ray.
('That' cannot be omitted.)

Object: I saw the car (that) Mr Ray bought.
('That' may be omitted.)

The object form *whom* can also function as a relative pronoun introducing adjective clauses.

Example:

Here is the boy whom (or who) you wanted to talk to.

When the **adjectival** clause defines a place, time or reason, we use *where, when* and *why* in place of the relative pronoun. These words are called 'relative adverbs' because besides introducing an adjective clause they also function as adverbs.

We visited the house where Mahatma Gandhi was born. (place)

At a time when prices are high, we must reduce our expenditure. (time)

Could you tell me the reason why he has resigned? (reason)

The possessive form *whose* can also introduce a relative clause.

Example:

Here is the man whose house was burgled.
The man whose house I bought wants to buy it back.

Exercise 1

Make meaningful sentences from these tables:

a

A cobbler is a man This is the boy I want a servant Where is the shop What is the problem	who whose whom that which	I can trust completely. worries you? works on leather. father has been appointed collector. sells second-hand books?

b

The thief took the police to the place We asked the doctor the reason May is the month The tired traveller was looking for a place	why where when	the patient's temperature wasn't coming down. he could rest. it is hottest in Hyderabad. he had buried the stolen articles.

Exercise 2

Combine each of the following pairs of sentences into one sentence, turning the italicized sentence into an adjectival clause. The first three are done for you as examples.

1 *A lady composed this poem.* She is visiting **us** today.
Answer: The lady who composed this poem is visiting **us** today.

2 *You took some books from me.* Have you read them?
Answer: Have you read the books you took from me?

3 I bought a watch. *It shows the date.*
Answer: I bought a watch which shows the date.
4 *A thief broke into my neighbour's house.* He has been caught.
5 *You borrowed a dictionary from me last week.* Would you please return it?
6 *A man used to come here every day to beg.* He was found to have Rs. 5,000 in the bank!
7 *You suspect the man.* The police find no reason to suspect him.
8 This is Mr Chowdhury, the great artist. *One of his pictures was sold recently for Rs.* **10,000** (Use: *one of whose.*)
9 *You sent me a boy yesterday.* I am impressed with him.
10 *You sent me some books.* I found them very informative.
11 The man was the first principal of this college. *His portrait adorns the library.*
12 The grammar book has run into five editions. *He wrote it.*

Exercise 3

Look at these sentences:

A friend of mine is coming to see me today.

I worked with him in the Secretariat.

We can combine these sentences as follows:

A friend of mine with whom I worked in the Secretariat is coming to see me today.

[Note that *him* has been changed into the relative pronoun *whom* and the preposition *with* is placed before this relative pronoun.]

Combine each of the following pairs of sentences turning the second sentence into an adjectival clause, as shown above:

1 I walked towards a bench in the park.
Some boys were sitting on it.
2 The thief carried away the box.
We had kept our clothes in it.

3 The officer cancelled the licence of the ration shop.
There were several complaints against it.

4 In front of the office you will see a receptionist.
You can get the information from her.

5 The boys climbed a tree.
They were able to watch the match from there.

6 He gave me a book.
There were some very interesting stories in it.

7 He introduced me to a person.
I was able to contact the Minister through him.

8 He gave me a key.
I opened my box with it.

Look at this sentence:

I want to buy a watch which will show the day and the date.

In this sentence the adjectival clause answers the question: 'which (or what kind of) watch?' This type of clause is called a defining adjectival clause.

Now look at this sentence:

Raju has gone to stay with his father, *who is now in Delhi*.

In this sentence the adjectival clause (in italics) does not answer the kind of question that the defining clause does. It only *adds* some information about the noun that it refers to. Often it is not essential to identify the noun it follows.

An adjectival clause of this kind is called 'a non-defining' adjectival clause.

[Note that a comma separates the clause from the rest of the sentence.]

Exercise 4

Combine each of the following pairs of sentences, turning the sentence in italics into an adjectival clause, separating the clause by a comma or commas where this is necessary:

1 Cricket is played in several countries.
It is called the king of games

2 Mihir Sen was the first man to swim the Palk Straits.
He was born in Purulia in West Bengal.

3 My uncle sent me a lovely birthday present.
He likes me very much.

4 Saturday is named after Saturn.
It is the last day of the week.

5 Mrs Rao introduced me to her husband.
I had not seen him before.

Adverbial Clauses

Adverbial clauses are of different kinds. They modify the verbs to which they are connected in meaning.

1 *Adverbial Clause of Time*

Look at the sentences in this table.

(1) *Main Clause*	(2) *Conjunction*	(3) *Adverb Clause*
I found the house locked	when	I reached home.
The children clapped	as	the clown entered the circus ring.
Some persons in the audience were asleep	while	the speaker was speaking.
Wait here	till/until	I come back.
The train had left	before	we reached the station.
I have not met him	after	he became Principal.
The game was resumed	as soon as	it stopped raining.
I paint	whenever	I get free time.
He hasn't written to us	since	he left home.
Companions will crowd around one	as long as	one has money.

The clause in each of the sentences in the table is an *adverbial clause of time*. It denotes or specifies the time when the action expressed by the main clause takes place. Each of the sentences in the table is a complex sentence. In column (1) of the table you have the main clause, in column (3) the adverb clause and in column (2) the subordinating conjunction joining the adverb clause to the main clause. In the sentences in the table, the adverb clauses come after the main clause. They can also come before the main clause in several cases: e.g.

When I reached home, I found the house locked.
As the clown entered the circus ring, the children clapped.

Exercise 5

Combine each pair of sentences given below into a complex sentence containing an adverbial clause of time. Use the conjunction given in the brackets.

1 I will get ready. Wait till then. (till)
2 The sun comes out. Then the stars disappear. (when)
3 I gave up smoking. It is now ten years after that. (since)
4 The thief saw a policeman coming. Immediately he took to his heels. (as soon as)
5 I want to tell you something. I may forget it. (before)
6 Mr Thomas explained the poem twice. Only then did we understand it well. (only after)
7 He was taking his bath. He was humming a tune. (as)
8 Rome was burning. Nero was playing on his fiddle. (while)
9 I switched off the lights. I heard a knock at the door. (just when)
10 There should be unity in the country. Then no enemy dare attack us. (as along as)

2 *Adverbial Clause of Place*

Look at the sentences in this table.

(1) *Main Clause*	(2) *Conjunction*	(3) *Adverb Clause*
Put these keys	where	we can find them easily.
You may go	wherever	you like.

The clauses in column (3) are ***adverb clauses of place*** **and** the words in column (2) are the **subordinating conjunctions.**

Exercise 6

Combine each pair of sentences given below into a complex sentence with an adverbial clause of place. Use the conjunction given in the brackets.

1 The battle was the thickest at one place.
The prince was found there. (where)
2 I found the umbrella in a certain place.
I had left it there. (where)
3 You may like a certain place.
Sit there. (wherever)
4 We came from a certain place.
We shall go back there. (where)
5 You may go to any place.
I shall go with you. (wherever)

3 *Adverbial Clause of Purpose*

Look at this sentence.

The police officer went out in plain clothes *so that no one might recognize him.*

The clause in italics expresses a purpose and it is called an *Adverbial Clause of Purpose. So that* is the conjunction used in this kind of clause. In place of this we can also use *in order that* or simply *that*:

The police officer went out in plain clothes *in order that* no one might recognize him.

Speak more loudly *that* he may hear you.

Exercise 7

Express the idea in each of the following pairs of sentences in one sentence, turning the second sentence into an adverbial clause of purpose.

1 He built a fence round the garden. The purpose was to prevent stray cattle from getting in.

2 The police surrounded the house. They wanted to prevent the thief from escaping.
3 The doctor gave him a sleeping pill.
The patient might then sleep well.
4 He built an additional room.
His purpose was to accommodate guests.
5 Check the figures once again.
You can then be sure of their correctness.

4 *Adverbial Clause of Reason or Cause*

Study the sentences in the table:

(1) *Main Clause*	(2) *Conjunction*	(3) *Adverb Clause*
He will win the election	because	he is very popular.
I believe the story	since	it comes from you.
I didn't attend office	as	I was not well.
You can be punctual to school	now that	you have a school bus.

The clauses in column (3) are *adverbial clauses of reason* and the words in column (2) are the conjunctions.

The clause can also come before the main clause. e.g.

Because he is very popular, he is sure to win the election.

As I am not well, I am not attending office today.

Now that you have a school bus, you can be punctual to school.

Exercise 8

Combine each of the following pairs of sentences into one sentence turning the sentence in italics into an adverbial clause of reason.

1 I gave him the money.
He needed it. (because)
2 *He is honest and diligent.*
He will easily get a job. (since)

3 The strike was called off.
The management conceded the demands of the workers. (as)
4 *The rain has stopped.*
We can resume play. (now that)
5 The meeting had to be postponed.
There was no quorum. (as)

5 *Adverbial Clause of Result or Effect*

Study the sentences in the table.

(1) *Main Clause*	(2) *Conjunction*	(3) *Adverb Clause*
Our soldiers fought so bravely	that	the enemy suffered a crushing defeat.
It rained very heavily for two days	so that	the rivers and lakes were flooded.
The police took such prompt action	that	the riots were quelled in a short time.

The clauses in the third column express the results or consequences of the actions expressed in the main clauses. They are adverbial clauses of result/effect/consequence. The conjunctions used are: so . . that, so that, and such . . that.

The conjunction *that* is sometimes understood and not expressed:

He spoke so softly we could not hear him.
He was so weak he could not even sit up in bed.

Exercise 9

Combine each of the following pairs of sentences using *so... that.*

Example:

He was very tired.
He could not walk any further.
He was so tired that he could not walk any further.

1 He was very nervous.
He forgot what he had wanted to say.

2 The box was very heavy.
I had to get a porter to carry it.
3 The compartment was very crowded.
We could not find a seat.
4 His offence was very serious.
The judge wanted to give him deterrent punishment.
5 He had prepared very well for the examination.
He was able to answer all the questions correctly.

Exercise 10

Combine each of the following pairs of sentences using *such ... that*. The first one is done for you as an example.

1 He used very bad words.
I don't wish to repeat them.
Answer: He used such bad words that I don't wish to repeat them.
2 The boy has very fine manners.
Everyone likes him very much.
3 I had a very heavy lunch.
I don't want my tea.
4 Our soldiers fought with great courage.
The enemy suffered a crushing defeat.
5 He speaks with great eloquence.
He can get anyone to his side.

6 *Adverbial Clause of Condition*

Look at this sentence.

If you take exercise regularly, you will keep fit and healthy.

The clause in italics tells the conditions or circumstances that will keep you fit and healthy. It is an *adverbial clause of condition*. The conjunction generally used to express an adverbial clause of condition is *if*.

Here are some more examples.

If he apologizes to me, I shall forgive him.
If the weather is fine, we will go for a picnic.

The adverb clause can also express a negative condition.

If you don't come in time, you will be marked absent.
If you don't take a taxi, you will miss the train.

Negative conditions can also be expressed with the conjunction *unless*.

Unless you take exercise regularly, you will not keep fit and healthy.

Unless you really love children, they will not obey you.

The adverb clauses in these sentences express conditions that may or can be fulfilled.

[Note that the *if/unless* clause is in the simple present tense although the main clause refers to what will happen in the future.

Note also that the *if/unless* clause can come after the main clause.] e.g.

I shall forgive him if he apologizes to me.

If the adverb clause comes before the main clause, put a comma at the end of the clause. No comma is necessary if this clause comes after the main clause. The adverb clause of condition may also be introduced by the phrase *in case*. Look at these sentences.

Take an umbrella with you, in case it rains.

I took down his telephone number, in case I had to speak to him again.

We generally use *in case* to introduce a condition or eventuality, when the main clause refers to the action to be taken to meet that condition or eventuality.

Exercise 11

Combine each of the following pairs of sentences into a complex sentence, turning the first sentence into an adverb clause with an appropriate conjunction: *if*, *in case*.

Examples:

Take exercise regularly.
Then you can keep fit and healthy.

Answer: If you take exercise regularly, you can keep fit and healthy.

You may need more money. Take this cheque with you.

Answer: Take this cheque with you, in case you need more money.

1 Get one hundred marks.
Then you will get a prize. (if)
2 Cut down your expenses.
Then you can save something. (if)
3 Read a large number of books.
Then you can improve your English. (if)
4 Take another step.
You are a dead man. (if)
5 Are you likely to go to the post office?
Then please post these letters for me. (in case)
6 Electricity may fail.
So keep a few candles at hand. (in case)

Exercise 12

Rewrite the following sentences using *unless* in place of *if*.

Example:

If you don't work hard, you cannot hope to pass.
Unless you work hard, you cannot hope to pass.

1 If you don't go in your uniform, you will not be admitted into the grounds.
2 How can I attend the function if I am not invited?
3 If there is no quorum, we cannot hold the meeting.
4 You are likely to be punished, if you don't express your regret.
5 Our petition will not be considered if all of us do not sign it.

Hypothetical or Imagined Condition

The adverb clauses of condition illustrated above express conditions which may or may not be fulfilled.

Look at this sentence:

If I had a lot of money, I would build a house and buy a car.

The sentence expresses the probable result of a certain condition which is hypothetical or assumed. The condition is generally not one that is expected to be fulfilled.

[Note that the verb in an *if*-clause of this kind is in the simple past tense and the verb phrase in the main clause is *should/would/could/might + verb*.]

Though the verb *had* is in the past tense, it does not refer to the past, but to the present time.

Here are some more examples.

> If he changed his views, we could elect him.
> (But he won't change his views.)
> If I had the money, I would help him.
> (But I haven't got the money.)

The *if*-clause can also be used to express a purely imagined and untrue condition. e.g.,

> If Raju were here, he would support me.
> (But he is not here.)
> If I were you, I wouldn't put up with this insult.
> If Gandhiji were alive, what a difference it would make to the country!

[Note the use of *were* in such clauses, and also the past tense form of the verb in the main clause.]

Exercise 13

Supply the correct tense forms of the verbs given in brackets.

1 If he (agree), we shall elect him as our president.
2 Take my advice. If you do so everything (go off) well.
3 I don't know how to operate this machine. If I (know) it, I would show you how to do it.
4 I am not hungry. If you (be) hungry, you may eat.
5 If I (be) you, I would not undertake a journey in the present circumstances.
6 If Gandhiji (be) alive, he (be) unhappy to see the violence in the country.
7 If you got a lakh of rupees in a lottery, tell me what you (do).
8 If he (eat) more, he will be sick.

Unfulfilled Condition in the Past

Look at these sentences:

> *If he had pleadea guilty* he would have been given a lighter punishment.
> *If he hadn't wasted his time*, he would have passed.
> *If he had asked me*, I would have helped him.

The adverbial clauses in these sentences express an unfulfilled condition relating to the past. Note the use of *the past perfect tense* in the clause, and the use of *would have* + *past participle* in the main clause.

The three sentences above mean:

> He did not plead guilty; and he was given a heavier punishment.
> He wasted his time; and he failed.
> He did not ask me; and I didn't help him.

[Note that we also use in the principal clause in such sentences, *could have*, *might have*, or *should have* in place of *would have*, depending on the meaning we wish to express.]

Exercise 14

Rewrite the following sentences putting the verb in brackets in the correct tense.

1 If he (work) hard, he could certainly have passed.
2 If you had come a little earlier, you (get) a ticket.
3 If the fire engines (arrive) an hour earlier, the building could have been saved.
4 If he (be) more alert, he could have avoided the accident.
5 If he (strictly follow) the doctor's instructions, he would not have had a relapse.
6 If I had known you were coming, I (met) you at the station.

7 *Adverbial Clause of Concession*

a. Look at these sentences:

1 *Although he was ill*, he attended to his office work.
2 *Though he hadn't eaten for several days*, he looked strong and healthy.

In each of these sentences the clause in italics expresses a concession; it admits a fact. In sentence (1) the fact conceded or admitted is: *he was ill.* In sentence (2) the fact conceded or admitted is: *he hadn't eaten for several days.*

Clauses of this kind are called *adverbial clauses of concession.* They begin with *although* or *though.* The sentences can be written with *but, still* or *yet.* That is, *although/though* as a subordinating conjunction is the equivalent of *but/still/that* as a co-ordinating conjunction.

He was ill, but/still/yet he attended to his office work.

Exercise 15

Rewrite the following sentences, turning the first sentence into an adverb clause of concession:

1 I had seen the picture twice.
Still I wanted to see it a third time.

2 He is past eighty.
His senses are still keen.

3 I read the poem several times, still I could not understand it.

4 He is not very rich.
Still he has been helping several needy persons.

5 It was threatening to rain.
Yet, they went out for a walk.

b Adverb clause of concession with *whether ... or.*

Look at this sentence:

Whether we win or lose, let us play the match.

The clause in italics expresses what we may call alternative condition and concession.

The sentence means:

We might win or we might lose, but let us play the match.

Exercise 16

Rewrite the following sentences turning the sentences in italics into a clause with *whether ... or.*

1 *He may accept our invitation. He may not accept our invitation.* We shall invite him.
2 *I may win a prize. I may not win a prize.* I shall try my luck.
3 *He might attend. He might not attend.* We must go ahead with the meeting.
4 Let us submit our proposals. *They may be accepted. They may not be accepted.*
5 *His parents may agree. They may not agree.* He is determined to marry this girl.

8 *Adverbial Clause of Manner*

a Look at these sentences:

Do *as I tell you.*
Plants breathe *as animals do.*

The clauses in italics are called *adverbial clauses of manner.* They express the manner in which the action expressed by the verb in the main clause is done or is to be done.

b Look at this sentence.

He speaks *as if he knew about everything under the sun.*
He trembled with fear *as if he had seen a ghost.*

The clause in the first sentence means: as he would speak if he knew about everything under the sun (which is not the case). The clause in the second sentence means: as he would have trembled if he had seen a ghost. The implication is that he had not seen a ghost.

Note the use of the past or the past perfect tense in the clause. We can also use *as though* in place of *as if.*

Exercise 17

Express the idea in each pair of sentences below in one sentence using *as if* or *as though.*

Example:

He screamed in great fear.
One might think he had seen a ghost.

Answer: He screamed in great fear as if he had seen a ghost.

1 He started ordering all the servants in the house.
One might think he was the master of the house.
(But he wasn't.)

2 He spoke to us discourteously.
One might think we had gone to him to beg.
(But we hadn't gone to him to do so.)

3 He described the shooting of the bison very vividly.
One might think he saw it himself.
(But he hadn't seen it.)

4 He walked with unsteady steps.
One might think he was drunk. (But he wasn't.)

5 Look at the way that man walks.
One might think he is the monarch of all he surveys.
(But of course he isn't.)

9 *Adverbial Clause of Comparison*

Look at these sentences:

He is not so stupid *as he looks.*
Ravi doesn't work as hard *as Raju does.*
He is older *than he looks.*
He speaks much better *than he writes.*

The clauses in italics are ***adverb clauses of comparison.*** They are introduced by *as* or *than.* *As* is used when the adjective or adverb in the main clause is in the positive degree. *Than* is used when it is in the comparative degree.

Exercise 18

Look at these sentences:

The red sari costs Rs. 250.
The blue sari costs Rs. 300.

We can compare the cost of the saris and say:

The red sari is not as expensive as the blue sari.
The red sari is less expensive than the blue sari.
The blue sari is more expensive than the red sari.

Write three sentences as shown above, for each of the following pairs of sentences. Use the adjective or adverb given in the brackets.

1 The one-room house costs Rs. 20,000.
The two-room house costs Rs. 30,000. (expensive)
2 The bed-room is twelve by twelve.
The drawing room is fourteen by fourteen. (big)
3 The blue box weighs ten kilos.
The white box weighs fifteen kilos. (heavy)
4 The market road is twenty feet wide.
The hospital road is thirty feet wide. (wide)
5 My watch gains five minutes a day.
Your watch gains seven minutes a day. (fast)

The Noun Clause

Look at these sentences:

a The teacher told me *that I was wrong.*
We knew *that the plan was impractical.*

The clauses in italics are *noun clauses* introduced by the conjunction *that.* They function as the objects of the verbs in the main clauses, *told* and *knew.*

b *That he will be appointed to the job* is certain.
That he is the most qualified person will be admitted by everyone.

The clauses in italics are noun clauses, and they function as the subjects of the verbs: *is* and *will be admitted.*

c Our hope is *that he will improve in due course.*
Everybody's expectation was *that he would pass.*

The clauses in italics function as the complements of the verbs *is* and *was.*

d We were certain *that he would pass.*
I am hopeful *that he will agree to our proposal.*

The noun clauses in italics are the complements of the adjectives before them: *certain* and *hopeful.*

When the noun clause is an object or a complement, the conjunction *that* may be omitted.

I believed he was right.
I was sure he was right.

e The suggestion *that the meeting should be adjourned was* unanimously accepted.
The belief *that stars have some influence on our lives* is still common.

The noun clauses in italics are in apposition to the nouns before them: *suggestion* and *belief*. The suggestion and the belief are stated in the clauses that follow them.

Wh-*clauses as Noun Clauses*

Wh-clauses do all the five functions that *tnat* clauses do. But in addition to these, they can function as objects of prepositions.

Examples:

Subject	:	What you say is true. Where he lives is a mystery.
Object	:	I don't know what he would say to this idea.
		Do you know where he lives?
Subject Complement	:	The question is who will bell the cat. The problem is where the money will come from.
In apposition	:	My question, who is responsible for the loss, has not been answered.
Adjectival Complement	:	I wasn't sure whose mistake it was.
Object of Preposition	:	We were not aware of what they were doing.
		He is against whatever I want to do.

If/whether *clauses as noun clauses*

I asked him if/whether he can speak French.
I don't know if/whether he has been appointed or not.
I don't care whether he attends the meeting or not.
Whether he comes or not doesn't worry me.

[Note that in some cases both *if* and *whether* can be used, but in some only *if* and in others only *whether*.]

Exercise 19

Rewrite each of the following bits of conversation in indirect speech.

Example:

Pratap: Where are you going, Ravi?
Ravi : To the library.
Pratap asked Ravi where he was going.
Ravi said he was going to the library.

1 Ashok : Did you finish reading the book I gave you?
Mohan : Not yet, Ashok.

2 Ashok : Will you return it next week?
Mohan : I shall.

3 Leela : Where did you buy these bangles?
Kamala: I bought them in Hyderabad.

4 Leela : How much did a pair cost?
Kamala: Rupees ten only.

5 Leela : What stones are there on these bangles?
Kamala: They are a kind of imitation diamonds. You get them at some shops in Charminar, Hyderabad.

Exercise 20

Rewrite each of the following pairs of sentences as one sentence with a noun clause functioning as a complement.

Example:

He will improve in due course.
This is our hope.
Our hope is that he will improve in due course.

1 He may have lost his way.
That is my fear.
2 She hasn't got the money.
That is the fact.
3 The earth was flat.
This was the belief in very old times.
4 This year the harvest should be quite good.
That is our expectation.
5 We should drop the plan.
That is my suggestion.

Exercise 21

Combine each of the following pairs of sentences into one sentence with a noun clause functioning as a complement to an adjective.

Example:

He will agree to be the chief guest. I am hopeful.
I am hopeful that he will agree to be the chief guest.

1 He will be completely cured.
The doctor is hopeful.
2 The bridge will give way.
The engineers are afraid.

3 The management will concede our demands.
We can be certain.

4 The prices will go down hereafter.
You can be sure.

5 He will pass.
I am confident.

Exercise 22

Combine each of the following pairs of sentences into one sentence turning the first sentence into a noun clause as object of a preposition.

Example:

I told you something.
Have you given your thought to it?
Answer: Have you given your thought to what I had told you?

1 You have something.
Try to manage with it.

2 The radio announcement said something yesterday about licences.
Did you listen to it?

3 They have suggested something.
I am against it.

4 It is something you cannot have.
Don't long for it.

5 What happened in the library?
Tell me all about it.

Exercise 23

Combine each of the following pairs of sentences into one sentence turning one of the sentences into a noun clause functioning as subject.

Example:

You said something.
It is true.
What you said is true.

1 He said something.
It is not clear.

2 When will the elections take place?
This has not been announced.

3 Why were the appointments not made?
This is not known.

4 Who is going to organize the show?
This has not been decided.

5 Where will the tournament take place?
This has yet to be decided.

The Sequence of Tenses

1 He *said* that he *had* enough money for the journey.
I *asked* him when he *would be* back home.
He *said* he *would be* back home after two months.

When the verb in the main clause is in the past tense, the verb in the subordinate clause also is usually in the past tense.

2 Copernicus *proved* that the earth *moves* round the sun.
Shakespeare *said* that mercy *is* twice blessed, it *blesses* him that *gives* and him that *receives*.

A past tense in the main clause may be followed by a present tense in the subordinate clause when the subordinate clause expresses a universal truth.

3 I *suspect* Ravi *has stolen* the pen.
I *suspect* Ravi *stole* the pen.
I *shall prove* that Ravi *stole* the pen.

If the verb in the main clause is in the present or future tense, the verb in the subordinate clause may be in the past tense or present tense according to the context.

Exercise 24

Fill in the blanks with the correct tense of the verb or the auxiliary given in brackets.

1 He gave me as much money as I ———. (need)
2 Whenever I ——— you, I remember one of my classmates. (see)
3 He ——— see only if he wears glasses. (can/could)
4 Though he came first, he ——— the last to go. (be)
5 He walked so fast that we ——— not keep pace with him. (can/could)
6 Wherever Gandhiji went, people ——— in thousands. (gather)
7 We took a guide with us so that we ——— our way. (not lose)
8 There is a much larger audience here than I ———. (think)
9 Fools ——— in where angels fear to tread. (rush)
10 His speech proved to be much better than I ———. (expect)
11 Keep these documents in your locker so that they ——— be safe. (may/might)
12 He walks as if he ——— a little lame in one leg. (be)
13 He hasn't turned up, just as I ———. (expect)
14 Just as I ——— into my bed the telephone rang. (get)
15 You can sit wherever you ———. (like)

APPENDIX 1

EXERCISES IN SYNTHESIS

Exercise 1

Combine each group of sentences into one simple sentence using infinitives. The first two are done for you as examples.

1 The poem was very difficult.
I could not understand it.
Answer: The poem was too difficult for me to understand.

2 I have some books from the library.
I must return them today.
Answer: I have some books from the library to return today.

3 He ran away from this place.
He wanted to escape arrest.

4 I can't buy that house.
I don't have the money.

5 He doesn't listen to any advice.
He hasn't the patience.

6 He has a large family.
He must support it.

7 I heard of your father's death.
I was sorry.

8 He heard the news of his son's success.
He was very happy.

9 Everyone should do his duty.
Our country expects this.

10 She saw a snake in her room.
She was frightened.

Exercise 2

Combine each pair of sentences into a simple sentence using a present, perfect or past participle. The first two are done for you as examples.

1 I heard a loud noise on the road.
I went out.
Answer: Hearing a loud noise on the road, I went out.

2 He left his job.
He was not satisfied with the salary.
Answer: Not being satisfied with the salary, he left the job.

3 We saw a girl guide.
She was leading a blind old woman.

4 I was very tired.
I soon fell asleep.

5 Hundreds of tourists come to India every year.
They just wish to see the Taj.

6 He served the company for forty years.
He chose to retire.

7 She opened the cage.
She let the bird fly away.

8 The manager was pleased with my work.
He gave me an advance increment in my salary.

9 He was occupied with some important business.
He refused to see us.

10 I looked out.
I saw a huge crowd.

Exercise 3

Combine each pair of sentences below into a simple sentence using a noun or noun phrase in apposition. The first one is done for you as an example.

1 Mr Purandar is our principal.
He is an eminent educationist.
Answer: Mr Purandar, our Principal, is an eminent educationist.

2 His uncle is a rich merchant.
He has promised to send Gopal abroad for his higher education.

3 Tourists seldom miss visiting the Taj.
It is one of the wonders of the world.

4 My uncle built this bridge.
He is an engineer in the P.W.D.
5 Tagore was awarded the Nobel Prize for *Gitanjali*.
It is a collection of beautiful poems.
6 Hampi is now a city of ruins.
Once it was the capital of the Vijayanagar kingdom.
7 Mr Dimri is the manager of the firm.
He was a clerk ten years ago.
8 Last year our Association staged *The Merchant of Venice*.
It is a comedy by Shakespeare.

Exercise 4

Combine each pair of sentences below into a simple sentence using the absolute construction. The first one is done for you as an example.

1 The captain was killed in battle.
The soldiers were in a state of panic.
Answer: The captain having been killed in the battle, the soldiers were in a state of panic.
2 The Chief Engineer went on leave.
The Assistant Engineer was put in charge of his duties.
3 The main road was closed for traffic.
We had to take a round-about route.
4 The river was in spate.
We could cross it only by boat.
5 The holidays have ended.
The students are returning to college.
6 He was very happy.
His son secured a scholarship to go abroad.
7 The rains stopped.
The sky became clear.
8 The prosecution failed to prove the charges.
The judge acquitted the accused.
9 The sun sets.
The flower closes its petals.
10 Rain has been abundant this year.
The price of rice is bound to come down.

Exercise 5

Combine each pair of sentences below into a simple sentence using *a preposition + a noun or a gerund*. Use the words or phrases given in the brackets.

1 The team has such a splendid record.
It is difficult to beat it. (with such a)
2 He was given the best medical care.
Still his condition steadily grew worse. (in spite of)
3 You helped him.
Otherwise he would have been bankrupt. (but for)
4 The boys are making a great deal of noise.
The teacher is absent. (in the absence of)
5 You turn these knobs.
You can then open the box. (by turning)
6 There was lack of funds.
The work on the dam had to be stopped. (for lack of)
7 The mill had to be reopened.
The public pressed for it. (owing to)
8 The pilot was warned not to land.
Still he chose to land. (in spite of)
9 He has lost his job.
He has also to face the charge of misappropriation of public funds. (besides)

Exercise 6

Combine each set of sentences below by using an adverb or adverb phrase.

1 The army was required to surrender.
They were not to lay down any condition.
2 The bridge has to be repaired immediately.
The cost does not count.
3 The dying man said something.
It was not distinct.
4 He hurt the boy.
He had no intention to do so.
5 He accepted my version of the event.
He did it without any reservation.

6 The patient is responding to treatment.
The response is gradual but steady.
7 He has succeeded.
The success is beyond my expectation.
8 He signed the petition.
He did this with some reluctance.
9 He will pass.
There is no doubt about it.
10 The fox kept jumping at the grapes.
He did not succeed.

Exercise 7

Combine each set of sentences below into a simple sentence.

1 He built a beautiful tomb over his wife's grave. It had lofty arches. It had a high blue dome.
2 He richly deserves our thanks. He has helped us a great deal. He did not expect anything in return.
3 A fire broke out near my house. It broke out last night. It caused great damage. It destroyed several shops.
4 A battle was fought. It was fought between Akbar and Hemu. It was fought at Panipat. It was in the year 1506. It was known as the second battle of Panipat.
5 Trees give us shade. They give us also fruit to eat. They give us wood for our furniture and fuel for cooking.
6 Gandhiji led the country to independence. It was a long struggle with the British Government. We call him the Father of the Nation.
7 The meeting ended in great confusion. It was convened by the President. It was convened to make certain amendments to the constitution of our club.
8 The guards were vigilant. But the thief managed to escape. He escaped at night. He scaled a wall at the back of the jail.

Combining simple sentences into compound sentences:

We have seen that a compound sentence is one in which there may be two or more main/independent clauses. There may or may not be any subordinate clauses.

The main clauses are connected by co-ordinating conjunctions.

Exercise 8

Combine each of the following sets of sentences into a compound sentence using an appropriate conjunction.

1 He is a man of his word.
He will return your money on the promised day.

2 She can sing.
She can play on the veena as well.

3 He is learning German.
He is leaving for Germany next month on a scholarship.

4 He is a millionaire. He is not proud of his wealth. He gives liberal contributions for worthy causes.

5 I expected only a bare pass for him. But he has secured a first class. This is more than I expected.

6 You may read in the library.
You may listen to the radio.
You should not be running about on the verandah.

7 The thieves were caught. I never got back the stolen goods. They were worth about ten thousand rupees.

8 I must catch the seven o'clock train. I have only fifteen minutes. Permit me to leave at once.

9 Your essay is well written. There are some spelling mistakes. With spelling mistakes in your writing you cannot get first class marks.

10 The aeroplane took off. Ten minutes later it developed trouble. The pilot landed it again. No damage was done to the aircraft.

11 Don't be a borrower. Don't be a lender. A loan often loses itself and the friend.

12 King Canute was seated on a chair placed on the shore. He ordered the waves to move back. But they rolled forward with greater force than before.

Combining simple sentences into complex sentences:

When we combine two or more simple sentences into a complex sentence, what we do is to retain the sentence which carries the main idea as the main clause. We change the other clause or clauses into adjectival, adverbial or noun clauses. We use relative pronouns, relative adverbs or subordinating conjunctions.

See Chapters 19 and 20 for the way sentences are combined, with regard to each type of subordinate clause.

Exercise 9

Combine each set of sentences below into a complex sentence.

1 He is very efficient. Every one in his office says this.
2 He will soon be appointed manager. Everyone expects this.
3 I have seen you somewhere. I cannot remember where.
4 Don't overeat. You will be ill.
5 He told a lie. He was beaten by his father.
6 Come home before nine. Otherwise Father will rebuke you.
7 The doctor gave me just three doses of a medicine. He was able to cure my disease. I had been suffering from it for several years.
8 I attempted to move. I could not stir. My arms and legs were strongly fastened on each side to the ground. My hair was tied down in the same manner.
9 He says one thing. He does another. How can you rely on such a man?
10 Every member should give a day's salary towards the Famine Relief Fund. That was my suggestion. The suggestion was unanimously accepted.

APPENDIX 2

WORD-FORMATION

A form of word to which a process of word-formation is applied is called a *base*. The chief processes of word-formation are the following:

a assigning the base to a different part of speech without changing its form (examples: rescue, wish, bite, which can be used both as nouns and verbs)

b adding a prefix to the base with or without a change of part of speech (examples: *dis*content, *sur*charge)

c adding a suffix to the base with or without a change of part of speech (examples: driv*er*, friend*ship*, arriv*al*)

d compounding, that is, adding one base to another (examples: goldsmith, pickpocket)

Sometimes a base that has undergone a word-formation may become the base for the formation of a third word and a fourth word. (examples: friend, friendly, unfriendly, unfriendliness).

A Assigning the base to a different part of speech:

There are numerous words in English which can be assigned to different parts of speech.

Look at the use of the word *milk* in the following sentences:

1 *Milk* is good for health.
2 The servant-maid *milks* our cow.
3 I gave the baby a *milk* chocolate.
4 He wore a *milk* white turban.

In sentence (1) *milk* is a noun. In sentence (2) *milks* is a verb. In sentence (3) *milk* is an adjective. In sentence (4) *milk* is an adverb.

We see the same word assigned to or converted into different parts of speech. This kind of word-formation is called conversion. Here are some examples of conversion.

a Verb to noun conversion

He *desires* to be an engineer. (verb)
My *desire* is to be a doctor. (noun)

I *doubt* his honesty. (verb)
I have *doubts* about this honesty. (noun)

Take care, he will *cheat* you. (verb)
Take care, he is a *cheat*. (noun)

b Noun to verb conversion

Please get me a *bottle* of milk. (noun)
The milk is *bottled* in a factory. (verb)

A *nurse* is looking after my son. (noun)
A lady is *nursing* my son. (verb)

c Adjective to noun conversion

They are playing the *final* match today. (adjective)
They are playing the *finals* today. (noun)

'The Hindu' is a *daily* newspaper. (adjective)
'The Hindu' is a *daily*. (noun)

He loves to read *comic* books. (adjective)
He loves to read *comics*. (noun)

d Noun to adjective conversion

The hut is made of *mud*. (noun)
He lives in a *mud* house. (adjective)

The children are going to *school*. (noun)
They are *school* children. (adjective)

The chair is made of *steel*. (noun)
This is a *steel* chair. (adjective)

e Adjective to verb conversion

The people were not *calm*. (adjective)
The speaker tried to *calm* them. (verb)

The classroom is very *dirty*. (adjective)
Who *dirtied* it? (verb)

He had a lot of wealth, but was *humble*. (adjective)
The sudden loss of his wealth *humbled* him. (verb)
The pot is still not *empty*. (adjective)
Empty it. (verb)

f Other types of conversion

The Taj is a *must* for all tourists.
(auxiliary *must* to noun)
Don't ask me the *why* of it.
(interrogative *why* to noun)
In life we have to face *ups* and *downs*.
(adverbs to nouns)
He doesn't support communism, socialism or any other *ism*. (suffix to noun).

Exercise 1

The following nouns are used both as nouns and verbs. Write sentences using them first as nouns and then as verbs.

colour	delay	favour	mistake
crowd	demand	form	notice
control	end	group	place
damage	experiment	judge	point
question	reason	request	water

Exercise 2

The following verbs are often used both as verbs and nouns. Write sentences using them both as verbs and nouns.

attack	command	dress	guess	smile
arrest	cook	drink	drop	hurry
shout	attempt	cry	fall	hope
start	call	cut	fear	limit
support	cause	cover	turn	play

B Adding prefix to the base

A *prefix* is a word or syllable placed in front of a word to add to or change its meaning or function. Prefixes are of three kinds.

1 Prefixes that change the meanings of the bases.
2 Number prefixes.
3 Conversion prefixes, that is, prefixes which change the part of speech.

1 *Prefixes that change the meanings of the bases*

These prefixes can be sub-divided into various kinds:

a Prefixes that reverse or negate the meanings of words

a : (lack of) used with nouns and adjectives: amoral, asymmetry, atheist.

contra : (against) used with nouns or adjectives: contrasuggestion, contrasuggestible.

de : (to reverse the action, to get rid of) used with nouns and verbs: decode, deform, decompose, devaluation, deforestation, decentralization.

dis : (the opposite of) used with verbs, nouns and adjectives: dislike, disappear, disallow, disability, displeasure, discomfort, dishonest, disobedient.

-im -in
-il -ir : (the opposite of) used with nouns and adjectives: inability, impossibility, illogical, invisible, illegitimate, irresponsible, inaccurate, irreligious.

non : (not) with adjectives, nouns, verbs non-vegetarian, non-co-operation, nonsense, non-gazetted.

un : (the opposite of) used with verbs and adjectives: unnecessary, unhappy, undesirable, unexpected, uncover, untie.

b Prefixes of degree and size

arch : (highest, worst) with nouns: arch enemy, archbishop.

extra : (more than) with adjectives: extraordinary, extracurricular.

hyper : (extra, specially) used with adjectives and nouns: hypersensitive, hypercritical, hypertension.

mini : (little) used with nouns: mini-car, mini skirt.

out : (to do something better, faster etc.) used with intransitive verbs to form transitive verbs: outgrow, outlive, outweigh.

semi : (half) used with nouns: semi-circle, semi-darkness.

super : (above, more than, better) used with nouns and adjectives: supermarket, supernatural, superhuman

sub : (under, lower than) used with adjectives, nouns and verbs: subnormal, subhuman, sub-inspector, subordinate, sublet, subdivide.

ultra : (over and above) used with adjectives: ultra-violet, ultra-modern.

under (too little) used with verbs: underestimate, undervalue.

c Prefixes of time and order

fore (before) used with verbs and nouns: foretell, forecast, foreknowledge.

pre : (before) used with nouns and adjectives: pre-school, pre-war, pre-marital, pre-ordained.

post : (after) used with nouns and adjectives: post-war, post-graduate.

ex : (former) used with nouns: ex-principal, ex-president.

re : (again, back) used with verbs and nouns: rebuild, rewrite, recall, rehearsal, resettlement.

vice : (deputy) used with nouns: vice-principal, vice-president.

d Prefixes of attitude

co : (with, accompanying) used with verbs and nouns: co-operate, co-exist, co-author, co-operation, co-existence.

counter : (against, in opposition) used with verbs and nouns: counteract, counter-revolution.

anti : (against) used with nouns and adjectives): anti-government, anti-social.

pro : (for, on the side of) used with nouns: pro-communist, pro-American.

2 *Number prefixes*

uni : (one) used with nouns and adjectives: unisex, unilateral, uniform.

mono : (one) used with nouns and adjectives: mono-syllable, mono-acting, monolingual.

bi : (two) used with nouns and adjectives: bi-weekly, bicycle, bifocal, biceps.

tri : (three) used with nouns and adjectives: triangle, tricycle, tripartite.

multi : (many) used with nouns and adjectives: multipurpose, multi-lingual, multi-millionaire.

3 *Conversion prefixes*

These prefixes are used in order to change the part of speech of a base.

be : noun to participial adjectives: bespectacled, bedevilled.
adjectives and nouns to verbs: becalm, bewitch.

en, em : nouns to verbs: empower, endanger, enslave.

C Adding a suffix to the base

A *suffix* is a word or syllable placed after a word to add to or change its meaning or function. Suffixes frequently change the part of speech of the base.

Example: happy (adjective), happiness (noun).

Noun to noun suffixes

-ster, -eer	:	gangster, trickster, engineer, profiteer.
-er	:	teenager, three-wheeler.
-let	:	booklet, leaflet, rivulet.
-ess	:	lioness, actress.
-hood	:	boyhood, priesthood.
-ship	:	friendship, headship, membership.
-dom	:	kingdom, officialdom.
-ocracy	:	democracy, autocracy, mobocracy.
-ery, -ry	:	slavery, drudgery, foolery, machinery.
-ful	:	mouthful, handful, plateful.

Noun/adjective to noun/adjective suffixes

-an, -ian	:	republican, Indian.
-ese	:	Chinese, Japanese.
-ist	:	flutist, loyalist, Buddhist, socialist, communist.
-ism	:	Buddhism, idealism, absenteeism, communism.

Verb to noun suffixes

-er, -or	:	writer, driver, employer, waiter, receiver, silencer, actor.
-ant	:	inhabitant, consultant, informant.
-ee	:	payee, employee, nominee.
-ation	:	exploration, starvation, organization.
-ment	:	judgement, postponement, payment, agreement.
-al	:	arrival, dismissal, proposal.
-ing	:	swimming, painting, gardening.

Adjective to Noun suffixes

-ness	:	happiness, kindness, neatness.
-ity	:	seniority, diversity, activity.

Verb suffixes

-ify	:	beautify, classify, modify, simplify.
-ize	:	sympathize, memorize, hospitalize, modernize.

-en	:	widen, broaden, quicken, strengthen, lengthen.

Noun to adjective suffixes

-ful	:	beautiful, useful, helpful.
-less	:	harmless, childless, tactless.
-ly, -like	:	manly, cowardly, brotherly, childlike, statesmanlike.
-y	:	sandy, hairy, creamy, misty.
-ish	:	boyish, foolish, selfish.
-esque	:	picturesque, statuesque.
-some	:	troublesome, burdensome.
-worthy	:	praiseworthy, seaworthy.
-arian, -ean	:	authoritarian, Shakespearean.
-al	:	cultural, natural, philosophical, psychological.
-ic	:	heroic, emphatic, specific.
-ive	:	expansive, attractive, explosive.
ious, -ous, -eous	:	ambitious, virtuous, famous, riotous, beauteous.

Other adjective suffixes

-able, -ible	:	readable, pardonable, commendable, memorable, laughable, **convertible**
-ish	:	bluish, longish, tallish.
-ing	:	running, hunting, crying.
-ed	:	hunted, charred, spotted, walled, blue-eyed.

Adverb suffixes

-ly	:	greatly, easily, happily.
-ward(s)	:	downwards, toward(s), upward(s), homewards(s), heavenward(s).
-wise	:	clockwise, moneywise.

D *Compounding*

A *compound* is a unit consisting of two or more bases. A compound may be a noun, a verb or an adjective:

flashlight (noun)
fireproof (adjective)
daydream (verb)

A compound may be written as one word, as a hyphenated word or as two words:

headache (one word)
book-keeping (hyphenated word)
hydrogen bomb (two words)

There is no hard-and-fast rule to guide us when we are in doubt as to which of the three classes a compound noun belongs to. The dictionary is the best guide if you are in doubt.

1 *Noun compounds*

Noun+noun	:	motorcycle, steam engine, hydrogen bomb, silkworm, tear gas, honey-bee, cane sugar, gaslight, sawdust, telephone receiver, cartwheel, window-pane, man-servant, oak tree, pussy-cat, cowshed, flowerbed, coffee time.
Adjective+noun	:	blackboard, short-hand, blueprint.
Noun+verb	:	daybreak, rainfall, earthquake.
Noun+verb+er	:	taxpayer, game keeper, language teacher.
verb+noun	:	glow-worm, watchdog, driftwood, drawbridge, push-button, scarecrow.
verb -ing (participle)+noun	:	washing machine, sliding scale, flying-fish.
Noun+gerund	:	sightseeing, dressmaking, letter-writing.
Gerund+noun	:	dining table, living room, walking stick, sun-bathing, sleepwalking, handwriting.
Adverb+noun	:	overload, postscript, after-thought.
Adverb+verb	:	output, outburst, over-throw, upstart, outlet, outcast.
Pronoun+noun	:	he-goat, she-devil.
Possessive noun+noun	:	stone's throw, hair's breadth, child's play.

Noun/verb + adverb : breakdown, run-away, passer-by.

2 *Adjective compounds*

Noun + adjective : homesick, knee-deep, waterproof, noteworthy, brick-red.

Noun + present participle : breath-taking, fact-finding, life-giving, time-saving, record-breaking.

Noun + past participle : moth-eaten, home-made, thunder-struck, heartfelt.

Adjective + past participle : true-born, broad-based.

Adjective + noun : four-horse (carriage), ten-rupee (note).

Adjective + adjective : socio-economic, deaf-mute, Anglo-Indian.

Adverb + past participle : far-fetched, well-meant, widespread.

3 *Verb compounds*

Noun + verb : brainwash, lip-read, housebreak, housekeep daydream, typewrite, spring-clean.

Adverb + verb : outdo, outlive, overcome, overlook, undermine, underestimate, uphold, upset.

APPENDIX 3

COMMON ERRORS

Some of the errors in grammar usually found in Indian learners have been gathered and classified here under different categories: errors in the use of the articles, errors in the use of the tenses, etc. The first column gives the incorrect sentence and the second column the corrected one. In each sentence there is only one kind of error and the word/s in which the error occurs and the corrected version of the word/s have been put in italics.

1 THE USE OF ARTICLES

Incorrect	*Correct*
The rice is the staple food of people in the South.	*Rice* is the staple food of people in the South.
Rice that I bought yesterday is bad.	*The rice* that I bought yesterday is bad.
The cars are made in India.	*Cars* are made in India.
Mangoes you gave me were very good.	*The mangoes* you gave me were very good.
Mr Menon has invited me to *the dinner* today.	Mr Menon has invited me to *dinner* today.
I enjoyed *dinner* Mr Menon gave me.	I enjoyed *the dinner* Mr Menon gave me.
I play *the cricket* at college.	I play *cricket* at college.
The Queen Elizabeth II recently visited Japan.	*Queen Elizabeth II* recently visited Japan.
My brother is going to *U.S.A.* for higher studies.	My brother is going to *the U.S.A.* for higher studies.
He will stop for a week in *U.K.* on his way.	He will stop for a week in *the U.K.* on his way.
Sikkim is now a state in *Union* of India.	Sikkim is now a state in *the Union* of India.
I live in *the Mint Street* in Madras.	I live in *Mint Street* in Madras.

The first satellite was launched by *Russians*.	The first satellite was launched by *the Russians*.
There is a school for *deaf* in the city.	There is a school for *the deaf* in the city.
Moon is a crescent today.	*The Moon* is a crescent today.
Thomas reads *Bible* every day.	Thomas reads *the Bible* every day.
Raju is *cleverer* of the two brothers.	Raju is *the cleverer* of the two brothers.
My brother is in *Air Force*.	My brother is in *the Air Force*.
Both his sons go to *the school*.	Both his sons go to *school*.
I went to *hospital* to visit my sick uncle.	I went to *the hospital* to visit my sick uncle.
They performed a yagna for the welfare of *the humanity*.	They performed a yagna for the welfare of *humanity*.
This year *the Deepavali* falls on a Sunday.	This year *Deepavali* falls on a Sunday.
I watched the film from *the beginning to the end*.	I watched the film from *beginning to end*.
He reached *the home* at ten in the night.	He reached *home* at ten in the night.
He can play *sitar* very well.	He can play *the sitar* very well.
Ganga flows through Varanasi.	*The Ganga* flows through Varanasi.
I am going to Delhi by *the train*.	I am going to Delhi by *train*.
He worked all *the day* and is tired.	He worked all *day* and is tired.
The man is the only creature that can laugh.	*Man* is the only creature that can laugh.
Ravi is *tallest* boy in the class.	Ravi is *the tallest* boy in the class.

Indefinite Article

Child cries when he is hungry.	*A child* cries when he is hungry.
I paid *hundred* rupees for this racket.	I paid *a hundred* rupees for this racket.

What *beautiful* building the library has!	What *a beautiful* building the library has!
I have never seen such *idiot.*	I have never seen such *an idiot.*
If I get a promotion I will get *higher* salary.	If I get a promotion I will get *a higher* salary.
We have never had *a such* hot summer.	We have never had *such a* hot summer.

2 AGREEMENT WITH VERB AND SUBJECT

One of my teachers *are* leaving for the U.S.A. today.	One of my teachers *is* leaving for the U.S.A. today.
A thousand rupees *are* all the money I need.	A thousand rupees *is* all the money I need.
'Steps to English Literature' *are* published by a reputed company.	'Steps to English Literature' *is* published by a reputed company.
The family living next door often *quarrels* among themselves.	The family living next door often *quarrel* among themselves.
The cow and calf *are* the emblem of the Congress party.	The cow and calf *is* the emblem of the Congress party.
The majority of the boys *is* against your proposal.	The majority of the boys *are* against your proposal.
Either those children or my son *have* damaged this window.	Either those children or my son *has* damaged this window.
Either you or I *are* to attend the meeting.	Either you or I *am* to attend the meeting.
The president as well as the members *are* responsible for the loss.	The president as well as the members *is* responsible for the loss.
Five times five *are* twenty-five.	Five times five *is* twenty-five.
Nobody, not even the committee members, *is* here.	Nobody, not even the committee members, *are* here.
Mumps *are* a bad disease.	Mumps *is* a bad disease.
The news of the air crash *are* shocking.	The news of the air crash *is* shocking.

There *is* plenty of jobs these days for qualified young men.	There *are* plenty of jobs these days for qualified young men.
The footwear on that rack *are* pure leather.	The footwear on that rack *is* pure leather.
All my luggage *have* been weighed.	All my luggage *has* been weighed.
Some of the milk *were* spilt.	Some of the milk *was* spilt.

3 THE TENSES

The earth *is moving* round the sun.	The earth *moves* round the sun.
I *am going* to school by bus every day.	I *go* to school by bus every day.
My uncle *writes* a novel.	My uncle *is writing* a novel.
I *am seeing* a bus coming.	I *see* a bus coming.
I *have slept* for eight hours last night.	I *slept* eight hours last night.
He *has had* his scooter repaired yesterday.	He *had* his scooter repaired yesterday.
He *is studying* English for three years.	He *has studied* English for three years.
They have lived in this house *since ten years*.	They have lived in this house *since* ***1966***.
I *did not see* him since last Monday.	I *have not seen* him since last Monday.
I have not played cricket since I *have left* college.	I have not played cricket since I *left* college.
I will talk to him when I *will see* him.	I will talk to him when I *see* him.
If I *will have* the time, I shall visit the zoo.	If I *have* the time, I shall visit the zoo.
He *didn't* yet complete his assignment.	He *hasn't* yet completed his assignment.
I *shall look* forward to seeing you.	I *look* forward to seeing you.
It is high time that we *leave* the place.	It is high time that we *left* the place.
I'd rather you *will stay* home.	I'd rather you *stayed* home.

The English alphabet is *consisting* of 26 letters.	The English alphabet *consists* of 26 letters.
Mr Sen *is owning* two houses.	Mr Sen *owns* two houses.
If I *tell* the truth, no one would believe me.	If I *told* the truth no one would believe me.
If he *worked* hard, he would have passed.	If he *had worked* hard, he would have passed.

4 THE USE OF THE INFINITIVE

The teacher made the boy *to do* the sum again.	The teacher made the boy *do* the sum again.
The boy was made *do* the sum again.	The boy was made *to do* the sum again.
We felt the whole building *to vibrate.*	We felt the whole building *vibrate.*
I know *to operate* that engine.	I know *how to operate* that engine.
He enjoys *to tell* stories to children.	He enjoys *telling* stories to children.

5 REDUNDANT PRONOUNS, PREPOSITIONS, CONJUNCTIONS, ETC.

I found the book that I lost *it* yesterday.	I found the book that I lost yesterday.
They gazed at the statue *to* which the guide was pointing to.	They gazed at the statue, which the guide was pointing to.
We shall meet tomorrow to discuss *about* the subject.	We shall meet tomorrow to discuss the subject.
Although he was ill, *but* he attended his office.	Although he was ill, he attended office.
Because he damaged the chair, *so* he was fined.	Because he damaged the chair, he was fined.
My brother lost his wife *since* five years ago.	My brother lost his wife five years ago.

6 THE USE OF CORRELATIVES

He *not only cheated me but also my friend.*	He cheated *not only me but also my friend.*

He *neither cares for his wife nor his children.*	He cares *neither for his wife nor his children.*
He is neither honest *or* efficient.	He is neither honest *nor* efficient.
The thief *both carried away my wife's clothes and my own.*	The thief carried away *both my own and my wife's clothes.*

7 WORD ORDER

What *you are* saying?	What *are you* saying?
Where *he is* going?	Where *is he* going?
Why *you can't* come?	Why *can't you* come?
Tell me *where is the post office.*	Tell me *where the post office is.*
Ask him *why does he want* a hundred rupees.	Ask him *why he wants* a hundred rupees.
No sooner he *had received* the telegram than he started crying.	No sooner *had he received* the telegram than he started crying.
She bought a *blue long* ribbon.	She bought *a long blue* ribbon.
He carried his clothes in a *black heavy steel* trunk.	He carried his clothes in a *heavy black steel* trunk.
Seldom *I have* spoken to him	Seldom *have I* spoken to him.
Rarely *he has* discussed the subject with me.	Rarely *has he* discussed the subject with me.
We *all were* happy to hear the news.	We *were all* happy to hear the news.

8 THE USE OF PRONOUNS

I and Mr Karthik work in the same office.	*Mr Karthik and I* work in the same office.
The principal wants to see *you and I.*	The principal wants to see *you and me.*
All the students except *I* are going for the picnic.	All the students except *me* are going for the picnic.
Myself am going to the post office to post this letter.	*I am* going to the post office to post this letter.

The principal desires to see *yourself* and Sekhar.

The principal wants to see *you* and Sekhar.

I cursed *me* for going late to the station.

I cursed *myself* for going late to the station.

It was Rahul *who* broke the chair.

It was Rahul *that* broke the chair.

This is the best film *which* I have ever seen.

This is the best film *that* I have ever seen.

If the child cannot bite the apple, *it* should be cut into pieces.

If the child cannot bite it the *apple* should be cut into pieces.

This is the gentleman *whose all sons* are in the army.

This is the gentleman *all of whose sons* are in the army.

One must keep *his* word.

One must keep *one's* word.

Where is the man *whom* you said insists on seeing me?

Where is the man *who* you said insists on seeing me?

Your's is the best painting in the exhibition.

Yours is the best painting in the exhibition.

He insisted on *me to accompany* him.

He insisted on *my accompanying* him.

9 THE USE OF PREPOSITIONS

I told him *on* his face that he was a liar.

I told him *to* his face that he was a liar.

The principal has entrusted this work *upon* me.

The principal has entrusted this work *to* me.

I hope to spend the summer *at* Kashmir.

I hope to spend the summer *in* Kashmir.

They sat *under* the shade of a tree.

They sat *in* the shade of a tree.

This cloth is superior *than* the cloth we saw in the last shop.

This cloth is superior *to* the cloth we saw in the last shop.

I prefer going for a walk *than* seeing a film.

I prefer going for a walk *to* seeing a film.

The child died *from* jaundice.

The child died *of* jaundice.

The Executive Committee consists *in* eleven members.

The Executive Committee consists *of* eleven members.

Happiness consists *of* contentment with one's lot.

Happiness consists *in* contentment with one's lot.

The boy is standing *besides* his mother.	The boy is standing *beside* his mother.
Beside a son by his second wife, he has a daughter by his first wife.	*Besides* a son by his second wife, he has a daughter by his first wife.

10 MISCELLANEOUS ERRORS

One of *his family members* is a brigadier.	One of the *members of his family* is a brigadier.
Mr Prabhu is the *eldest* citizen of the village.	Mr Prabhu is the *oldest* citizen of the village.
You are coming with me, *isn't it*?	You are coming with me, *aren't* you?
I picked up a *ten-rupees* note from the road yesterday.	I picked up a *ten-rupee* note from the road yesterday.
I bought four *dozens* mangoes.	I bought four *dozen* mangoes.
My health is *alright* these days.	My health is *all right* these days.
I have never spoken to him *nor* his brother.	I have never spoken to him *or* his brother.
She did not see me *nor* my friend.	She did not see me *or* my friend.
He is my *cousin brother.*	He is my *cousin.*
Having read the book, *it was returned.*	Having read the book *I returned it.*
Walking through the jungle a snake bit him.	*As he was walking through the jungle* a snake bit him.
He is *too* healthy.	He is *very* healthy.
I have disposed *off* my house.	I have disposed *of* my house.
The house is under *repairs.*	The house is under *repair.*
My *circumstance* does not allow me to leave my village.	My *circumstances* do not allow me to leave my village.
Though he worked very *hardly*, he failed.	Though he worked *hard*, he failed.

Composition

I LETTER WRITING

Read the two letters given below, carefully.

A letter to your younger brother sending him birthday greetings:

40, Krala Khud,
Second Bridge,
Srinagar.
May 2, 1976.

Dear Raj,

I apologize for the delay in replying to your last letter which everyone enjoyed reading repeatedly. Mother shed tears of joy on hearing of your brilliant performance in class. Congratulations!

This letter is written from all of us to you on a very special occasion. Next Monday is your 10th birthday and everybody here (including Kitty) wishes you many happy returns of the day. We all wish you were here to celebrate it with us but we know you cannot come away for another six weeks. Father is sending you a parcel whose contents must remain a secret until you open it on the big day. And Rita and I have bought you something to remind you of the last holidays we spent together. Pappu sends you kisses because she has no money for presents. Mother sends you all good wishes and looks forward to 15th June when you'll be home. I too look forward to that day. Do look after yourself. Love.

Yours affectionately,
Raman

2 A letter to a friend of yours you met by chance after many years:

26 Tarnaka,
Hyderabad.
20th August 1975.

Dear Virendra,

Thank you very much for your letter which I've just received.

You are perfectly right about my memory for names — it is very poor indeed. But in this case I don't blame myself very much; after all, we met after about seven years and the meeting was so unexpected. In fact, it took me quite some time to realize that you always used to call me Subbu. No one dares call me by that name except you, of course! Let me tell you a secret. As soon as I got back here, I rushed into our store room and got hold of my favourite album. And once I opened it, I was back in the good old days. How I wish they could come back! What fun we had together and how happy we could be even with tests and examinations to worry us! Everyone used to envy us and most of them thought we were twins.

Well, things have changed, but it was great meeting you after so long. I know you travel a lot more than I do. So if you happen to come this way again, do make it a point to break your journey at least for a day. I shall look forward to that day.

For now all the best.

Yours sincerely,
Subramanian (Subbu!)

These two letters are *personal letters,* which one writes to friends and relations. Personal letters are one of the kinds of letters that we write. Note the parts of the two letters.

1 *The heading*

This is the writer's own address and the date written at the top right hand corner. Note the order of the details in the address: number or name of the house, name of street and town or city. Don't write your name over the heading. You may, if you wish, write it on the top left-hand corner.

The date can be written in more ways than one: for example, January 16th, 1974 or 16th Jan. 1974 or 16-1-1974.

2 *The salutation*

The forms for letters to relations usually are: My dear Father/Mother, My dear Uncle/Aunt, My dear Brother/Sister, Dear Raju.

The forms for letters to friends usually are: Dear Virendra, Dear Mr Rao, Dear Mrs Raman, Dear Miss Smith, Dear Dr Kamath.

[*Note*: We do not begin a letter with *Dear friend*. We use names instead, e.g. Dear Prem, Dear Radha, etc.]

3 *The body of the letter*

This usually has three parts: an introduction which gives the reason for the letter, a message which includes the main information and a conclusion which always contains a polite wish (e.g. I hope to see you soon, for now all the best, etc.).

A good personal letter must read true. You should imagine that the person is near you and you are talking to him. The letter must also show your interest in the friend or relative you are writing to. The interest can be shown in different ways. Keep in mind the likes and dislikes, interests and tastes of the person you are writing to. Do not, for example, talk of tennis to a friend who has never seen or touched a tennis racket. Secondly, make your style personal and intimate, using informal and conversational language, and whenever possible using contracted forms (e.g. ' you've ' for ' you have ') and expressions of friendliness and intimacy. If you have to give reasons for anything, for example, your inability to accept an invitation to a dinner, wedding etc., make sure that they are good, sensible and convincing reasons.

4 *The subscription*

This is written below the body of the letter to the right. The forms to friends usually are: *Yours sincerely*, *Yours very sincerely*. The forms to relatives are: *Yours affectionately*, *Your loving son/daughter/brother*, etc. [Note that there is no apostrophe (') for *yours*.]

5 *The address*

Write the address neatly and legibly on the envelope. Make it clear, correct and full to help the postman deliver it to the person it is meant for.

If you are writing to a person outside your State, note the name of the State too (e.g. Kerala, Tamil Nadu, Karnataka). If you are writing to someone who is abroad, write the name of the country too at the end (e.g. U.S.A., U.K., U.S.S.R.).

If you write the PIN code, you can be sure of your letter reaching the addressee without delay.

A. Personal Letters

Here are some personal letters given as examples:

1 You hold two complimentary tickets for a variety entertainment. Write a letter to a friend of yours inviting him to accompany you.

15 University Road,
Hyderabad.
10th August, 1975.

My dear Murali,

Many thanks for your kind letter of 31st July. I am very sorry it has taken me long to send this reply. The day I received your letter I left for Guntur to play in the State Football Tournament. I hope you will excuse me for my long silence.

On my return from Guntur I find two complimentary tickets for a Variety Entertainment waiting for me. The show is coming off on Sunday next and is being organized by the local Youth Club. I shall be most happy if you can come with me to the show.

Some of the city recreation clubs, and music and dance sabhas are presenting very interesting items and the show is bound to be entertaining. The highlight of the show, I am told, is a scene from Kathakali presented by the Kerala Club. I know how interested you are in this art form and I hope you will find it convenient to come. Please drop me a line in reply.

My regards to your parents.

Yours sincerely,
Prasad

2 You quarrelled with a friend of yours and now you feel sorry for it. Write a letter to him requesting him to forget about it and inviting him to tea.

27 Market Road,
Guntur.
September 10, 1975.

Dear Srinivas,

Perhaps this letter will come to you as a surprise.

I have been very upset and uneasy ever since we parted last Sunday. Having been very good friends all these years. it was indeed very unfortunate that we quarrelled over what appears to me now a very silly matter. How difficult it is sometimes to control one's temper! Indeed I am sorry I lost mine and I feel very bad about it. If Ranjit had not intervened, things would have got worse, I guess. Let me express my regret for the way I behaved. Let's forget all that happened and be friends again. May I suggest that we meet at the Three Aces Restaurant on Monday and have tea together? Do come.

Yours as ever,
Ramesh

3 Write a letter to your father about your experience at college after admission.

Room 4, B Hostel,
Government Arts College,
Rajahmundry.
8th July, 1975.

My dear Father,

I have been at college a week now and I know how eagerly you will be waiting to hear from me.

For a day or two after admission I felt a little uneasy, this being the first time I am away from home. But I may now say I can look forward to a happy time here.

One thing that strikes me is the excellent discipline maintained in this college, something that I had really not expected. We have an efficient principal and a team of earnest and devoted teachers. Regular work started the day after I joined and the classes are now in full swing.

My life in the hostel is just a little disappointing. I have been put in an extension which is nearing completion. And the food is not quite to my taste. But I hope I will soon get used to it. As you have often told me one should learn to adjust oneself to circumstances.

The college has, however, a very nice programme of extra-curricular activities, all very well organized. I propose to join the Tennis Club. That is something I have looked forward to.

With love to everyone at home,

Yours affectionately,
Sankar

4 You receive information that a friend of yours is in hospital after meeting with an accident. Write a letter expressing your concern.

30 College Road,
Warangal.
20th September, 1975.

My dear Prema,

It was with a shock that I learnt just this morning that you met with an accident while returning from college yesterday and that you were rushed to hospital. I am distressed and worried to hear the news. Father told me the news but did not give any details.

I am sure the doctors will do all that they can for you. I have a test in English today and on my way back from college I shall visit you.

With all good wishes for your speedy recovery,

Yours very sincerely,
Renuka

5 Write a letter to a friend of yours telling him about your future plans after leaving college.

24 Station Road,
Secunderabad.
July 28, 1975.

Dear Savithri,

Thank you very much for your kind letter of July 20th. It was such a pleasure to hear from you after a long time.

I wonder how you found time to write to me in the midst of your preparations for your final examination.

You ask me what I intend to do after I take my B.Sc. degree. It has all along been my ambition to study medicine and become a doctor. But I am not sure whether I'll get a high enough rank to qualify me for admission. If I don't join a medical college I would like to join the Library Science Course in the University. I can complete this course in a year and can be sure of a job too. That would be a great relief to my father who is to retire two years hence.

You didn't tell me what your plans are. How about applying for research in your field of study?

With kind regards,

Yours sincerely,
Seethalakshmy

Learn how personal letters are begun and concluded. Here are a few ways of beginning them. You should always think of one that is appropriate to your context:

Many thanks for your kind letter dated.......
Thank you very much for your kind letter of..... 1975.
It is a long time since I heard from you.
This letter may perhaps come as a surprise to you.
I am sorry I have not yet heard from you in reply to my letter......
It was with a shock that I heard.....
It is with great pleasure that I inform you that......
Let me at the outset apologize for the delay in replying to your letter.....
You will be glad to know that.....

Here are a few ways in which you can conclude your letters: You should say what is appropriate to your situation.

With kind regards,
With warm and affectionate regards,
Please give my love/regards to your parents......
More when we meet,
Wishing you the best of luck,

With good wishes for your/your brother's speedy recovery...
Wishing you many happy returns of the day,
Thanking you for all your help/co-operation,
With love,

Exercises

A Write a letter:

1 to your friend thanking him for the birthday present he sent you.
2 to your cousin/friend who is in another town inviting him to spend the Diwali holidays with you and your family.
3 to a friend thanking him for the hospitality extended to you during the holidays.
4 to your father telling him about the career you would like to choose after graduation, and why.
5 to your mother telling her about your progress at college.
6 to your father asking for an increase in your monthly allowance, giving reasons.
7 to your uncle telling him how your cousin (his son) is getting on at college.
8 to your father's friend who forgot his umbrella in your house. Say you will have it sent to him on Sunday.
9 to your cousin telling him about the new bicycle you have bought and why you like it.
10 to your neighbour, complaining about the noise his radio makes and the problem it creates for you and your brother who is preparing for his B.A. examination.
11 to your brother, describing your visit to a museum or zoo.

B 1 You had a minor accident while riding a bicycle. You received a very anxious letter of enquiry from your father. Write a letter to him about the accident asking him not to worry.

2 Write a letter to your younger brother telling him that you are not satisfied with his progress at school and asking him to pay more attention to his studies.
3 Your neighbour left the town, locking up his house. A thief broke into the house but you noticed this in time and the thief ran away. Write a letter informing your neighbour of this incident.

B Professional or Business Letters

Read these letters carefully:

1 A letter to a book-seller ordering some books:

15/26 Ashok Nagar,
Hyderabad 20.
September 17, 1975.

To

The Manager,
Messrs College Booksellers,
Madras 600002.

Dear Sir,

Please send me a copy each of the following books per V.P.P.:

1 Bhandari and Ram
English Composition, Book 2, Orient Longman Ltd., India.
2 Pereira
Modern Mathematics, Frank Brothers, Delhi.
3 Sud and Bhatia
One Act Plays, Macmillan, India.
4 Hornby and others
The Advanced Learner's Dictionary of Current English. O.U.P., London.

Early action will be appreciated.

Yours faithfully,
Mubarik Hussain.

2 A letter to the editor of the local daily complaining about the neglect of the roads and drains in your locality:

16 Mahatma Gandhi Road,
Guntur,
Andhra Pradesh.
20-9-1975.

To
The Editor,
The Deccan Chronicle,
Secunderabad.

Sir,

I would like to bring to the notice of everyone who values cleanliness something extremely worrying about our locality. All the roads in our street have remained unswept for at least two weeks, with the result that all of us have to suffer an ever-growing foul smell. The bye-lanes are, one and all, full of stagnant water since most drains stopped working weeks ago. The result is millions of mosquitoes and flies. Our only park which used to be a sight for sore eyes will soon become an eyesore; no one pays any attention to it.

Sir, many of us believe that it will soon be too late to save the situation. Will the authorities wake up to it?

Yours truly,
V. Rukma Rao

These two letters belong to a second category of letters called professional or business letters. They are also called official letters. Such letters are written to a company, or a person holding some official position. The addressees are often very busy persons and hence these letters should be clear and concise.

In this category of letters are included letters to editors of newspapers, applications for jobs, applications for leave of absence, representations and petitions to authorities such as chairmen of municipalities, presidents of panchayat boards, the postal department, the police department, etc.

Study the parts of this type of letter:

1 *The heading*

This is the writer's address written at the top right-hand corner, as in personal letters. To the left and a little below the level of the date, write the designation (Manager, Chairman, President, Inspector of Police, the Post-master etc.) of the person you are writing to together with the address of the company, business concern, office etc.

2 *The salutation*

To companies, business houses, etc.:
Dear Sir, Dear Sirs, Gentlemen.

To officials:
Sir, Dear Sir, Madam.

To persons in official or business positions who are addressed by name:
Dear Mr Mathur, Dear Mrs Francis, Dear Miss Sakuntala, Dear Shrimati Janakiamma, Dear Shri Nanavati, Dear Kumari Padma.

3 *The body*

This usually consists of three parts:

a *Reference or introduction*
In this you refer to a letter, advertisement, etc. which caused you to write.

b *Information*
In this part you give the relevant information, if any is asked for, or the purpose of writing the letter.

c *Conclusion*
You conclude your letter appropriately with a request, assurance, etc.

4 *Subscription*

For companies, business houses, etc.:
Yours faithfully, Yours truly

For person addressed as Mr———, Mrs———, Shri ———, etc. Yours sincerely, Yours very sincerely,
Editor of newspaper. Yours truly,
Headmaster, Principal: Yours obediently,

5 *The address*

Write the address clearly on the envelope giving details of district, state, country, etc. wherever necessary.

Note the positioning of the address in the letters addressed to companies, officers, etc.

Here are some specimens of professional and business letters:

1 You ordered some books from a book-seller, but you found some of the books damaged on opening the parcel and two books were missing. Write a letter to the book-seller asking for replacement of the damaged books and the despatch of the missing ones.

40 Sankar Matt Road,
Hyderabad 13.
10th September, 1975.

To

The Manager,
India Book Store,
Fort, Bombay.

Dear Sir,

The books that I ordered on 15th August arrived yesterday. Many thanks for the prompt execution of my order.

I regret, however, to inform you that three of the books I ordered were found to be badly damaged when the parcel was opened. The damage may be due to defective packing or careless handling. The books are not in a condition for use. I attach a list of these books.

Secondly, the following books were not in the parcel:

1 Complete Works of Shakespeare: Globe Edition.
2 David Copperfield: Charles Dickens.

I request you to replace the three damaged books and also send the two missing books. I shall arrange to return the damaged books on hearing from you.

Yours faithfully,
Pramila Rao

Enclosed: list of damaged books.

2 Write an application for the post of a typist-clerk in response to an advertisement in the newspapers:

12/K Sanjeevi Nagar,
North Extension,
Secunderabad.
1st August, 1975.

To

The Manager,
The Co-operative Urban Bank Ltd.,
Jawaharnagar,
Nellore.

Sir,

I understand from your advertisement in the Deccan Chronicle of 25-7-1975 that you require two typist-clerks in your bank, and I submit this application for one of the posts.

I have passed the Intermediate Examination of the Board of Intermediate Education, A.P., obtaining a first class. While studying in the Intermediate Course, I learnt type-writing too and passed the Higher Grade Examination held in April last. I can type 50 words per minute.

I am at present working in a pharmaceutical firm in a temporary capacity and the management has agreed to relieve me at a week's notice, in case I wish to leave.

I am aged 19 years and possess good health.

I enclose two testimonials, one from my principal and the other from the local Magistrate.

Should you be pleased to appoint me, I shall do my best to give you complete satisfaction in my work.

Yours faithfully,
V. S. Raghavulu.

3 Write a letter to the editor of a newspaper on the reckless driving you have witnessed on the roads of your town or city.

56, Tilak Road,
Indiranagar,
Nellore.

To
The Editor,
Indian Express,
Vijayawada.

Sir,

I wish to draw, through the columns of your esteemed paper, the immediate attention of the police authorities to the several instances of reckless driving I have been witnessing in recent times on the roads of Nellore.

The principal offenders are the lorry drivers and the auto-rickshaw drivers. Only yesterday, I was a witness to a serious accident in which a lorry hit a cart while overtaking it. The cart was badly damaged; the cartman luckily escaped serious injuries. It was a case of sheer recklessness on the part of the driver.

The auto-rickshaws usually exceed all speed limits and are a real hazard to pedestrians and other users of the road.

Will the police and the traffic authorities take immediate steps to see that the rules of the road are obeyed by all users, so that accidents are avoided?

Yours truly,
Manya Janaki

4 Some thefts and instances of house-breaking have occurred in your street. Write a letter to the Sub-Inspector of Police drawing his attention to this.

27 Main Road,
Musheerabad,
Hyderabad 20.
7-1-1976.

To
The Sub-Inspector of Police,
Musheerabad Police Station,
Musheerabad,
Hyderabad 20.

Sir,

I write to draw your immediate attention to the several instances of house-breaking and theft that have been occurring in my locality in recent weeks.

Only yesterday a daring house-breaking incident occurred in one of the flats in broad daylight. The inmates had gone out locking the door. Two or three persons seem to have got in through a back door, breaking open the lock. Last week, some persons broke open the door of a Hanuman temple in our locality and took away some silver vessels used for the poojas. A few other thefts too have taken place. We have reason to believe that a gang is operating in the locality and it is committing these thefts.

I request you to arrange for frequent patrolling of the streets by policemen, especially at night and also investigate the cases referred to.

Yours faithfully,
K. P. Upendran

5 You have moved into a new house. Write a letter to the postmaster informing him of the change of address.

'Prasanti Nilayam,'
20 Hospital Road,
Vijayawada.
10th October, 1975

To

The Post-master,
Vijayawada Post-Office,
Vijayawada.

Sir,

I write to bring to your notice that my parents and I have moved to a new house the address of which has been given at the top. We were hitherto residing at:

202 Bull Temple Road,
Girinagar,
Vijayawada.

I request that all letters, registered letters, parcels etc. intended for me and my parents and addressed to our old address may kindly be redirected to our new address.

Thanking you,

Yours faithfully,
V. K. Sukumaran

Exercises

1. Write a letter to the manager, R.T.O., complaining about the bad behaviour of a bus conductor.
2. Write a letter to the Director of Public Instruction requesting him to preside over the College Day Celebrations. (You are the president of the School Union.)
3. Write a letter to the police inspector of your town describing the street accident that you saw last evening.
4. Write a letter to the Editor of a newspaper complaining about the non-availability of your Non-detailed Reader.
5. Write a letter to a dealer in sports goods ordering half a dozen cricket bats and balls.
6. Write a letter to a shop-keeper complaining against the bad hold-all he sold you.
7. Write a letter to the manager, Regal Hotel in Madras, asking for a single room for you for three days.
8. The timings of the bus do not suit you and other school-going children. Write a letter to the transport authorities suggesting more suitable timings.
9. The walls in your town are frequently disfigured by the sticking of ugly posters. Write a letter to the police authorities expressing your disapproval and giving alternative suggestions.
10. An important man in your town, known for his philanthropy, has passed away. Write a letter to the Editor of a newspaper praising his services to the community and suggesting a suitable memorial for him.

11 'Wanted: A library assistant for the Municipal Central Library. Apply to the Commissioner, Nellore Municipality.' Write an application in response to this advertisement.

12 You have to accompany your sister to Delhi and you will be away for a week. Write an application for leave, addressed to your Principal.

C Social Letters

There is a third type of letter, namely, *social letters*. These include invitations (also acceptance or inability to accept an invitation), letters of congratulation or condolence, and letters to thank someone for presents, favours done, hospitality shown, etc. In short, these are letters one has to write, being a member of a society or community and in fulfilment of certain social obligations.

Social letters can be formal or informal, depending on the person we address or the occasion for writing the letter. Generally the formal ones are written using the third person and the informal ones, the first person. Study the specimens given below:

1 *A Formal Invitation and its Acceptance*

Invitation:

Sri Nageswara Rao
and
Shrimati Pappamma Rao
request the pleasure of Dr and Mrs Subba Rao's
company at buffet lunch
on Monday, 16th January 1976, at 1 p.m.

RSVP 24 Rajaji Road,
Hyderabad 500007
Tel: 82453

Acceptance:

C.S. Subba Rao and Mrs Subba Rao have pleasure in accepting Prof. Nageswara Rao and Mrs Rao's invitation to lunch at 1 p.m. on 16th January 1976.

23/11 Banjara Hills,
Hyderabad.

Refusal:

C. S. Subba Rao and Mrs Subba Rao thank Prof. Nageswara Rao and Mrs Rao for their kind invitation to lunch but regret that a prior engagement prevents them from accepting it.

23/11 Banjara Hills,
Hyderabad.

2 *An Informal Invitation*

10 Ashok Nagar,
Hyderabad.
March 30, 1976.

Dear Dr Rajan,

Shobha and I would feel delighted if Mrs Rajan and you would join us at dinner on Saturday, 2nd April 1976, at 8 p.m. I am sorry for giving such short notice but hope you can come nevertheless.

Warm regards,

Yours sincerely,
K. V. Reddy.

Acceptance

21 Sarojini Devi Road,
Secunderabad.
March 31, 1976.

Dear Shri Reddy,

Thank you very much for your kind invitation. Radha and I shall be pleased to join Mrs Reddy and you on Saturday at dinner. We look forward to seeing you after such a long time.

All good wishes.

Yours sincerely,
S. K. Rajan

Refusal

21 Sarojini Devi Road,
Secunderabad,
March 31, 1976.

Dear Shri Reddy,

I have just received your kind invitation to dinner, for which many thanks. We would have accepted it gladly but unfortunately Radha has a bad cold and I have to be away in Waltair for the week-end. So neither of us can join you and we regret it. Radha joins me in sending our warm regards to your wife and your mother.

Yours sincerely,
S. K. Rajan

3 Your principal is camping in the holiday station where you are spending the vacation. Write on behalf of your parents, inviting him to a meal in your house.

'Prasanthi,'
Mount Pleasant,
Ootacamund.
4th April, 1976.

Dear Sir,

I am K. J. George, a student of the Junior Intermediate class of St. Thomas College. My parents and I arrived here on the first of this month and are spending the summer here.

From a letter that a friend of mine has written to me, I understand that you are camping in this town and are likely to stay here for a week. I was very glad to receive this information. My parents too are very glad to learn that you will be here for a few days. They have asked me to write to you inviting you to lunch on any day that is convenient to you. I am, therefore, writing this letter to you on their behalf and on my own behalf. We shall be delighted if you find it convenient to come. Kindly let us know when you will give us the pleasure.

With respectful regards,

Yours obediently,
K. J. George

Exercises

1 Write a letter to your class teacher inviting him to lunch on your birthday.

2 Your brother is in the U.S.A. An American friend of his is visiting India and is in Delhi at present. Write a letter inviting him to your town and telling him what interesting places he can visit in and near your town.

3 You are the President of the Students' Union. The Union has decided to give a party to a retiring professor. Prepare a formal invitation from you and the Students' Union to the members of the staff to attend the party.

4 Write a letter of congratulations to a student of your college who has won the first prize in an inter-collegiate elocution competition.

5 You have been selected to represent your college at a Students' Conference in Delhi. You have received messages of congratulations from numerous friends. Prepare a letter of thanks in the third person to be put up on the College Notice Board.

2 EXPANSION

In an exercise in expansion you are generally given a well-known saying, a proverb, a maxim or a quotation. Though these sayings, etc. usually consist of a brief statement, they are nevertheless packed with meaning. Here are some examples:

A stitch in time saves nine.
Rome was not built in a day.
The early bird catches the worm.
Penny wise, pound foolish.

What you are required to do is to *expand* the statement, that is, to give, through a process of elaboration, reasoning, etc., the full meaning and significance of the statement. You can also cite examples or illustrations to support the statement. Your final product should be a closely-knit piece of writing which has unity of thought and is an integrated and complete piece of composition.

The exercise is useful in stimulating your thought and strengthening your powers of expression.

Here are some helpful directions for doing this exercise.

1 Spend some time thinking over and getting at the meaning, significance and implications of the statement given to you.
2 Write down the important points you should include, in the order in which they are to be developed.
3 Think of one or two illustrations if possible to support the main idea.
4 Put your thoughts in simple language, linking them appropriately. If a limit has been set, do not exceed it. Usually the length set is a page of ordinary writing.
5 Avoid beginning with sentences such as the following: This statement means.......The meaning of the proverb is.......This is a well-known proverb ....
6 Revise what you have written correcting errors of spelling, grammar, punctuation etc.

Study the following examples which illustrate how a statement can be expanded:

1 *Make Hay while the Sun Shines*

Main points:

a explanation
b uncertainties of life
c opportunities seldom come
d illustration
e conclusion.

It is common knowledge that farmers have to depend on the weather for their operations. For instance they have to wait for bright sunshine to dry the hay after the harvest; and if they miss it, the hay will be ruined by exposure to mist or rain.

All of us are in the same position as the farmer. Life is as uncertain as the weather. There are several unpredictable factors in life. No one can predict when death will snatch him away. Health, wealth, help, co-operation of friends and relatives are all uncertain factors. Opportunities for education, employment, progress, etc. are also unpredictable. That man is, therefore, wise who seizes a situation, an opportunity, etc. when it comes along and makes the fullest use of it, to achieve his ends in life. He will fail in life if he is not vigilant and lets slip these opportunities.

We see these days a number of young persons in schools and colleges frittering away their energies and wasting their time on things other than their studies. They let slip their opportunities in their formative years and later repent for their folly.

It is, therefore, necessary that we seize opportunities when they come to us and use them to the best advantage.

2 *A Stitch in Time Saves Nine*

Very often an article of dress or a piece of cloth gets a little torn, but with just a stitch or two done without delay we can mend the tear. But if we postpone doing this, the tear will become larger and we may have to put in a number of stitches to mend it, or worse still, it may not be possible to mend it at all, and the article gets useless.

What is true of a piece of cloth is true of several situations of life. A damage to an article of daily use, a piece of furniture, a building etc., can be repaired with just a little effort and expense if attended to promptly, but if neglected, the repair will entail much effort and expenditure.

The statement is very pertinent in regard to a person's health. If he has a minor ailment it can be easily cured with just a visit to the doctor, but if neglected it may develop into serious trouble requiring prolonged treatment and numerous visits to the doctor.

Bad habits such as smoking are to be 'nipped in the bud' or they will get beyond correction or control.

Any damage, therefore, to property, health, etc. should be attended to immediately after it is detected.

3 *Peace hath her Victories no less Renowned than War*

If you turn over the pages of history books, you will find the waging of wars filling a major part of these books. The exploits of soldiers such as Alexander, Hannibal, Napoleon, Timur, the Duke of Wellington, are described at great length and these men receive high praise. But we forget what a great deal of destruction to property and men has been caused by wars. In contrast to this the achievements of mankind during times of peace, which receive very bare treatment in history books, are much more valuable to the world. These have brought peace, prosperity and happiness for man.

For instance, the conquest of disease by medical scientists such as Louis Pasteur, Alexander Fleming, and Sir Ronald Ross. As a result of their discoveries, human suffering has been reduced and man can now hope to live longer than before. There is, again, the array of scientific inventions such as the telephone, the radio, the television which have enriched man's life. Equally significant are the works of art and architecture, which are the great achievements of man's spirit. Aren't these victories at least as worthy of praise as the achievements of renowned conquerors?

4 *Sweet are the uses of Adversity*

Man as a rule longs for a life of peace and happiness. He dreads all sorrows, misfortunes and calamities such as failures in examinations, loss of money, deaths in the family and suffering from disease. Life should be for him a continuous flow of success, peace and prosperity.

But man does not realize that adversity has its own advantages. It is during moments of great stress, suffering and misfortune that the best faculties in man have shown forth. It is during such times that he turns contemplative and philosophical and becomes a believer in divine forces. When Kunti, the mother of the Pandava princes, was asked by Krishna to choose a boon, she promptly asked for a life of adversity, which alone would fix her mind on God. Long ago there was a great Sanskrit scholar who, afflicted with a serious attack of paralysis, sought the grace of the Lord and composed over a thousand masterly verses in His glory. Instances can be multiplied to prove that great things have been achieved by man in times of suffering and adversity.

Exercises

Expand the idea contained in each of the following:

1 A rolling stone gathers no moss.
2 Rome was not built in a day.
3 All that glitters is not gold.
4 A bird in the hand is worth two in the bush.
5 Blood is thicker than water.
6 Too many cooks spoil the broth.
7 Familiarity breeds contempt.
8 A new broom sweeps well.
9 People who live in glass houses should not throw stones.
10 Little strokes fell great oaks.
11 God helps those who help themselves.
12 Penny wise, pound foolish.
13 The early bird catches the worm.
14 Variety is the spice of life.
15 One man's meat is another man's poison.
16 Slow and steady wins the race.
17 The path of duty is the way to glory.
18 Beggars cannot be choosers.
19 As you sow, so shall you reap.
20 Do unto others as you wish them to do unto you.
21 It is never too late to mend.
22 Charity begins at home.
23 The hand that rocks the cradle rules the world.
24 Prosperity gains friends, adversity tries them.
25 An empty vessel makes the greater noise.
26 One crowded hour of glorious life is worth an age without a name.
27 Necessity is the mother of invention.
28 Failures are stepping stones to success.
29 One swallow does not make a summer.
30 Birds of a feather flock together.
31 Bad workmen quarrel with their tools.
32 A little learning is a dangerous thing.
33 Fortune favours the brave.
34 Fools rush in where angels fear to tread.

3 PRECIS-WRITING

A precis is a summary or a restatement in shortened form of the main or essential ideas of a piece of writing.

Precis-writing (also called epitomization) is a very rewarding exercise in composition. In the first place, you learn to *read* a passage competently. You learn to *understand* its essential ideas through concentration of attention. Secondly, you learn to *express* your ideas precisely and effectively. You learn to choose your words carefully so that they express what you want to say fully and at the same time briefly.

Precis is a French word derived from the Latin word *Praecissus,* past participle of *Praecidere,* 'to cut off,' 'to be brief,' and is connected with the English word *precise.* Another word for *precis* is the Greek word *epitome,* 'to cut upon'.

Characteristics of a Good Precis

1 A good precis is not merely a list of the main ideas of a passage unrelated to one another. The ideas are to be organized or interrelated and expressed in logical sequence, so that the precis reads as an original piece of composition by itself.

2 A good precis should contain all the essential ideas in the original, omitting non-essential ideas, examples, etc. The ideas should be as far as possible in the same order as in the original.

3 The language of a precis should be clear, brief, and precise, maintaining at the same time the style and spirit of the original.

4 A good precis should, as far as possible, be in the writer's own words.

5 It should not exceed or fall short of the length prescribed by too large a margin. Usually, the limit set for a precis is a third of the original in length. That is, the number of words used should be a third of the number on the original.

6 Direct speech should, as a rule, be changed into indirect speech.

Steps for the Writing of a Precis

Here are some suggested steps that a learner may follow in mastering the art of writing a good precis.

1 Read the given passage carefully, several times if necessary, until you understand it *as a whole*, until you grasp the central idea of the passage and what the author wants to say. If you succeed in this, you will be able to hit on a suitable heading for the passage, if you are required to provide one.

2 Write down the main ideas or points of the passage leaving out unimportant or incidental details, so as to form a framework for your precis. If you have grasped the central idea, you will be able to distinguish between what is important and what is unimportant.

3 Write down a preliminary draft, having in mind the number of words prescribed. You should try to condense not by omitting certain phrases, sentences, etc. which you consider unimportant, but by remodelling the sentences altogether. Do not put in any fresh ideas either, when so remodelling.

4 Rewrite your draft carefully checking whether you have put in all the main ideas and whether what you have written reads smooth. Check the number of words in the final draft and bring it to the limit prescribed. Correct mistakes if any, in spelling, grammar, punctuation, etc.

5 Write out the fair copy under the heading you have chosen.

A few examples have been given here to **demonstrate** how a precis is written. Study them closely.

I

In spite of rigorous precautions against accidents, many people are injured every year in factories and elsewhere. In addition, some people are born with physical disabilities. They are either blind or deaf or in some way deformed from birth. Up to quite recent times, little planned action was taken to fit handicapped people for employment. A number of charitable organizations tried to help them in cases of hardship; but few seriously held the idea that these people might still have abilities in other directions.

Only during the last few decades has society slowly come to acknowledge its responsibilities and to recognize that handicapped people can be trained to play a useful part in economic as well as social life. The second world war gave impetus to this. During the 1939–45 war, pressure on resources of labour compelled all fighting nations to call on the services of handicapped people for tasks adapted to, and within the limits of their capacities. A man might have lost the use of his legs, but still be able to use his hands with skill. Another person might have lost his sight, but still be capable of training in ways in which his other senses could be employed effectively in furtherance of the war effort.

In recent years, scientific inventions and discoveries have lessened the disabilities of deafness, some forms of paralysis, and other physical handicaps. Scientists working in association with engineers have devised methods by which handicapped people can take up work again, thanks to the invention of mechanical limbs, the improvement of hearing aids and so on. (263 words)

From *Man in Our Modern World*
Odhams Press Ltd., London (Adapted)

The Main Points

1 Many people in the world suffer from physical disabilities.
2 Charitable organizations help them, but do not utilize the abilities they may have.
3 Efforts in the last few decades to provide employment for the handicapped people.
4 Scientific inventions have come to the aid of the handicapped in several ways.

First Draft

Many people suffer from physical handicaps such as loss of limb, blindness or deafness caused by accidents or existing at birth. Till recent times, there have been several organizations engaged in helping them and lessening their suffering, but no thought has been given by these organizations to employing them and utilising the abilities that they may still have. During the last few decades, especially during World War II when labour was scarce, ways and means came to be devised of discovering and appropriately utilizing the abilities that the handicapped may still have, and making them useful members of society. Scientists in collaboration with engineers have also developed instruments such as mechanical limbs and hearing aids to lessen the suffering of the handicapped and increasing their working efficiency. (132 words)

Final Draft

Many people suffer from physical handicaps such as loss of limb, blindness or deafness. Till recently, there have been organizations engaged in lessening their sufferings, but no thought has been given to utilizing the abilities that they may still have, and making them useful members of society. During the last few decades, especially during World War II, ways and means came to be devised of utilizing their abilities. Scientists and engineers have also invented instruments to lessen the suffering of the handicapped and increasing their efficiency. (86 words)

Here are some phrases and sentences deleted in the final draft either because they are details or because they are examples illustrating a point or idea.

......In spite of rigorous precautions against accidents.....
......In addition, some people are born with physical disabilities.................
......In cases of hardship...............
......A man might have...................
.................with skill.
Another person might have................
................the war effort...........
......Some forms of paralysis.......................

Secondly, note how the first three sentences of the second paragraph have been remodelled and condensed.

Suggested title

Rehabilitation of the Handicapped

II

One of the outstanding features of the century has been the improvement of living conditions of the working man — greater political power, more wealth and leisure, and better facilities for health, security and education.

In early civilizations, most communities were sharply divided into two classes, those who laboured and those who did not. The small number of rulers — kings, priests, military leaders — lived in great comfort, and did very little work. The vast majority of the population enjoyed very few comforts, did most of the work, and had scarcely any political power. In some societies, there was an even more wretched class, the slaves, who had no rights at all.

The Industrial Revolution of Europe led to the production of vast quantities of goods, and workers began to be dissatisfied with their poverty. The factory owners needed skilled workers, and gradually they realized that they must show good-will to their workmen, in order to stay in business. As in many other reforms, some enlightened employers began to treat their workers better, and the idea slowly spread that workers were entitled to some consideration. Since men were free to work for any master they chose, good masters soon had the pick of the workers, and old-fashioned employers found themselves with a factory full of lower-grade workmen. Such a situation soon led to an all-round improvement in standards, and good employers tried to raise working conditions still higher. These improvements were speeded up by the increased organization of workers in Trade Union movements, particularly in low-standard factories, where the owner often had to deal with strike action by dissatisfied workers.

Now that the working classes are getting better and better working conditions, the need to strike has lessened considerably; and employers and workers alike have come to realize that they depend on each other for their livelihood. (306 words)

The Main Points

1 Working classes have better living conditions in the present century.

2 The big gap in earlier civilizations between the conditions of kings, etc. and those of the majority.
3 The effect of the Industrial Revolution on the lot of the working classes.
4 The starting of Trade Unions.

First Draft

An important feature of this century is the improvement in the living conditions of the working classes, in the form of more power, wealth, leisure and security. At one time, kings, leaders, priests, etc. lived in comfort doing little or no work while the majority did all the work, at the same time enjoying fewer comforts and rights. In some countries there were slaves who had no rights at all. During the Industrial Revolution of Europe, production increased and workers started feeling dissatisfied. Employers were induced to improve working conditions so as to improve production. Some even felt workers had a right to better conditions. Clever employers selected the best workers. This led to competition and improvement of working conditions. Soon Trade Unions were organized to fight for rights or even to start strikes. Now employers and employees have come to realize their mutual dependence and strikes are disappearing. (150 words)

Final Draft

An important feature of this century is the improvement of the lot of the workers. In earlier civilizations, kings, priests, etc. lived comfortably doing little, while the majority worked hard with few comforts and rights. Some societies had slaves too. During the Industrial Revolution, production increased and workers started feeling dissatisfied. Employers attracted the best workers with better conditions to improve production. Some thought workers had a right to better conditions. Soon Trade Unions were organized to fight for workers' rights with strikes if necessary. Now, there is increasing realization of the mutual dependence of employers and their workers. (100 words)

Note the deletion of the following phrases, sentences, etc.:

......Greater political power, wealth, etc..........

......Most communities were sharply divided into two classes................
......Had scarcely any political power ....
......Old fashioned employers found themselves with a factory full of lower-grade workmen...........
......Such a situation ....
.... still higher.

Note also how almost all the sentences have been remodelled and condensed.

Suggested title

The Working Class Comes into its Own.

III

Interdependence is and ought to be as much the ideal of man as self-sufficiency. Man is a social being. Without inter-relation with society he cannot realize his oneness with the universe or supress his egotism. If man were so placed or could so place himself as to be absolutely above all dependence on his fellow-beings, he would become so proud and arrogant as to be a veritable burden and nuisance to the world. Dependence on society teaches him the lesson of humanity. That man ought to be able to satisfy most of his essential needs himself is obvious; but it is no less obvious that when self-sufficiency is carried to the length of isolating oneself from society, it almost amounts to sin. A man cannot become self-sufficient in respect of all the various operations from the growing of cotton to the spinning of the yarn. He has at some stage or other to take the aid of the members of his family. And if one may take the help from one's own family, why not from one's neighbours? Or otherwise what is the significance of the great saying, ' The world is my **family** '? (195 words)

— M. K. Gandhi

The Main Points

1 Interdependence as much man's ideal as self-sufficiency.
2 Independence makes man arrogant. Dependence instils humanity.

3 Self-reliance is good, but isolation is sinful.
4 Man has to depend on his family. Why not depend on his neighbours too?

First Draft

Man is a social being. Interdependence should be as much his ideal as self-sufficiency, as it will help him to fight his ego and realize his oneness with the world. If man should become independent, he would get proud and arrogant and be a burden to the world. Dependence instils humanity in him. Man should no doubt be self-reliant, but totally isolating himself is sinful. Man has to depend upon relatives, for instance, if he is engaged in growing and spinning cotton. If that is the case, he could seek the help of friends and neighbours too. If he fails to do this the saying that the world is one family becomes meaningless. (113 words)

Final Draft

Interdependence should be as much man's ideal as self-sufficiency. Through interdependence he will realize his oneness with others. Independence will make him arrogant while dependence will instil humanity. Self-reliance is indeed desirable, but isolation is sinful. Man is dependent on his family for several things. Why not, then, seek his neighbours' help? After all, is not the world one family? (66 words)

Note how the following phrases and sentences have been deleted, because the ideas expressed by them are expressed in other ways.

......Man is a social being......................
......He cannot suppress his egotism...................
......As to be a veritable burden and nuisance to the world..................................

Note how most of the sentences have been recast and condensed.

Suggested title

The Interdependence of Men.

Exercises

Write a precis of each of the following passages in about one third of its length, and suggest a suitable heading for it.

1 In every country people imagine that they are the best and the cleverest and the others are not so good as they are. The Englishman thinks that he and his country are the best; the Frenchman is very proud of France and everything French; the Germans and Italians think no end of their countries and many Indians imagine that India is in many ways the greatest country in the world. This is all conceit. Everybody wants to think well of himself and his country. But really there is no person who has not got some good in him and some bad. And in the same way there is no country which is not partly good and partly bad. We must take the good wherever we find it and try to remove the bad wherever it may be. We are of course most concerned with our country, India. Unhappily it is in a bad way today and most of our people are very poor and miserable. They have no pleasure in their lives. We have to find out how we can make them happier. We have to see what is good in our ways and customs and try to keep it, and whatever is bad we have to throw away. If we find anything good in other countries we should certainly take it.

—Jawaharlal Nehru; from *Autobiography*
Messrs John Lane, The Bodley Head, Ltd

2 The Indian culture of our times is in the making. Many of us are striving to produce a blend of all cultures which seem today to be in clash with one another. No culture can live, if it attempts to be exclusive. There is no such thing as pure Aryan culture in existence in India today. Whether the Aryans were indigenous to India or were unwelcome intruders, does not interest me much. What does interest me is the fact that my remote ancestors blended with one another with the utmost freedom and we of the present generation are a result of that blend.

I do not want my house to be walled in on all sides and my windows to be stuffed. I want the cultures of all lands to be blown about my house as freely as possible. But I refuse to be blown off my feet by any. I would have our young men and women with literary tastes to learn as much of English and other world-languages as they like, and then expect them to give the benefits of their learning to India and the world alike like a Bose, a Ray or a Tagore. But I would not have a single Indian forget, neglect or be ashamed of his mother tongue, or to feel that he or she cannot think or express the best thoughts in his own or her vernacular. Mine is not a religion of the prison-house.

—*M. K. Gandhi*

3. All who have gone before you have submitted to the stroke of death. All who come after you shall undergo the same fate. The great and good, the prince and the peasant, the renowned and the obscure travel alike the road which leads to the grave. At the moment when you expire, thousands throughout the world shall, with you, be yielding up their breath. Can that be held to be a great calamity which is common to you with everything that lives on earth—which is an event as much according to the course of nature, as it is that leaves should fall in autumn, or that fruit should drop from the tree when it is fully ripe?

The pain of death cannot be very long, and is probably less severe than what you have at other times experienced. The pomp of death is more terrifying than death itself. It is to the weakness of our imagination that it owes its chief power of dejecting the spirits; for when the force of the mind is roused, there are few passions in our nature that have not been able to overcome the fear of death. Honour has defied death; love has despised it; shame has rushed upon it; revenge has disregarded it; grief has a thousand times wished for its approach. Is it not strange that reason and virtue cannot give strength to surmount that fear, which, even in feeble minds, so many passions have conquered? What inconsistency is there in complaining so much of the evils of life, and being at the same time so afraid of what is to terminate them all! Who can tell whether his future life might not teem with disasters and miseries as yet unknown, were it to be prolonged according to his wish?

—*Hugh Blair*

4 There are hundreds of superstitions which survive in various parts of the country, and the study of them is rather amusing. We are told, for example, that it is unlucky to point to the new moon or to look at it through glass, but if we bow nine times to it we shall have a lucky month!

Nearly all superstitions are concerned with 'luck'. Good luck is associated with black cats, horseshoes, the finding of a pin, the threepenny bit in the Christmas pudding, the old shoe flung at a wedding party, and the dark man who is the first to step over the door-step on New Year's Day. Ill luck is associated with the howling of dogs, the spilling of salt, the crossing of knives, sitting down thirteen to a table, meeting a cross-eyed woman, walking under a ladder, the falling of a picture from the wall, the breaking of a mirror, and scores of other things.

When the fire is reluctant to burn, a servant-girl will often place a poker upright before the bars. She does not know why she does it. She has seen her mother and grandmother do it. But centuries ago a sulky fire was attributed to witchcraft, and the upright poker against the bars (which made the sign of the cross) was thought to have power to destroy the evil spell.

Now suppose you tell a scientist that you believe a certain superstition — let us say, that the howling of a dog is a sign of death. The scientist will immediately require evidence before he can accept your belief. He will want figures to prove it. It will be useless to quote two or three cases; he will want hundreds. He will want also to know (a) if it ever happens that the howling of dogs is not followed by a death, (b) if every person's death is predicted by the howling of dogs. The answer to the former question is in the affirmative, and to the latter in the negative. Your superstition will not bear investigation. It may impress an ignorant person, but it cannot face the light of facts. Your case would not carry conviction in a court of law.

Apart from this process of testing by results, however, any intelligent man will want to know the 'reason why'. What connection can there be between a howling dog and an approaching death? Can it be cause and effect? Can it be that the dog has a gift of foreseeing such events? Or is the dog the instrument employed by some uncanny power that moves invisibly in our midst?

5 Ariosto tells a pretty story of a fairy, who, by some mysterious law of her nature, was condemned to appear at certain seasons in the form of a foul and poisonous snake. Those who injured her during the period of her disguise were forever excluded from participation in the blessings which she bestowed. But to those who, in spite of her loathsome aspect, pitied and protected her, she afterwards revealed herself in the beautiful and celestial form which was natural to her, accompanied their steps, granted all their wishes, filled their houses with wealth, made them happy in love and victorious in war. Such a spirit is Liberty. At times she takes the form of a hateful reptile. She grovels, she hisses, she stings. But woe to those who in disgust shall venture to crush her! And happy are those who, having dared to receive her in her degraded and frightful shape, shall at length be rewarded by her in the time of her beauty and her glory!

There is only one cure, for the evils which newly-acquired freedom produces; and that cure is freedom. When a prisoner first leaves his cell, he cannot bear the light of day; he is unable to discriminate colours or recognise faces. But the remedy is, not to remand him into his dungeon, but to accustom him to the rays of the sun. The blaze of truth and liberty may at first dazzle and bewilder nations which have become half-blind in the house of bondage. But let them gaze on, and they will soon be able to bear it. In a few years men learn to reason. The extreme violence of opinions subsides. Hostile theories correct each other. The scattered elements of truth cease to contend, and begin to coalesce. And at length a system of justice and order is educed out of the chaos.

Many politicians of our time are in the habit of laying it down as a self-evident proposition, that no people ought to be free till they are fit to use their freedom. The maxim is worthy of the fool in the old story, who resolved not to go into the water till he had learnt to swim. If men are to wait for liberty till they become wise and good in slavery, they may indeed wait for ever.

—*Macaulay*

6 It had long been suspected that there was some connection between the abundance of mosquitoes and the occurrence of malaria, since both were at their worst in the same regions and at the same seasons, but what the connection was had not been understood. Sir Patrick Manson, reasoning from the state of things discovered by him in another disease happily unknown to us in this country, made the suggestion that the parasite might be conveyed into the human body by the mosquito in the act of biting.

Following this suggestion, Major Ronald Ross made a set of experiments in India by feeding all the different kinds of mosquito procurable on the blood of malaria patients, and then dissecting and examining every part of their bodies to see if there was any trace of the parasite. Hundreds of mosquitoes were thus laboriously examined, but for two years there was no result. Still the tireless investigator persevered and finally he found a species the blood of which showed certain characters in common with the blood of malaria patients. He was soon able to prove that all the mosquitoes of that particular kind fed on the blood of malaria patients became infected with the parasite which causes the fever.

The life-history of the parasite is difficult to follow, but it is sufficient for us to understand the general results gained so far. Malarial fever in man is due to a very minute parasite living in the blood. This parasite may go on living and multiplying in the blood of man for an indefinite time, unless it is killed by drugs, but it does not go through any further stage of its life-history, and cannot infect other human beings.

A mosquito biting an infected person receives some of the parasites into its own blood; there they go through a further stage of development, and finally, the infected mosquito passes on the fully developed parasites to the next persons it bites, and these soon show symptoms of malarial fever.

But the last part of this story had still to be proved, and that no doubt might remain, an enthusiastic student of science, who had not been in a malarious country since his childhood, deliberately allowed himself to be bitten by infected mosquitoes brought to London from Rome. He took malaria, and the case was proved.

7 Few doctors have any time for the study of philosophy, for their profession is an exacting one, and it is all they can do to keep abreast of its advances. What is true of medical science is also true of the whole civilized world. Men at the present time, are so engrossed in their various occupations, in manufacturing goods, in buying and selling, in accumulating wealth, or in struggling merely to maintain themselves, in altering their environment, in building for the future, and rushing hither and thither, that they have no time left to wonder what it is all about.

Up till recently there has existed an excuse for this failure on the part of civilized man to inquire into the why and wherefore of his existence. The way of prosperity that followed the industrial revolution, the triumphant progress of science, man's impressive conquest of the external world all created a feeling of optimism. Man was marching forward to a glorious future. With the fate of man assured what need was there for him to interrupt his labours in order to inquire about his nature? Speed was the key to success and those who moved fastest and crammed most activities into each fleeting hour would arrive first. There was no time to think.

But disillusionment has come, and we begin to doubt whether material prosperity is necessarily synonymous with successful living. We are discovering that much is wrong with the form of civilization that we have invented. Hitherto we have prided ourselves on our education, but in practically any country we find a decrease, rather than an increase, in the intellectual and moral culture of those responsible for our public affairs. Despite the immense hope we placed on it, our civilization has failed to develop men of intelligence and culture who are capable of guiding us along the dangerous road that we are treading. We can no longer rest satisfied with ourselves, or our leaders, and some of us are pausing for a moment and wondering whether the optimistic opinion of the world is any longer justified.

—*Kenneth Walker*

8 I take it that most people who talk glibly of science, including our great industrialists, think of science merely as a kind of handmaiden to make their work easier. And so it is. Of course, it does make their work easier. It adds to the wealth of the nation and better conditions. All this science does do. But, surely, science is something more than that. The history of science shows that it does not simply better the old. It sometimes upsets the old. It does not merely add new truths to the old ones, but sometimes the new truth it discovers disintegrates some part of the old truths, and thereby upsets the way of men's thinking and the way of their lives. Science, therefore, does not merely repeat the old in better ways, or add to the old, but creates something that is new to the world and to human consciousness.

If we pursue this line of thought, what exactly does the spirit of science mean? It means many things. It means not only accepting the fresh truth that science may bring, not only improving the old, but being prepared to upset the old if it goes against that spirit. It also means not being tied down to something that is old because it is old, because we have carried on with it, but being able to accept its disintegration; it means not being tied down to a social fabric, or an industrial fabric, or an economic fabric, if it goes against the new discovery.

I find a curious hiatus in people's thinking. I find it even in the thinking of scientists, who praise science and practise it in the laboratory, but discard the ways of science, its method of approach and the spirit of science in everything else they do in life. They become completely unscientific. If we approach science in the proper way, it does some good and there is no doubt that it will always do some good. It teaches us new ways of doing things. Perhaps it improves our conditions or industrial life; but the basic thing that science should do is to teach us to think straight, to act straight and not to be afraid of discarding anything or of accepting anything, provided there are sufficient reasons for doing so.

—*Jawaharlal Nehru*

9 Slow-motion photography is often used in newsreels to show exactly how a horse jumped or a sportsman played a stroke.

If you want to film a scene in slow motion you run the camera twice as fast as usual, which sounds, ridiculous but isn't. When a film camera is running at normal speed, it takes twenty-four pictures a second. When the film is run through the film-projector in the camera twenty-four pictures a second appear on the screen. This is because the camera which took the pictures and the projector which shows them run at the same speed. If you are filming in slow motion, however, the camera runs at twice the normal speed, yet, in spite of this, the projector which shows the film will be run at the normal speed, and this means that the projector will show the film at half the speed at which it was photographed. On the screen everything appears at half the speed at which the camera recorded it when it was filmed. In other words, things will seem to be done in 'slow motion'.

This trick can also work the other way round. In a film comedy it sometimes looks very funny if all the characters suddenly move very fast. The director may want to tell his audience in an amusing way that life in a particular city is lived at a tremendous pace. He shows a shot of the city streets in which men and women seem to be darting about at top speed.

To get the effect you do just the opposite of what you did to get 'slow motion'. Instead of running the film camera at twice the normal speed you run it at half the normal speed instead. The projector in the cinema is, as usual, run at the normal speed. This time the projector shows the film at twice the speed at which it was photographed, since the camera was run at half the normal speed.

You may find this difficult to work out at first. But the thing to remember is that a projector in the cinema always runs at the same speed, so if the action is to be slowed down, the projector must be showing things which have been taken by a camera that was moving faster than usual. If the projector is to show things speeded up, it must be showing things which have been taken by a camera whose speed was slower than usual. Either way the people who appear in the scene will have been acting at a perfectly normal pace.

—*Barbara Vereker*

10 How to convert salt water into fresh water, for a long time the worry only of ancient mariners, is becoming increasingly the worry of modern land dwellers.

In fact, if someone really wants to make a large packet of money, he should settle down, work out and then patent a really cheap conversion method. By cheap I mean that taking the salt out of salt water should cost no more than 3s. 6d. a thousand gallons.

Already 18 salt water conversion plants have been erected in the world. They use a wide variety of methods, and no one knows yet which system is the best. This uncertainty about the future method is matched by one absolute certainty that in the future there will be thousands of these plants.

Europe still has plenty of water, but countries like the United States are getting shorter and shorter of it. When they have tapped all flood water, all subterranean reservoirs and all land-based supplies, they will have to turn to the sea. There is nowhere else for the stuff to come from.

The latest conversion plant to be built is near Freeport, Texas. It is the first of five units which the United States Office of Saline Conversion is building to demonstrate new techniques. It sucks up water from the Gulf of Mexico and, by means of 12 evaporators, delivers it fresh at the other end. The price of this pure water? Seven shillings a thousand gallons. Engineers hope and think they can cut this price in two.

There is now a town in the United States, Coalinga, California, which gets all its water from the sea. It has to pay 14s. a thousand gallons for this water, but this is better than before when it had to be transported there and was much more expensive.

Even without transport costs fresh water does not come free. In the United States the general price is about 2s. 6d. a thousand gallons, and so salt water conversion is not so much more costly.

But as soon as it can become a little bit cheaper, as soon as someone has had a really bright idea, I predict a tremendous surge in conversion plants all over the world. There are 18 plants now, but there will be tens of thousands very soon.

—*Anthony Smith*

11 Men who have studied the ways of ants tell us strange things about their social life. Just as in ancient days men kept slaves to work for them, so some ants raid the homes of other ants, and, making them captives, bring them back to their own nests and compel them to work for their captors. Ants, indeed, are by no means the only inhabitants of ants' nests. We are told that several hundreds of other small creatures, such as beetles and crickets, make their homes with ants. Some of these creatures are useful to the ants, and clean up the nests and do other duties, while others seem to be mere boarders, and to do nothing for their keep. Why the ants allow them to stay no one knows. Is it sheer good nature?

Ants, we are told, play games; that they nurse their sick, bury their dead and that everyone does its share of the work, and that no one is allowed to be lazy. All this seems to show that ants have some form of reasonable government. A celebrated naturalist tells how he captured an ant and covered it with a piece of clay so that only its head showed. For some time the little captive was not discovered, then one of its fellow-ants found out what had happened and tried to set it free. But this task proved too much for one ant, and very soon it hurried away, to return in a few minutes with a dozen companions who at once set to work and in a very short time set the captive free.

The same naturalist tells another tale of how ants show what he thinks may be reasoning powers. A column of ants had to cross a small stream, and the only bridge was a small branch with just enough room for the ants to cross in single file. This, however, was too slow for the ants, who by clinging to each other and to the branch, soon widened the bridge until three or four ants could cross the stream abreast over the bodies of their living companions.

Is this reason? It is difficult to say, but it certainly does show a desire to work together for the general good.

—*C. B. Rutley*

4 ESSAY-WRITING

Essays may be divided into four main types:

1 Descriptive
2 Narrative
3 Expository or reflective
4 Argumentative

In college you will be required to learn each of these. The hints and suggestions given below are meant to help you with all four types of essays. Study them carefully.

A First, some general guidelines:

Every essay is written for a reader. A good essay must hold the reader's attention. For this it must have the following qualities.

1 It must be based on your own thinking and experience. An essay presents the writer's views from his personal

standpoint. Do not therefore write what other people say about the topic; think your own thoughts about it and express them in your own language. Also, remember the following. To learn how to write an essay is like learning good manners. We study the best models (as one studies the best behaved persons) and learn from them.

2 An essay must possess unity and coherence. (This is equally true of a good paragraph.) To give it unity we must put together our thoughts according to a clear plan. To give it coherence we must, in addition, use the words and other devices that help the sentences and the paragraphs to stick together. For this purpose we must learn to use the linking words and phrases appropriately. They include:

a Words: and, or, but, still, however, therefore, also, yet, nevertheless, first, next, last, then, firstly, secondly. . .lastly, finally, consequently, accordingly, before, after, now, then, soon, later, meanwhile, moreover, however, etc

b Phrases: on the other hand, on the contrary, in addition, in conclusion, in other words, to sum up, in brief (short), as a result, etc.

Your study of good essays and good writings in general will help you learn the best use of these devices as well.

3 Every essay has its structure — a beginning, a body and a conclusion. The beginning, also called the introduction, need not be long but it ought to be striking. Since well begun is half done, a good introduction may largely decide your reader's reactions to your essay. Here are a few possible ways in which to begin an essay:

a We may begin with a definition (e.g. to begin an essay on 'Inflation': Inflation may be defined as rise in prices brought about by expansion of the supply of money...) and then try to illustrate it or support it with facts.

b We may begin with one or more questions both to provoke our reader and to prepare him for the answer that we supply in the essay. (e.g. for an essay on 'The choice of a career': What is a career? Is it merely an occupation or a profession or is it much more?)

c We sometimes begin with a quotation, e.g., for an essay on 'Misfortune', we may begin with the following words from William Shakespeare: 'When sorrows come, they come not single spies, but in battalions'. But quotations should be used only if we are absolutely sure that we remember them correctly and that they are clearly related to the subject of the essay.

d We may begin with an incident or experience of our own This is often done in narrative or biographical essays. (E.g. for an essay on 'An accident I witnessed,' we may begin with: 'It was a warm Sunday afternoon last June. I was riding my new bicycle which Daddy had given me as a birthday present.')

e Lastly, we may begin with a brief description to create the atmosphere for the main event. This will naturally vary from one type of essay to another. What is important, however, is that every essay must be introduced in such a way that it excites its reader's attention and makes him look forward to what follows.

The introduction is followed by the body of the essay which contains the main points — arguments, illustrations, details—and is thus the core of the essay. The body of the essay must always be based on an outline plan which forms the basis of every good piece of writing.

The third and the last part of an essay is the conclusion. Like the introduction, it too varies from subject to subject.

a The conclusion provides a brief and clearly written summary of the main points of the essay. This may be done either to bring together the ideas to prove the main argument or to give the reader an opportunity to relate the different points.

b The conclusion, especially in descriptive or narrative essays, may contain the most memorable event/incident of the story/description etc.

c One may conclude an essay by drawing a lesson or moral from it.

d Lastly, the conclusion may be used to raise a related question (or questions) for the reader to think about.

In all cases, we must attempt to conclude the essay on a suitable as well as striking note.

B Here now are a few hints on the types of essays you will learn to write.

1 A **descriptive essay** attempts to describe a place, an event or happening, a person or a natural phenomenon. A few examples are:

a places — Charminar, Nehru Zoological Gardens, the Museum

b natural phenomena — volcanoes, an earthquake, a flood

c things — a helicopter, television set, a newspaper, a book

d events — a fire, an accident, a street scene

e persons — the author I like best, the policeman, a good neighbour

To write a description, make sure what is the central idea or impression you want to convey. This will help you to relate everything in your essay and thereby give it unity. Having decided on the central idea, you must do two things: **one**, work out the details of the essay and two, proceed systematically from a general statement on your subject (in the introduction) to the details (in the body) in an ordered way. Always remember that a good essay is an organic whole; all its parts are related one to the other.

2 A **narrative essay** gives an orderly account of an event or happening, real or imagined. A few examples are:

Gandhiji's childhood, the cigarette that burnt six houses, a day without water, the inter-school tournament (of 1975), my first visit to Kashmir/Kodaikanal.

To narrate is to give an account of something — to tell a story, to talk of one's adventures or experiences, to describe events that took place. Every event, whatever its nature, has a beginning which is followed by one or more happenings. And all these happenings take place in an order that can be defined. The most important thing to remember, therefore, is the order in which the different happenings occur. Your outline must be prepared with this order in mind.

Two other things require particular attention:

a Every narrative has a main event. Your essay must highlight this main event and show its central importance.

b A good narrative is one that succeeds in keeping the excitement of the event to the very end. Do not therefore end your essay on an uninteresting note. The end must be striking and significant.

3 An **expository** or **reflective essay** contains the thoughts of its author on a certain subject. Often, it also explains or expands the topic. The discussion is usually based on the author's knowledge, experience or imagination. This type of essay is written on abstract subjects (e.g. truth, friendship, bravery, honesty, malice) and on social, political and religious and economic questions (e.g. caste system, democracy, female education, joint families, Christianity, Hinduism).

The most important part of a reflective or expository essay is a clear understanding of what is involved in the topic. This is so because such essays lend themselves to different types of treatment; they can be interpreted in different ways. What you must decide on is the aspect that you consider as the most important. This may in part depend on the aspects that interest you most or the ones that are related to your experience. Make sure that you write on what you know best.

4 An **argumentative essay** is usually one through which the author tries to persuade or convince the reader in

order to make him accept his point of view. Such essays are therefore based on facts rather than on imagination. In them the writer argues for or against something and, in most cases, proposes a solution to a problem. Very often the topics for argumentative essays may be the same as those for reflective essays. The difference lies mainly in the approach.

This being so, the most important part of an argumentative essay is its convincing presentation. For this you must remember the following:

a It always pays to organize your facts. They must support each other. A few facts, carefully selected and well organized, can do much more than a large number of facts badly organized.

b Build your essay on proved facts — facts that are acceptable and well defended.

c Lastly, since an argument is always for or against something, be fair to the opposite viewpoint. Your reader must never get the impression that what you are saying is biased or partial. Never invent a fact to prove yourself right.

C In addition to the helpful hints we have given you under A and B you should remember the following. They are true of all forms of good writing:

a Always begin with an outline plan. The outline plan is your essay in a nutshell. To prepare it you must think of the different aspects of the topic and then note the main points in a definite order. If necessary, revise your plan to give it fullness and correct order.

b Write your essay in short paragraphs. Each paragraph must add a fresh point to your essay and it must be related to the one that precedes it and the one that follows it.

c Never spend too much time on one idea at the expense of another. And if you find it helpful to give illustrations or examples to defend your point, make them brief and to the point.

d Your essay must show balance. For this it is important to pay attention to all the important ideas. Of course, you must highlight your main ideas.

e A good quotation, a proverb or saying may be in place in some types of essay. But since an essay is based on the writer's personal thinking and experience, it is wrong to use too many quotations.

f Avoid repetitions and be brief and clear.

g Lastly, remember your essay is a piece of personal writing. So never try to use words and expressions that you are not fully familiar with. Also, avoid the use of difficult words in place of simpler ones. Avoid long and involved sentences.

h Always go over your essay to make sure it does not contain any mistakes in spelling, punctuation, grammar and usage.

D Specimen Essays.

1 *Patriotism*

(Outline plan: What is it? Why should one be patriotic? How is one's patriotism expressed? Its advantages and limitations — a good compromise.)

Patriotism or love for one's country is one of the noblest sentiments of man. It is love that comes from one's gratefulness to the land where one is born, the country that provides everything that makes life worth living — food, clothing and shelter, families, friends and the way of life of its people. Or, in other words, it is our country that gives us all that we enjoy and all that makes man's life different from and richer than that of all other animals. That is why patriotic feelings are natural to man.

Every country has its special ways of expressing this noble sentiment. In our country we have songs in praise of our motherland or the mother-country. Some people prefer to call their country the fatherland. 'Nothing, not even

Heaven, is superior to our motherland,' is the main theme in much of our literature, both old and new. And the same theme is expressed in all sorts of ways in fiction, in heroic tales in poems, in folklore and in film songs.

Patriotic songs are only one way of expressing this sentiment. Especially in times of war and natural calamities, a patriot is judged in other ways. A flood or famine, a drought or epidemic disease in one part of the country calls for help and assistance from citizens in the rest of the country. A patriot is always in the forefront on all such occasions. He offers his services or sends generous donations through different agencies. And when, in times of external aggression, the call of the country reaches his ears, he does not hesitate to lay down his life for his motherland. A patriot places his country well above his personal interests.

But even this fine and noble sentiment can at times be misused or abused. There are people who begin to accept the idea of ' my country, right or wrong '; that is patriotism without conscience. They defend their country even if it does things that are obviously wrong. There are others who go further. For them patriotism means hatred for other countries even more than love for one's country. This type of patriotism is an evil and it should be condemned because in today's world man belongs to the whole world as much as he belongs to a country. We must love mankind as we love our fellow citizens. Patriotism is a noble sentiment which ought never to be abused.

2 *My First Day in College*

(Outline plan: The first day feeling; the atmosphere and my reaction to it; the day's events and how I felt at the end. As I now see it.)

Our college began on the first day of July. It was a wet morning when I left home to catch the bus. And as I walked towards the bus stop, my mind was full of hopes and fears.

The first hour at college passed without any notable event. We got through the admission formalities, paid the term's fee, and waited for the introductory lecture.

Then something happened which shook me out of my confidence. As I was walking towards the auditorium for the principal's address, a group of boys stood in my way. They asked me a whole lot of questions and whether I answered them correctly or not, made fun of both what I said and how I said it. Then one of them, a tall and stout boy, ordered me to sing and dance. I tried to explain that I was a bad singer and had never learnt how to dance. But he had such force and authority in his voice that refusal was impossible. The senior boys who were led by this tall fellow thoroughly enjoyed making fun of my voice and movements. I felt like crying but restrained myself to save face.

This torture would have gone on for much longer but for the arrival of a lecturer who asked the boys to report at the auditorium immediately. On the way I saw a number of other first-year boys who had suffered similar treatment. Some of them were in tears and a few others were shouting in anger and disgust.

That was the worst hour of college on that first day. For, as soon as we entered the auditorium, we were given a warm and friendly reception by the Principal, the teaching staff and members of the College Union. First the Principal spoke. He told us about the facilities that would be made available to us, invited us to participate fully in the life of the college and briefly described our duties and rights as college students. The next to speak was the Union President. He apologized for the excesses of 'ragging,' assured us of friendly behaviour from the seniors and invited us to join him for an afternoon's entertainment and get-together. Some other brief speeches followed his.

The meeting concluded with a sumptuous tea where the seniors made us feel at home as equals. Some of the students who had misbehaved and treated me so badly in the morning were now all smiles and friendly. A few of them apologized or explained why they had behaved as they did.

The whole afternoon was spent in outdoor games. The senior students had organized a number of matches which included a half-day cricket match, several hockey and football matches and several other group games. A number of us participated in some of these and enjoyed ourselves thoroughly.

The day ended with two things. First, the Vice-Principal gave us a brief talk on the first week's time-table and co-curricular activities. Then, the Principal hosted a tea with biscuits. The day which had begun with hope and apprehension and led to fear and frustration, thus ended much better than any of us had expected. Looking back at it after several months have passed I now find that even the unpleasantness was less harmful and humiliating than I found at that time. The first day at college was a highly rewarding day in more ways than one.

3 *Women must be Equal but not Identical Partners with Men* (or *Equality of Sexes, not their Identity*)

(Outline plan: The need to liberate women; women's neglect costs the nation dearly. Women excel men in certain spheres of life. Essential to have equal opportunities and rewards. But there are differences; these to be accepted/acknowledged. Utilize both to maximum advantage.)

All over the world there is today a movement which seeks to liberate the woman. In some countries it is taking more extreme forms — processions, protests and agitations against man and man-dominated society.

Women must be liberated in the sense that they should be enabled to play responsible roles in different walks of life. In most countries women continue to be neglected; in general there are far fewer women than men who have had the benefits of higher education or suitable careers. In some parts of the world a woman's place is still in the kitchen. Man supports the family economically, the woman serves him and looks after the children.

The neglect of one half of mankind costs the world a great deal both in economic and in social terms. A family without an educated mother is, in most cases, a poorer family than one in which everyone is educated and can earn a living. A family of the former kind may suffer in other ways too, because the mother is unable to help the children in their education and training for life. An educated and enlightened mother can make all the difference to the family fortunes. This must be equally true of nations with or without enlightened women.

In today's world we know something else which strengthens our belief in the liberation of women. It is that given equal chances and opportunities women can do as much and as well as (if not better than) the best of men. The world today has several women Prime Ministers and Presidents, a growing number of women scientists and scholars and numerous women leaders in different walks of life.

Nor need women lag behind in sport or adventure. Recently a Japanese mother and housewife conquered Mount Everest and not so long ago a woman tennis player beat a male world-class tennis champion. Women have begun to serve in the police force and the Americans are recruiting large numbers of women in their armed services.

Everything seems thus to justify the need to give equal opportunities to women. The liberation of women is essential for the liberation of mankind.

But this raises a question: should enlightened women be the same as enlightened men? This question is difficult to answer. If by equality we mean that women should do exactly what men do and avoid doing what men do not attempt, this may create more problems than it can help solve. The two sexes come to this world with different strengths and different potentialities. Each should be allowed to do what it can do best. There are professions where both men and women must play equally important roles (e.g. medicine and research). There are others where women, given equal opportunities, appear to excel men (e.g. teaching and some kinds of social service). But there are also tasks and roles which require man's physical strength rather than woman's sensibility, delicacy and quiet perseverance. It will be wrong and uneconomical to force the one to attempt the tasks that suit the other.

Equal opportunities need not mean identical training. It should mean training that provides equally rich possibilities for growth and development. For the good of mankind and our future on this earth men and women must march forward together, each contributing his/her mite to the common cause — a better and more human world.

4 *Diwali*

(Outline plan: What it is and when it is celebrated. Some important events of the day. A few less desirable happenings. My view of Diwali.)

In this country of many faiths and myriad beliefs almost every week a festival is celebrated. Each has its own significance and each is associated with some special celebrations.

Diwali falls in the month of October or November and it comes off about three weeks after another Hindu festival— Dussehra. Diwali is held sacred to the goddess of wealth, Lakshmi, but it also marks a big event in Hindu mythology — the return of Sri Rama from his fourteen-year-long exile. Hindus in almost all parts of the world celebrate this festival. It is a festival of joy and gaiety, of abundance and generosity.

In many parts of India preparations for Diwali begin a week before the festival day. Housewives clean their houses and the children enjoy decorating the rooms with pictures and toys. Diwali is the year's big day for businessmen and shopkeepers. They whitewash and clean their shops and premises and prepare in a big way for the day of the goddess of wealth. Most business houses and shops close their old account books and open new ones on the day of the festival.

Diwali also marks the beginning of a new season — winter. On this day most people who can afford it wear their best clothes. Most households also shop for utensils and children's toys. But the thing that is in great demand is sweets of all kinds including sugar toys of different sizes. It is a day when sweets are exchanged and distributed, the beggars too receiving their share of sweets from generous shopkeepers and housewives. Diwali does bring sweetness into many homes.

Everyone looks forward to Diwali evening — the evening of lights and lamps. The streets, especially in larger cities, are illuminated and there are impressive displays of fireworks. Rows upon rows of earthen lamps and rows of lighted candles are a sight worth seeing. Many rich men's houses and business premises are illuminated with electric lamps and some have trees and walls full of lighted lamps or candles. In almost every Hindu home at night the goddess Lakshmi is worshipped. There are hymns and songs and prayers for health, wealth and happiness. It is a day of prayer and thanksgiving, a day of smiles and generosity, but above all, it is a feast of sweets and lamps.

In some parts of the country a small number of people misuse the day for wrong purposes. They indulge in gambling and drinking and not only waste their money and spoil their health but also become a public nuisance. This often results in street brawls and violence, in unpleasant and unwanted scenes.

Diwali is a religious festival and it ought to be celebrated as such. But over the years it has also become a social festival, full of joy and happiness. I should like to see it used as a day of good deeds also. On this day those who can afford it ought to help the poor and the needy and feed the hungry. That would make it a truly enjoyable day, a day that brings sweetness in the name of the goddess of wealth.

5 *Dignity of Labour*

(Outline plan: What does it mean? What are its problems? What can we do to make it work? A world where labour is virtue.)

Labour, says the dictionary, is work and this includes both bodily and mental work. But when one calls for or works towards the dignity of labour one always refers to work with the hands rather than work that mainly occupies our minds. Why is this so?

The main reason is that whereas most men consider mental work respectable and dignified, manual labour is looked down upon as something unsuited to an intelligent man. A white collar worker who spends most of his time at a desk signing papers and writing notes is looked up to as a man of achievement. The manual labourer who dirties his hands doing difficult tasks is thought of as a man who has failed to do better things.

If now we look at the work done by the two categories of people in terms of its relevance to social needs, we shall arrive at an entirely different picture. Life's basic essentials

— food, clothing and shelter—require manual labour much more than mental labour. To grow food we need the farmers' work—tilling, sowing, protecting and harvesting. And all this is manual work. To build a house or to make cloth for garments, we once again depend on manual labour — the work done by carpenters, builders and masons or the work done by carders, weavers and tailors. For all essential goods we depend on work done with the hands. It cannot therefore be anything but dignified.

But there can be a possible opposite argument. It is that the higher-order tasks require mental rather than manual work. Behind the builder stands the architect and the engineer, behind the garment maker the master tailor and designer, and behind the successful farmer the scholar researcher. Without their help these artisans cannot get good results.

This argument is wrong on two counts. It makes the adviser more important than the performer. The architect's plans require the builder's skill and abilities before they result in a building. The adviser requires the practitioner as much as the latter requires him. Secondly, it is wrong to consider the engineer, the architect, the designer or the researcher as purely mental workers. To be good they too must combine action with thinking and work with their hands as well as their minds. And in all cases it is only in a sound body that we find a sound mind. If all this is true, there is need to raise and answer another question. How can we guarantee the dignity of labour in our society? The short answer is: 'By improving our schools and the education they give.'

Schools must become places where children learn how to work. And this work must be work with the hands as well as mental work. Schools must provide training in the practical aspects of all the subjects. They must make arts and crafts central to their time-tables. They must help all the learners to build strong bodies. Above all, they must teach respect for work with the hands. After all, our hands are meant to work as much as our hearts and heads. Work is really the best type of worship.

6 *The Day When Everything Went Wrong*

(Outline plan: How the day began, the journey from home to the airport, disappointment, the return journey. The last event.)

Last October I spent the Pooja holidays in Madras mainly because my aunt invited me to her daughter's wedding. I spent ten delightful days at my aunt's place, but, like all good things, they ended **much too soon.**

The first of November was the college reopening day. I wanted to return to Hydèrabad by train on 30th October but my aunt refused to let me do so. Instead she bought me an air ticket and advised me to fly to Hyderabad on the morning of the reopening day.

It was a wet Saturday morning when I woke up about half an hour later than I should have. The plane was to take off at 6 a.m. and I got up at ten minutes to six. When I looked at the clock on the drawing room wall, I felt helpless and wanted to cry. The alarm clock had let us down.

Fortunately for me my uncle walked into the room at just that time. On hearing what had happened, he rang up the airport to find out if the plane had already left or was about to leave. A very polite lady at the enquiry desk informed him that the plane would take off half an hour late **owing** to engine trouble.

My uncle decided to drive me to the airport in his own car in spite of my aunt warning him against it. We left home at five past six and he drove fast for about ten minutes. We were about half way there when we heard a big noise. It was a puncture in one of the front wheels. 'We have a flat tyre and I do not know how to replace it,' my uncle told me sadly.

A taxi driver who was returning home from the airport helped us to change the wheel but it took him about 20 minutes to do so. By that time it was a little past 6.30 a.m.

My uncle drove very fast to the airport and he assured me that I would be able to board the plane in spite of the time lost on the way. And I thought he was right until I reached the counter to check in. I handed in my ticket at the counter only to hear that the plane was on the runway about to take off for Hyderabad. This time I actually cried.

To help overcome my disappointment, my uncle got the 50% refund on my unused ticket and rushed back to the sales counter to buy me a ticket for that evening's flight. 'Sorry sir,' said the ticket clerk, 'we have no seats for this evening's flight. There is a large group of M.P.s travelling to Delhi on that flight.' Nor was he able to assure us a place on the next morning's flight. He could place my name on the waiting list and let me know about it in the evening.

After a cup of bad coffee at the airport restaurant we returned to the car. And what did we find there? My uncle had forgotten to lock the car and someone, having noticed this, had stolen the car radio.

There was nothing we could do about it and so my uncle started the engine. And there was nothing we could do once again when at about the place where the tyre had punctured, a man ran madly towards our car. He obviously wanted to commit suicide. Luckily the brakes worked and we got away without manslaughter on our hands.

When we reached my aunt's place my grandmother informed us that a servant had sneezed just as we were leaving. So she had been worried about us all the time.

Essay Outlines

1 *College Day*: Big event – sports and fun on all sides; inter-class matches – tea and snacks, great enthusiasm – joyful shouts; races, throws, jumps – prizes; the cultural evening dances, songs, plays.

2 *A Flight to Delhi*: Won a prize – Rs. 1,000 or a week-end in Delhi; chose the latter; the take-off; things look small and strange from above; passed cities, rivers; jerks at one time – felt uneasy; a smooth landing. Enjoyed the flight; 2 hours' journey instead of two nights and one day.

3 *The Public Library*: What is it? (books, journals, magazines, a reading room); how the books are indexed (card catalogues, the decimal system); rules of the library – x books for x days, late fee etc; the librarian – a friend and helper; the people who visit the library – different types, age groups and persons with different tastes (describe these); one of the best places to visit.

4 *Christmas*: The biggest Christian festival – 25th December – the birth of Christ commemorated; houses decorated, shops full of gifts, toys, cards, shops gaily decorated; people exchange visits, gifts, cards, greetings; morning prayers; evening parties – turkeys, puddings, games and amusement; songs and dances.

5 *Honesty*: Definitions – freedom from deceit; honesty in different aspects of life – in studies, at home, at work, etc., honesty and dishonesty in business – adulteration, black marketing, smuggling; dishonest professionals – doctors, engineers, executives – hide income from tax inspectors, make false statements; honesty in difficult circumstances, to help the needy, to save the poor; an honest man the best example to emulate.

6 *Salar Jung Museum*: Where situated, when founded and by whom; a one-man collection – the best in south-east Asia; the variety of collections – countries, periods of origin; which rooms impress one most and why – comparison with other museums; the Jade Room, the children's room; the total impression – a tribute to the founder's taste and dedication.

Essays for you to write

Narrative Essays

1 The Absent-minded Professor
2 The Day I Won my First Prize
3 How We Caught a Pick-pocket
4 The Cigarette Butt (end) that Destroyed a Whole Street
5 My Favourite Hill-station
6 That Scooter Accident

7 The Day of the Earthquake
8 The Night of the Robbery
9 The Birthday Party you Enjoyed Most
10 The Unforgettable Dream.

Descriptive Essays

1 A Good Teacher
2 When the Train Arrives at the Platform
3 Football
4 Telugu Films
5 Examinations
6 Hobbies
7 Floods
8 A Morning Walk
9 The College Tuck Shop
10 How to Make Friends.

Reflective (expository) Essays

1 Pride
2 Superstitions
3 Poverty
4 Bad Manners
5 Democracy
6 Early Rising
7 Rash Driving
8 The Telephone
9 Electricity
10 Malaria.

Argumentative Essays

1 The Pen is Mightier than the Sword
2 Village Life is Healthier than Town Life
3 Hard Work always Pays
4 Dowry is the Worst Social Evil
5 Cats make Better Pets than Dogs
6 It is Bad to Feed a Snake
7 There Should be Equal Pay for Equal Work
8 'Women's Lib' is Bunk
9 Cricket is a Better Game than Hockey
10 Everyone Must Pay the Same Taxes.